Emma Catherine Embury

The Poems

Emma Catherine Embury

The Poems

ISBN/EAN: 9783744771399

Printed in Europe, USA, Canada, Australia, Japan

Cover: Foto ©Andreas Hilbeck / pixelio.de

More available books at **www.hansebooks.com**

THE
POEMS

OF

EMMA C. EMBURY.

FIRST COLLECTED EDITION.

NEW YORK:

PUBLISHED BY HURD AND HOUGHTON

Cambridge: Riverside Press.

1869.

RIVERSIDE, CAMBRIDGE:
PRINTED BY H. O. HOUGHTON AND COMPANY.

PREFACE.

HOUGH the claim of Mrs. Emma C. Embury to a place among the poets of our land has long been established, no complete edition of her poetical works has ever before been published.

The compilation of the present volume has been altogether a labor of love, and no revision nor emendation of the poems has been attempted.

They are published in the order in which they were written, with the exception of two of the " Sketches from History," which, although written at a later date, are included with those published with " Guido " in 1828, under the *nom de plume* of " Ianthe."

In the years which have elapsed since the publication of that volume, the pen has become familiar to woman's hand, and crowds of aspirants now claim the meed of fame that was then awarded to but few. The poetic taste of the age has changed also, and we have more poems of the intellect than of the affection ; but many hearts will still respond to the glowing strains of her who has been not unaptly styled " The Hemans of America ; " for in her own expressive words, prefacing a little volume entitled " Love's Token-Flowers," published in 1854, " However changed may be the tone which now echoes from the

b

world's great heart, there are some chords in human nature that must ever vibrate to the soft and gentle touch of affection."

Mrs. Emma C. Embury, the gifted author of this volume, was the daughter of Dr. James R. Manly, an eminent physician of New York, distinguished not only for professional ability, but also for his quick sensibilities and fine conversational powers. From him his daughter doubtless inherited that peculiar sensitiveness, which combined with her rarer gifts to form a woman of ardent sympathies and brilliant genius. As a child she was most precocious, and learned to read almost intuitively. She early developed a talent for compositions, and her juvenile productions are remarkable for their graceful and flowing rhythm. Under the pseudonym of " Ianthe," she contributed to the periodicals of the day, and may be considered among the pioneers of female literature among us. She married early, and in her married life was singularly happy. Her husband, the late Daniel Embury, Esq., of Brooklyn, was a gentleman of fine talents and rare intellectual attainments ; as a mathematician, he ranked second to none in the country, while his extensive reading, courtly manners, and genial hospitality, rendered his companionship at once delightful and instructive. He appreciated fully the peculiar talents of his wife, and in every way encouraged their development ; together they drew around them the charmed circle of refinement and intelligence, and doubtless many still remember, with regretful pleasure, those delightful reunions which the elegant hospitality and brilliant conversation of the gifted host and hostess, rendered occasions of rare enjoyment. It was an oft repeated remark of Mrs. Embury, " Unless she read, she could not write," and her earlier poems were doubtless toned in harmony with the poets she loved the best ; later, her originality asserted itself, and her productions glow with self-enkindled fire. The peculiar melodiousness of her verse rendered her one of the most graceful of song writers, while the impassioned earnestness of her nature, her scorn of injustice, her quick sympathy with the oppressed, found expression in her poems, and running like an electric thread throughout them, awaken the deeper and higher emotions of the soul. In prose writing she confined herself, almost entirely to magazine writing ; her stories were extremely popular ; they were easily written, of sound moral purpose, and sparkled with wit and fancy. As a conversationalist, Mrs. Embury has rarely been excelled ; possessing a trenchant wit and a keen sense of the ridiculous, there were a few who feared while they admired her, but these few did not know of the warm and quick sensibilities that lay beneath, and that would not willfully inflict a wound. Her reading was extensive and varied, her memory retentive, her adaptation rapid, and her language forcible and graceful. The centre of a large circle, which numbered among its members many of the brightest names in literature, she shone, even as " a bright, particular star." The head of a well ordered household, a tender and devoted wife and mother, an active and sympathizing friend, she passed many years in a constant discharge of her varied duties, her energy and executive ability rendering her fully equal to all emergencies. For her to resolve and to act was almost simultaneous ; to hear of distress was to relieve it ; to sympathize with friends, was to assist them by counsel, by cheer, by tender pity, by whatever they seemed most to need, that she could give them. In the midst of this useful and brilliant career she was stricken down by an illness from which she never rallied, and for the last few years of her life she became an invalid, totally withdrawn from the world ; but she had not waited until the waning sun warned of the coming night, to begin her work ; in her own beautiful words, she began to

> "Labor on while yet the light of day
> Shed abroad its pure and blessed ray,"

and so, when the sudden gloom overshadowed her, she was not found idly over her task ; her work was taken from her hands, but not until she had inscribed her name high up upon life's scroll, and done her part to "-rouse the world's great heart " to higher aspirations, leaving behind her, in the spirit of prophecy, the impressive teaching, —

> "Diverse though our paths in life may be,
> Each is sent a mission to fulfill ;
> Fellow workers in the world are we,
> While we seek to do our Master's will.

> "Fellow workers are we ; hour by hour
> Human tools are shaping Heaven's great schemes,
> Till we see no limit to man's power,
> And reality outstrips old dreams ;
> Toil and struggle, therefore, work and weep ;
> In God's acre ye shall calmly sleep
> When the night cometh !"

CONTENTS.

POEMS.

—◆—

GUIDO.

A TALE.

"Dans le bonheur d'autrui je cherche mon bonheur."
CORNEILLE, *Le Cid.*

PART I.

THE halls were bright, and music echoed round,
   While merry feet responded to the sound,
   As light as is the gentle rustling heard
When the fresh leaves by evening's breath are stirred:
Aye, beautiful were those resplendent rooms,
All light, and flowers, and delicate perfumes;
While many a brilliant form swept gayly by,
With lofty step, and proudly flashing eye;
And many a knight, stern on the battle-field,
Taught by sweet woman's witchery to yield,
Was bowed to her capricious smile; and now
'Twas pleasant to behold the warrior brow
Bending before some gentle girl, as fair
And delicate as a thing all light or air.

Apart from the gay throng, a pale youth stood,
As, though 'mid thousands, still in solitude,

Holding a simple lyre: not his the form
That ladies love to look on and to charm:
Small, slender, boyish was his figure ; pale
His sunken cheek, that told a mournful tale
Of early suffering ; though his eye was proud,
And bright as flashes from the thunder-cloud ;
His thin and flexile lips seemed meant to pour
The wealth of song, but not the honeyed store
Of youthful love ; and though his raven hair
Fell on a lofty brow, yet early care
Had left its foot-prints on it. What doth he
Amid that joyous scene of revelry?

He was the castle's lord, and he in truth
Had tasted sorrow ; on his early youth
No parents kindly smiled ; their pride, their joy
Was centred in their younger, fairer boy.
The mother gazed upon the charms that dwelt
In Julio's noble face, until she felt
Her soul, almost with loathing, turn away
From Guido's pale and shrunken form: each day
Guido more keenly felt this ; his stern sire
Loved the proud boy who stood with eye of fire
To hear the tale of battles fierce and wild,
But turned in scorn upon his feebler child:
" What, comest thou, too? no, boy, thy woman's hand
Was never meant to grasp the blood-stained brand ;
Julio's high heart is vowed to chivalry,
But nursery legends are more fit for thee."
He little knew the being he despised !
Guido had not the gifts by warriors prized,

But genius o'er his soul had poured its light;
His was the poet's wreath, and O, how bright
It shone o'er wasted feeling's hopeless night!
Dearly the brothers loved each other: birth
Placed Guido first: but all men hold of worth,—
All that they deem the richest goods of heaven,
Love, beauty, honor,—were to Julio given;
While all the hapless elder-born could claim
Beyond his birthright, was a minstrel's fame.
Yet did they cling together: nought could speak
To Julio's heart like Guido's kindling cheek;
And praise might fall upon his ear in vain,
If that loved voice reëchoed not the strain;
While Guido felt as if not quite bereft
Of all life's joys, since Julio yet was left.

That sire was dead, that brother far away,
And Guido now must celebrate the day
When he first claimed his birthright; but how sad
Was his young heart while all around was glad!
He felt that to his noble name he owed
The homage of the gay and thoughtless crowd.
He knew that, had he been the younger born,
He had been deemed a thing that men might scorn;
And, now he stood apart from all, a smile
Of cold contempt curled his pale lip the while
That they, who bowed the castle's lord to greet,
Should think him duped by such scarce-veiled deceit.
But these unkindly feelings were not made
To dwell with poesy: his fingers strayed
Across his harp-strings, then, to still the throng
Of wayward thoughts, he calmed them thus with song:—

Nay, tell me not of woman's charms —
　Why should I heed though she be fair;
Bid me not mark those brilliant forms
　With step as light as summer air —
I dare not heed their witchery,
Since beauty was not meant for me.

I gaze upon the lofty brow —
　But changeless is its snowy hue;
I view the cheek where roses glow,
　The lip where love sips honey dew;
But lip, cheek, brow in vain I see,
Since beauty was not meant for me.

Yet I have dreamed of one whose cheek
　Upon my bosom might find rest;
Whose eye in love's sweet glance might speak,
　Whose lip might to mine own be prest;
But vain must all such visions be,
Since beauty was not meant for me.

As one might gaze on some bright star
　Lighting yon deep blue heaven above,
So I may worship from afar,
　But never dare to hope or love :
Love's star is bright — alas for me !
It shines not o'er my destiny.

The song had ceased; but still the minstrel seemed
Gazing on visions he too oft had dreamed;
Till the low tones of woman's voice awoke

New thoughts, new dreams; for of himself she spoke:
" And is he always thus — so sad and pale?
Surely that brow reveals a mournful tale."
He started — turned — O! years might not erase
The memory of that young and lovely face.
Her eye met his full gaze — a deep blush shone
O'er her fair cheek and brow — then — she was gone.
But those sweet words of kind and gentle feeling,
The look, that beamed on him so bright, revealing
All woman's pitying tenderness, now fell
On Guido's soul like some bewitching spell,
Bidding his wayward fantasies depart,
And chasing all the demon from his heart.

Where is he now? His simple lyre thrown by,
With joyous smile the bard is seated nigh
That graceful girl. E'en had she not been fair
Guido had found some trace of beauty there;
For he recalled the look, the low-breathed word
That with such new-born bliss his feelings stirred.
But she *was* beautiful; 'twas not the glow
Of simple beauty decked her cheek and brow;
For on her lofty forehead mind had made
Its visible temple; her thick tresses strayed
Down on her neck, as if they feared to rest
On that proud brow, but loved her gentler breast;
Her eye was dark as midnight, yet as bright
As if no tear had ever dimmed its light;
Lovely as love's first dream were her sweet lips —
Sweet as the honey that the wild bee sips
On famed Hymettus; the pale, pearl-like hue

Of her soft cheek was fair as if it drew
Its tint from purity: the oval face,
So like some sculptured statue's classic grace,
The nobly-arching brow, the veinèd lid,
'Neath which the full dark eye was scarcely hid,
The short, curved upper lip, — aye, Guido dwelt
On all these charms, until his spirit felt
As though it looked on some bright deity;
But O! what passing joy was his when she
Looked kindly on him, and, with gentle wile,
Sought to win back to his pale lip the smile!

The crowd have passed away, and, 'mid the sighs
Of dying odors, Guido lonely lies
Wrapt in fair dreams of beauty; but each thought
With the remembrance of one face is fraught:
He oft had fancied, but to-night ·he feels
How much of sweetness woman's look reveals.

PART II.

ALAS! alas for me! I cannot sing
Of happiness or joy's imagining;
I touch my wild and mournful lyre in vain,
It but returns the murmurings of pain;
Or if perchance I strike the chord of love,
It breathes the plaintive moanings of the dove
Who wails in loneliness her long lost mate:
I sing of love — but love left desolate!

Time passed away — how rapidly time fleets,
When every hour is redolent of sweets!
'Tis vain to trace the progress of love's power —
What eye can mark the springing of a flower?
All those impassioned feelings that so long
Were sealed in Guido's heart, the countless throng
Of early hopes and fancies, all were poured
Upon one altar. O, how rich the hoard
Of treasured love in such a heart must be!
And must its sole reward be misery?
'Tis vain to trace the progress of love's power —
Love was not here the plaything of an hour:
They walked together, and the lovely face
Of nature wore for Guido richer grace;
And e'en the breath of heaven more perfume cast,
When o'er Floranthe's cheek and lip it past;
They read together, and new beauties shone
Upon the poet's page, till then unknown.
Ah, woman's eye may charm, but there is nought
That with such peril to man's heart is fraught,
As when he breathes the poet's thoughts that burn
With passionate energy, and those eyes turn
With pleasure on him; or when both are stirred
With simultaneous feeling; though no word
Is uttered, yet the meeting look, the smile,
Betray how they have felt alike the while;
Or when, with gentle care, he leads her mind
To loftier energies and thought refined,
And she is blushing, half with shame to know
She needs such knowledge, half with joy, to owe
Its wealth to him: aye, Guido knew too well

How strongly this may aid love's powerful spell:
Within his breast self-love too had its part
(Ever an active spirit in man's heart):
He oft had known the voice of praise, but ne'er
Till now had heard its tones from lips so dear;
His song had called forth tears in those bright eyes,
And could the minstrel ask a richer prize?

And yet Floranthe loved him not — the pride
Of womanhood had taught her how to hide
Her struggling feelings; but she well had known
Those sorrows so peculiarly love's own.
So young, and proud, and beautiful, and born
To princely honors — could there be a thorn
Amid these flowers of life? The heart replies —
There dwells no balm in earthly vanities
To soothe a wounded spirit; and the sway
Of the wide universe can ne'er repay
One who beholds love's early hopes decay.
She was a high-souled woman: her proud race
Had ever won Ambition's loftiest place:
What marvel, then, that, from her childhood, she
Should dwell on the wild tales of chivalry?
She loved to roam alone through the rich halls
Where pictured shades of heroes decked the walls,
Until a dream was formed within her heart
Which no cold light of truth could bid depart:
A visioned form too beautiful to fade,
Within her breast its dwelling-place had made;
And e'en when lofty ones before her bowed,
She gladly turned from the adoring crowd

To meet her spirit-love. There was one name
She oft had heard breathed by the voice of fame ;
And half unconsciously her visions bright
Were linked with fancies of that wondrous knight.
At length a tournament was held, and fair
Was the array of youth and beauty there.
Queen of the festival Floranthe shone,
The palm of peerless beauty hers alone ;
And O, what feelings then her bosom swelled,
When first that youthful hero she beheld !
And O, how richly did her young cheek glow,
When first she placed upon his bending brow
The laurel crown ! The idol of her dreams,
Bright with the light of glory's sunny beams,
Now stood before her, and she felt how faint
Were fancy's tints a form like his to paint.
From that hour she was changed — the holy flame
Which long was fostered by the breath of fame,
Now, like the vestal's sacred fire, had won
A purer radiance from its parent sun :
That knight was Julio : hence it was that she
With pity looked on Guido's misery.
He was the brother of her love, and though
Nature had traced no beauty on his brow,
His voice, so like to Julio's, her heart stirred,
Like music o'er the moon-lit waters heard ;
And in his eyes she saw the same sweet light
That oft in Julio's glances shone so bright.

Why does my song thus linger ? The dark day
Of strife was gone, and peace resumed her sway.

E'en as the prophet's wand could once unlock
The hidden waters of the riftless rock,
So thou, sweet Peace, from iron hearts can bring
Th' unwonted freshness of affection's spring;
Till spurns the haughty chief his plumèd crest,
And clasps his smiling infant to his breast,
While the proud soldier turns from scenes of war,
Rejoiced to worship beauty's gentler star.
And 'mid the mailèd warriors Julio came,
His brow encircled with its wreaths of fame.
No more alone with Guido now were past
Floranthe's happiest hours; for Love had cast
His spell around them, and beneath his wing
Hope dared unfold her fragile blossoming;
For well could she, in Julio's eye, discern
(Ah, when was woman slow such tales to learn?)
The growing tenderness within his breast,
The love that made her all too wildly blest.
But where was Guido? Did not he too see
Within those tell-tale eyes Love's mastery?
One night there was a festival, and all
Of brave and lovely decked the joyous hall;
Guido beheld Floranthe's gentle hand
Meet Julio's in the graceful saraband;
Yet this was nothing; but when the light dance
Was ended, and he saw the thrilling glance
Exchanged between them, and her slender form
So tenderly upheld by Julio's arm,
While she repaid him with a timid look
Of soft confiding love, he could not brook
Longer to gaze upon that blasting sight;

Quickly he turned away — a mirror bright
Met his full gaze; reflected there, his own
Pale, sunken cheek, and wasted figure shone.
Then on his heart, like lightning flashes, came
The truth that woke despair's undying flame.
O! there are moments when the heart lives o'er
Ages of sorrow, when the eyes can pour
No gentle flood to ease the throbbing head;
But as if one among the mouldering dead
Should start to life, and vainly strive to burst
His prison-house, so that sad being, curst
With such o'erwhelming grief, in vain would find
A refuge from the horrors of the mind.

PART III.

IT was a lovely summer eve; the bay
As calmly as a slumbering infant lay:
Floranthe sat within her lonely bower,
Her heart filled with strange feelings; the calm hour
To her brought no tranquillity; the bright
And glowing west, the clouds of rosy light,
She gazed upon but saw not, and she heard
Not e'en a sound; altho' the mild breeze stirred
And made sweet music in the leaves, her ear
Was all unheeding; but there was one near
Who long had gazed on her; the breeze had fanned
The clustering ringlets from her cheek; her hand,

As delicate as a wreath of new fallen snow,
Was pressed against her wildly throbbing brow,
And, but that on her cheek there dwelt a flush
Like young Aurora's rosy-tinted blush,
And but for her bright lip, she might have seemed
A changeless statue; but she little deemed
He whom she loved to think on was so nigh.
Julio stood long and gazed on her; a sigh
Burst from her heaving bosom, and that eye,
Whose varying glance seemed meant but to express
The joy of love, the pride of loveliness,
Was clouded by sad tears; a moment more,
And Julio with bright cheek was bending o'er
The trembling girl — but why should I repeat
Love's follies? — words as gentle and as sweet
As the soft welling of the distant waves
Of ocean o'er his deep and hollow caves;
Or summer breeze that sweeps the trembling strings
Of the Æolian harp — sweet as when sings
Some rose-lipped cherub in the starry sky.
And O! how quickly can Love's thrilling sigh
Win all it seeks: when Julio vowed he ne'er
Would brook the lonely weight of life, a tear
Stood in her eye; he felt she was his own,
For she had paused to hear him, and the tone
Of her low voice grew fainter — they are gone.

That hour of deep, impassioned feeling past,
They sat within the hall; the moonbeam cast
A dim, sweet light through the thick orange-trees
That filled the casement, and the evening breeze
Was faint with their rich perfume. With a smile

That once could Guido's every grief beguile,
Floranthe bade him wake, in cheerful song,
Strains that to love and happiness belong:—

> 'Tis all in vain—I cannot sing
> The joys that happy Love may bring;
> I cannot win mirth's blooming wreath
> Its fragrance o'er my lyre to breathe.
> They say that in bright summer bowers,
> All redolent of buds and flowers,
> Young Love is dwelling; o'er his head
> The calmest, bluest skies are spread,
> And flowerets spring beneath his feet,
> As though to die by him were sweet;
> That some, with rapturous feeling, gaze
> Upon his brow's unclouded blaze,
> While others prize the gentler grace
> That glows around his half-veiled face,
> And all are happy—is it so?
> Does Love ne'er see a shade of woe?
> Ask not the smiling lip to tell
> The joys in Love's sweet home that dwell—
> Go ask the cheek where paleness sits
> If no cloud o'er that blue sky flits;
> If o'er those bowers so green and bright
> Grief's chilling breath ne'er throws a blight;
> If hope's young buds ne'er fade away
> Beneath the touch of slow decay.
> But pride may dye the faded cheek
> With hues that seem of joy to speak;
> And bright the eye may still appear,
> Though all its lustre be a tear.

Then wonder not that my sad lyre
Breathes not of fancy's thrilling fire:
The man who ne'er beheld the sun
Save when dark mists its face had shrouded,
Could never paint flowers shone upon
By summer skies and light unclouded.
Thus I must shun each brighter theme,
And still of wasted feeling dream;
Still tales of blighted love impart,
Because — I read them in my heart.

Floranthe little knew the thoughts that stirred
In Guido's breast; she knew not he had heard
Their plighted vows, her tender tones, when she
Confessed the love long cherished hopelessly.
Aye, Guido felt her falsehood had been bliss
To the wild thought she never had been his!
Is it not ever thus? O, who could brook
The knowledge that each gentle word, each look
Which hope had fancied filled with tenderness,
Was only meant cold pity to express?
O, surely it is far less grief to see
Upon the altered brow inconstancy,
Than still to view the loved eye's chilling beam,
Like sun rays glittering o'er a frozen stream.
Guido had seen his dearest hopes depart,
And now one high resolve filled his lone heart;
He knew her sire would ne'er bestow her hand
On one whose wealth was but his battle-brand;
Inly he vowed that not by him should she
Be doomed to long and hopeless misery:

The star of life had set — why should he care
For honors that Floranthe could not share?
On the next morning Julio sought to bear
His joyful tale to his loved Guido's ear,
But vainly did he seek — the orange bower,
The lonely grotto, and the ruined tower,
All his loved haunts, were silent now and lone;
His harp-strings, too, were broken, as if none
Might wake its gentle voice now he was gone.
They sought the chamber of his nightly rest —
It was untenanted, his couch unprest;
But on his ivory tablets he had traced
Words that a burning tear had half effaced:
" He loathed the false, deceptive world, and now
A cowl must hide his early furrowed brow;
And to the brother of his heart he gave
A name proud as Ambition's self could crave,
While for himself he sought an early grave."

O! there is never need of words to tell
To woman's heart that she is loved too well:
The glance, the sigh, in ill-dissembled hour,
Quickly betray the fullness of her power.
Haply Floranthe would not then unfold
Her every thought, while memory unrolled
Its darkened record, and her heart hung o'er
Each gentle look and tone unmarked before;
And haply, too, in after years, when prest
To her adoring husband's manly breast,
Floranthe felt she had not been thus blest
But for the self-devoted love which gave
Itself to be stern sorrow's veriest slave.

SKETCHES FROM HISTORY.

JANE OF FRANCE.

" Jeanne de France étoit fille de Louis XI. et sœur de Charles VIII. On la maria à l'âge de vingt deux ans avec Louis XII., l'an 1476. Elle en usa bien avec lui pendant qu'il étoit disgracié ; et ce fut elle qui, par ses prières, le fit sortir de prison, l'an 1491 ; mais cela ne fut point capable de balancer dans le coeur de son mari l'inclination violente qu'il avoit pour la veuve de Charles VIII. C'étoit Anne de Bretagne ; il l'avoit aimée, et en avoit été aimé avant qu'elle epousût Charles. Afin donc de contenter son envie, *il fit rompre son mariage*, et il promit tant de récompense au Pape Alexandre VI. qu'il en obtint tout ce qu'il voulut."

BAYLE, *Dictionnaire*.

PALE, cold, and statue-like she sat, and her impeded breath
    Came gaspingly, as if her heart was in the grasp of death,
While listening to the harsh decree that robbed her of a throne,
And left the gentle child of kings in the wide world alone.

And fearful was her look ; in vain her trembling maidens moved,
With all affection's tender care, round her whom well they loved ;

Stirless she sat, as if enchained by some resistless
    spell,
Till with one wild, heart-piercing shriek in their em-
    brace she fell.

How bitter was the hour she woke from that long dream-
    less trance ;
The veriest wretch might pity then the envied Jane of
    France ;
But soon her o'erfraught heart gave way, tears came to
    her relief,
And thus in low and plaintive tones, she breathed her
    hopeless grief : —

"O! ever have I dreaded this, since at the holy shrine
My trembling hand first felt the cold, reluctant clasp of
    thine ;
And yet I hoped — My own beloved, how may I teach
    my heart
To gaze upon thy gentle face, and know that we must
    part ?

"Too well I knew thou lovedst me not, but ah ! I
    fondly thought
That years of such deep love as mine some change ere
    this had wrought :
I dreamed the hour might yet arrive when, sick of pas-
    sion's strife,
Thy heart would turn with quiet joy to thy neglected
    wife.

2

"Vain, foolish hope ! how could I look upon thy glori-
    ous form,
And think that e'er the time might come when thou
    wouldst cease to charm?
For ne'er till then wilt thou be freed from beauty's
    magic art,
Or cease to prize a sunny smile beyond a faithful heart.

"In vain from memory's darkened scroll would other
    thoughts erase
The loathing that was in thine eye, whene'er it met my
    face :
O ! I would give the fairest realm beneath the all-see-
    ing sun,
To win but such a form as thou mightst love to look
    upon.

"Woe, woe for woman's weary lot if beauty be not
    hers ;
Vainly within her gentle breast affection wildly stirs ;
And bitterly will she deplore, amid her sick heart's
    dearth,
The hour that fixed her fearful doom — a helot from
    her birth.

"I would thou hadst been cold and stern — the pride
    of my high race
Had taught me then from my young heart thine image
    to efface ;
But surely even love's sweet tones could ne'er have
    power to bless
My bosom with such joy as did thy pitying tenderness.

"Alas! it is a heavy task to curb the haughty soul,
And bid th' unbending spirit bow that never knew control;
But harder still when thus the heart against itself must
  rise
And struggle on, while every hope that nerved the warfare dies.

"Yet all this have I borne for thee — aye, for thy sake
  I learned
The gentleness of thought and word which once my
  proud heart spurned;
The treasures of an untouched heart, the wealth of
  love's rich mine, —
These are the offerings that I laid upon my idol's shrine.

"In vain I breathed my vows to heaven, 'twas mock-
  ery of prayer;
In vain I knelt before the cross, I saw but Louis there:
To him I gave the worship that I should have paid my
  God, —
But O! should his have been the hand to wield the
  avenging rod?"

SCENES IN THE LIFE OF A LOVER.

Anne Boleyn, when maid of honor to Queen Catharine, was betrothed to Henry Percy, afterwards Earl of Northumberland, but at that time a page in the household of Cardinal Wolsey. The king, discovering their attachment by means of some gem, a love-gift from Percy to Anne, ordered him to be removed from court. The young lover, after beholding the object of his affection elevated to the highest station in the realm, was finally compelled, as one of the peers of England, to preside at her trial and condemnation. — Miss Benger's *Memoirs of Anne Boleyn.*

SCENE I.

WITHIN a green and flower-decked glade they
       stood ;
The harvest moon was shedding a rich flood
Of light around them, and revealed to view
The youth's bright glance, the deep and burning hue
That flushed the maiden's cheek ; her lover's arm
Was fondly clasped around her graceful form :
But half aside she turned ; she could not brook
The passionate fondness of his earnest look ;
And proudly did his o'er-fraught bosom swell
As there, to hide her blushing face, she fell.
Upon her brow he pressed one burning kiss,
And then in all the speechlessness of bliss
Stood gazing on her, till low murmurs broke
From her sweet lips, and his heart's pulses woke :
" Now am I thine, beloved one ; doubt me not
Amid the splendors of my courtly lot ;
For dearer far to me this little gem
Than e'er could be a queenly diadem ;
And when no more my bosom it shall grace, —
The sweet remembrance of this fond embrace, —

Then deem me faithless, Henry, and despise
The heart that only lives beneath thine eyes."
Then to her rosy lips the maiden prest
The gem with which his hand had decked her breast:
" Now fare thee well, beloved one, I must go
Once more to mingle in the heartless show
That fills yon haughty castle — one last kiss —
And shouldst thou doubt me, Henry, think on this."
She glided from his arms; her flying feet
Scarce from the violet pressed its fragrance sweet;
He was alone, and thus to music's spell
He joined the murmurs of his low farewell: —

Farewell to thee, dear;
    When I meet thee again,
Light hearts will be round us
    And pageantries vain;
But well do I know,
    In life's sunniest hours,
Thou'lt think of our meeting
    'Mid moonlight and flowers.

Farewell to thee, dear one,
    And O ! in thy dreams
When fancy sheds o'er thee
    Her loveliest beams,
Then think that thou rovest
    Through Percy's fair bowers,
And remember our meeting
    'Mid moonlight and flowers.

SCENE II.

HARK! hark to the tumult! the trumpets and drums
Are waking wild mirth as the pageantry comes;
'Mid knights and fair dames, see the king proudly ride,
While near him is borne in her glory his bride;
And never could England's proud diadem gleam
On a brow where more beauty and majesty beam.

There's a flush on her cheek like the deep crimson glow
That sunset sheds over the pure Alpine snow;
And her eye sheds a brightness more glorious by far
Than the splendor that beams from heaven's loveliest
        star;
There is joy in her heart, but does happiness speak
In the wildly bright eye, and the fever-flushed cheek?

'Tis she — 'tis the maiden! but where now is gone
The gem that so long on her bosom had shone?
Though diamonds are sparkling, and pearls rich and rare,
Yet the earliest offering of love is not there;
And the king at her side is not he on whose breast,
In that still hour of bliss, her sweet face had found rest.

Look, look to the queen! o'er her features are spread
A hue like the paleness that dwells with the dead;
Her wandering glance, as if urged by a spell,
Turned full on the form she had loved but too well;
And how did her heart with wild agony beat,
As she thought of those hours still in memory too sweet!

O ! sadly he looked on her robes rich and gay, —
He had seen that form fairer in simple array, —
And shuddering he gazed on her jeweled tiar
Less bright than her eye, once his loveliest star :
And his proud heart swelled high as he thought of past
     hours,
And remembered their meeting 'mid moonlight and
    flowers.

But vain such remembrance ; a tyrant's fierce love
Had broken the bonds young affection had wove.
The youth to another in sorrow is wed ;
In glory the maid as a queen is now led ;
And soon as a subject he humbly must bow
To her on whose lips he had breathed his love-vow.

SCENE III.

WITH black the stately hall was hung ; a cloud was on
    each brow
That gathered round the council board in solemn si-
    lence now ;
And pain and anxious doubt within each noble's bosom
    stirred,
For well they knew that life and death now hung upon
    their word.

With snow-white robes and veilèd brow, a female form
    drew nigh ;
With calm and stately air she stepped, while fixed was
    every eye ;

And 'mid the dark, stern visaged guards around her,
      she might seem
The being of a higher sphere, the creature of a dream.

Now like a criminal she stood, while plainly she could
      trace
The fearful workings of his soul upon each noble's face;
Yet was she calm; with queenly grace her veil aside
      was thrown —
Unhappy Percy! from thy lips burst that convulsive
      groan?

Well might his breast with anguish thrill! few years
      had passed away
Since that fair form within his arms in love's deep
      fondness lay;
Since then she moved the stately queen — now the dis-
      loyal wife,
For her deep treachery and wrong must answer with
      her life.

Yet she was innocent; O! none could gaze upon her eye
And deem that sin's dark stain within her bosom's
      depths could lie;
But who might dare assert her truth, when, wearied
      with her charms,
The tyrant had decreed that she should sleep in death's
      cold arms?

Now, placed 'mid England's haughty peers, must Percy
      seal the doom
That gave the creature of his love to fill a bloody tomb;

Too soon the fatal deed was done — though pure as un-
    sunned snow,
Yet must the fearful hand of death stamp guilt upon
    her brow.

He heard no more; but wildly from the judgment hall
    he rushed,
Too strong the tenderness within his anguished spirit
    gushed ;
Till worn by such resistless pangs, o'ermastered by the
    spell
Of demon thought, upon the earth in senselessness he
    fell.

Stately and calm the queen had sat, but when she heard
    his cry,
From her quick heaving bosom burst the half-convul-
    sive sigh.
One pleading look to heaven she cast, then spoke in
    murmured tone :
" Slight is the bitterness of death when spotless fame
    is gone."

Thus did she die — the young, the fair, the good, com-
    pelled to bow
Her graceful, swan-like neck beneath the headsman's
    heavy blow;
Her shining locks were dabbled in the blood that
    flowed like rain ;
But o'er the whiteness of her soul, e'en blood could
    leave no stain.

QUEEN ELIZABETH.

"Sir James Melvil tells us that this princess, the evening of his arrival in London, had given a ball to her court at Greenwich, and was displaying all that spirit and alacrity which usually attended her on these occasions: but when news arrived of the prince of Scotland's birth, all her joy was damped; she sunk into melancholy; she reclined her head upon her arm, and complained to some of her attendants, that the Queen of Scots was mother of a fair son, while she herself was but a barren stock."[1]

HUME's *History of England.*

COLDLY she sat, while graceful hands her stately
    form arrayed
  In silken robes, and wreathed her hair in many
    a jeweled braid;
But all a woman's vanity was in the vivid glow
That flattery's magic tones awoke upon her cheek and
    brow.

Beside her hung the pictured form of Scotland's match-
    less queen —
O! language would need rainbow hues to paint that
    glorious mien,
That face which bore the high impress of majesty, and
    yet
Where Love, as if to win all hearts, his fairest seal
    had set.

And bitter was the scorn that filled Elizabeth's proud
    eye,
As turning from her mirrored self, she saw her rival
    nigh;

[1] A slight, perhaps not unpardonable liberty has been taken with historical fact. The queen is supposed to be at her toilette, preparing for the ball.

But transient was the cloud, and soon she bent with
    smiles to greet
The graceful little page who now was kneeling at her
    feet : —

" Letters from Scotland " — eagerly she grasped the
    proffered scroll
Which sharper than a scorpion's sting could pierce her
    haughty soul ;
And timidly her maidens shrunk ; for quickly could
    they trace
Fierce passion in the darkening hue that gathered o'er
    her face.

The white foam stood upon her lip, and wildly beat
    her heart,
Till its convulsive throbbings rent her 'broidered zone
    apart :
" Away ! " she cried — awe-struck they stood to hear
    that anguished tone, —
" Away ! " — like frighted fawns they fled, and she was
    left alone.

O ! fiercer than the angry burst of ocean's tameless
    wave
Is woman's soul, when thus unchecked its maddening
    passions rave ;
But soon the storm was spent, and then like rain-drops
    fell her tears,
While thus the heart-struck queen bewailed her lone
    and blighted years : —

"All, all but this I could have borne — methought that
   queenly pride
Had checked within my woman's breast affection's
   swelling tide ;
But vainly has my spirit sought 'mid glory to forget
The youthful dreams whose faded light gleams o'er my
   fancy yet.

"And *she* has realized those dreams — aye, she whose
   gentle brow,
In all its graceful loveliness, is turned upon me now ;
Mary of Scotland ! gladly would my lofty heart resign
The pomps and vanities of power, to win such joy as
   thine.

"O ! dearer far than halls of state the humble cottage
   hearth,
Where childhood's joyous tones awake in all their reckless mirth ;
And happier far the meanest churl, than she, within
   whose breast
Affection's soft and pleading voice by pride must be
   represt.

"A mother's joy ! a mother's pride ! — O ! what is regal
   power
To the sweet feelings that are born in such a blissful
   hour ?
Now well art thou avenged, fair queen, of all my jealous hate,
For thou hast clasped a princely son, and I — am desolate ! "

THE DEATH OF QUEEN ELIZABETH.

A BALLAD.

COULD this be England's boasted pride?
  Where were her glories now?
  Where the rich jewels that were wont
To deck her princely brow?
Where were the pomps of regal state,
  The charms of lady's bower?
Not on such couch the island queen
  Should meet her dying hour.

In vain her anxious maidens decked
  Her bed of royal state ;
With finger pressed upon her lip,
  Upon the floor she sate ;
Sorrow had bowed her stately form,
  And time had blanched her hair ;
While her proud eye, now glazed and dim,
  Was filled with wild despair.

She took no heed of aught; her thoughts
  Were in the bloody grave
That her own hand had dug for him
  She would have died to save ;
And ever to her heart she pressed
  A ring, a trifling gem,
But far more precious to her now
  Than England's diadem.

It was a pledge of special grace —
   For hours had often been
When the proud dame could not forget
   The woman in the queen;
And to the hand of Essex then,
   In such an hour she gave
The ring, and promised any boon
   That with it he might crave.

And when they called him rebel chief,
   And told her he must die,
How long, how fondly did she wait
   To see that pledge brought nigh;
But time passed on, and it came not:
   Then, forced by harsh decree,
Her hand confirmed his doom, and sealed
   Her own deep misery.

Now when 'twas all too late, she learned
   How treachery and wrong
Around the noble earl had wove
   Their toils so deep and strong;
For he had sent the fatal ring,
   But ere it met her eye,
The hapless youth had sunk beneath
   The death that traitors die.

This was the fearful thought that weighed
   Upon her noble heart,
And never more could earthly pomps
   A ray of joy impart;

The crown her hand had decked with gems
  Oppressed her weary head,
And what cared she for princely power?
  It could not wake the dead.

Thus days passed on, while fixed she sat
  A statue of despair,
Unheeding aught save when arose
  The murmured voice of prayer;
Then slowly down her wasted cheek
  The gathering tear-drops stole,
But O! what human voice may speak
  The anguish of her soul?

Are there who smile that thus in age
  Affection should awake
And scorn to think a heart so late
  In hopelessness may break?
Go look upon the mountain stream —
  Its wild wave rushes by,
Till wasted by its own excess
  Behold the channel dry!

Aye, thus she suffered — she who scorned
  To share her envied throne;
She who had spurned a sceptered hand,
  Proud to but reign alone;
Now sunk beneath the fatal strength
  Of passion, and forgot
The glories of a stately queen,
  To die by woman's lot.

BOSCOBEL.

" By the Earl of Derby's directions, Charles went to Boscobel, a lone house, on the
borders of Staffordshire, inhabited by one Penderell, a farmer. To this man Charles
intrusted himself. Penderell took the assistance of his four brothers, equally honor-
able with himself; and having clothed the king in a garb like their own, they led him
into a neighboring wood, put a bill into his hand, and pretended to employ themselves in cutting fagots. For a better concealment, he mounted upon an oak, where
he sheltered himself among the leaves and branches for twenty-four hours. He saw
several soldiers pass by. All of them were intent in search of the king; and some
expressed in his hearing, their earnest wishes of seizing him."

HUME's History of England.

'TWAS sunset, and the forest trees
    Glowed 'neath the golden sky,
While evening's soft and dew-fraught
    breeze
    Awoke its gentle sigh.

Slowly the toil-worn woodman came;
    His glance was high and proud;
Though 'neath the fagots' painful weight
    His drooping form was bowed.

At length in weariness he cast
    His burden to the earth;
And never such a look could beam
    From one of lowly birth.

The peasant's summer toil seemed traced
    Upon his swarthy cheek;
But not more native pride than his
    A kingly eye could speak.

Aye, majesty upon his brow
  Its signet had imprest ;
And lofty was the heart that heaved
  Beneath the woodman's vest ;

For he was one of royal race,
  His heritage a throne :
What doth he in the pathless wood,
  Thus peasant-clad and lone ?

Beside the silver brook he threw
  His wearied limbs, and sighed :
" Alas ! must this then be the end
  Of Stuart's kingly pride ?

" Woe for the glorious hopes that once
  My lofty heart could fill !
The hand that grasped the warrior's sword,
  Now bears the woodman's bill ;

" The neck that never bent before,
  Now bows itself to wear
A burden that, in better days,
  My slaves had scorned to bear.

" Better, far better 'twere to die
  Beneath the assassin's knife,
Than thus drag on, 'mid toil and care,
  A painful load of life."

3

Hark to the sound of crashing boughs !
  A stranger's step is heard !
Again the love of life within
  The prince's bosom stirred.

With lithe and active limb he climbed
  An oak's majestic height ;
And, sheltered 'mid its clustering leaves,
  Looked on a fearful sight.

A band of fierce-eyed men were there ;
  Their swords were stained with blood ;
And they bent to lave their burning brows
  Within the crystal flood.

Then rose the ribald jest, the laugh,
  The tale of daily guilt ;
And, demon-like, the exulting boast
  Of blood their hands had spilt.

But still they sought one victim more —
  The Prince ! the Prince ! for him
With frantic haste they hurry through
  The forest-shadows dim.

He heard their cries of baffled rage ;
  He saw their eyes' fierce glare ;
He knew that he was hunted like
  A wild beast in his lair.

Then all death's bitterness was his ;
  And down his swart cheek rolled
Big drops of agony that well
  His soul's dread conflict told.

.   .   .   .   .   .

Night dews upon the green sward shed
  Full many a precious gem,
And on the midnight skies was seen
  Heaven's glorious diadem.

Stillness was on the peaceful earth,
  And beauty filled the grove,
While nature seemed too fair for aught
  Save gentleness and love.

A hallowed sound that stillness broke ;
  For, lowly kneeling there,
To pitying heaven the rescued prince
  Poured his unwonted prayer.

And O ! in after years, when placed
  On England's glorious throne,
The wealth and power of regal state
  Around him richly shone —

When pleasure o'er his fancy wove
  Her bright and powerful spell,
Did not the monarch's proud heart bless
  The shades of Boscobel ?

THE LAMENT OF COLUMBUS.

" Until now I have wept for others; have pity upon me, Heaven, and weep for me, earth! In my temporal concerns, without a farthing to give in offering; in spiritual concerns, cast away here in the Indies; isolated in my misery, infirm, expecting each day will be my last; surrounded by cruel savages, separated from the holy sacraments of the Church, so that my soul will be lost if separated here from my body! Weep for me whoever has charity, truth, and justice. I came not on this voyage to gain honor or estate; for all hope of that kind is dead within me. I came to serve your majesties with a sound intention and an honest zeal, and I speak no falsehood."

Extract of a Letter from Columbus.

" He looked upon himself as standing in the hand of Heaven, chosen from among men for the accomplishment of its high purpose. He read, as he supposed, his contemplated discovery foretold in holy writ, and shadowed forth darkly in the mystic revelations of the prophets. The ends of the earth were to be brought together, and all nations and tongues and languages united under the banners of the Redeemer."

IRVING's *Life of Columbus.*

" There is a fire
And motion of the soul which will not dwell
In its own narrow being .   .   .   .   .

.   .   .   .

And but once kindled, quenchless evermore,
Preys upon high adventure, nor can tire
Of aught but rest; a fever at the core,
Fatal to him that bears, to all who ever bore."

Childe Harold.

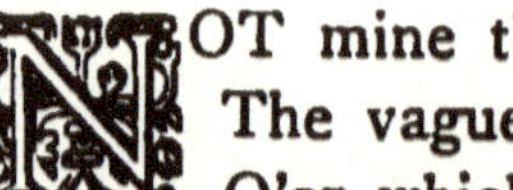NOT mine the dreams,
The vague chimeras of an earth-stained soul,
O'er which the mists of error darkly roll;
For Heaven-sent beams
Have chased the gloom that round my soul was flung,
And pierced the clouds that o'er creation's mysteries
hung.

From my youth up
For this high purpose was I set apart —

An unbreathed thought, it lived within my heart;
      And though life's cup
Was filled with all earth's agonies, I quaffed
Unmurmuring, for that hope could sweeten any draught.

      There were who jeered,
And laughed to scorn my visionary scheme;
They thought yon glorious sun's resplendent beam
      So brightly cheered
And vivified alone the spot of earth
Where they, like worms, had lived and groveled from
    their birth.

      But, called by God,
From home and friends my willing steps I turned;
Led by the light that in my spirit burned,
      Strange lands I trod;
And lo! new worlds, uncurtained by my hand,
Before th' admiring East in pristine beauty stand.

      And what was given
To recompense the many nameless toils
That won my king a new found empire's spoils?
      The smile of Heaven
Blessed him who sought amid those Eden plains
To plant the holy cross; but man's reward was chains.

      Forgot by all,
Amid a land of savages, I wait
From cruel, hostile hands my coming fate;
      Or else to fall

Beneath the grief that weighs upon my heart
While unaneled, unblessed, my spirit must depart.

How have I wept
In pity for my followers, when afar
O'er the wide sea with scarce a guiding star
Our course we kept;
But night winds only o'er *my* grave shall sigh;
For, bowed with cruel wrongs, on stranger shores, I die.

No selfish hope
Of fame or honor led me here again
To tread this weary pilgrimage of pain;
He who must cope
With treachery and wrong, until the flame
Of pure ambition dies, has nought to do with fame.

To serve my king
I came, with zeal unkindness could not chill;
To glorify my God, whose holy will
Taught me to fling
The veil of error from before my eyes,
And teach mankind his power as shown 'neath other
    skies.

Weep for me, earth!
Thou whose bright wonders I have oft explored,
Weep for me heaven! to whose proud heights has soared,
E'en from its birth,
My strong winged spirit in its might alone;
Lo! he who gave new worlds now dies unwept, un-
    known.

THE SHIPWRECK OF CAMOENS.

"On his return from banishment, Camoens was shipwrecked at the mouth of the river Gambia. He saved himself by clinging to a plank, and of all his little property succeeded only in saving his poem of the Lusiad, deluged with the waves as he brought it in his hand to shore."[1] — SISMONDI.

> " I saw him beat the surges under him,
>   And ride upon their backs; he trod the water,
>   Whose enmity he flung aside, and breasted
>   The surge most swoln that met him."
>
> *Tempest.*

CLOUDS gathered o'er the dark blue sky,
　　The sun waxed dim and pale,
　　And the music of the waves was changed
　To the plaintive voice of wail;
And fearfully the lightning flashed
　Around the ship's tall mast,
While mournfully through the creaking shrouds
　Came the sighing of the blast.

With pallid cheek the seamen shrank
　Before the deepening gloom;
For they gazed on the black and boiling sea
　As 'twere a yawning tomb:
But on the vessel's deck stood one
　With proud and changeless brow;
Nor pain nor terror was in the look
　He turned to the gulf below.

---

[1] He is described with his sword in his hand, upon the authority of his own words : —
　" N'huma maõ livros, n'outra, ferro et aço,
　　N'huma maõ sempre a espada, n'outra a pena."

And calmly to his arm he bound
    His casket and his sword;
Unheeding, though with fiercer strength
    The threatening tempest roared;
Then stretched his sinewy arms and cried:
    "For me there yet is hope;
. The limbs that have spurned a tyrant's chain
    With the stormy wave may cope.

"Now let the strife of nature rage,
    Proudly I yet can claim,
Where'er the waters may bear me on,
    My freedom and my fame."
The dreaded moment came too soon,
    The sea swept madly on,
Till the wall of waters closed around,
    And the noble ship was gone.

Then rose one wild, half-stifled cry;
    The swimmer's bubbling breath
Was all unheard, while the raging tide
    Wrought well the task of death:
But 'mid the billows still was seen
    The stranger's struggling form;
And the meteor flash of his sword might seem
    Like a beacon 'mid the storm.

For still, while with his strong right arm
    He buffeted the wave,
The other upheld that treasured prize
    He would give life to save.

Was then the love of pelf so strong
  That e'en in death's dark hour,
The base-born passion could awake
  With such resistless power?

No! all earth's gold were dross to him,
  Compared with what lay hid,
Through lonely years of changeless woe,
  Beneath that casket's lid ;
For there was all the mind's rich wealth,
  And many a precious gem
That, in after years, he hoped might form
  A poet's diadem.

Nobly he struggled till o'erspent,
  His nerveless limbs no more
Could bear him on through the waves that rose
  Like barriers to the shore ;
Yet still he held his long prized wealth,
  He saw the wished for land —
A moment more, and he was thrown
  Upon the rocky strand.

Alas! far better to have died
  Where the mighty billows roll,
Than lived till coldness and neglect
  Bowed down his haughty soul :
Such was his dreary lot, at once
  His country's pride and shame ;
For on Camoens' humble grave alone
  Was placed his wreath of fame.

LAMENT OF CAMOENS.

Donna Catharina de Atayde, a lady of rank and fortune, inspired Camoens with a love as deep as it proved lasting. He was her equal in birth, though destitute of riches. His poverty, however, in the opinion of her parents, was a crime which could be expiated only by exile; and as she was attached to the court, they found no difficulty in procuring from the sovereign a decree for his banishment. This summary mode of proceeding, though it separated the lovers, served but to increase their mutual affection, while it brought upon the unhappy Camoens misfortune and disgrace. After a lapse of years, during which he had suffered penury, shipwreck, and the loss of the little property he had accumulated in the East Indies, he returned to his native country, broken in health and in spirits, only to weep over the grave of his beloved Catharina, who had cherished her hopeless love for him to the last moments of her life. — *Life of Camoens.*

> "O when in boyhood's happier scene,
>   I pledged my love to thee,
> How very little did I ween
> My recompense would now have been
>   So much of misery!"
>
> CAMOENS.

M Y brow is wasted with its throbs of pain;
My limbs have worn the exile's heavy chain;
And now, in weariness of heart, I come
    To seek my home —
Alas! alas! what home is left me save
The marble stone that marks my Catharine's grave.

Amid the loneliness of banished years,
When every hour was traced in bitter tears,
When 'gainst itself my bosom learned to war,
    Thou wert the star
That o'er my path of dreary darkness shone,
My own sweet Catharine, and thou too art gone!

Too well thy faith, my gentle one, was kept;
The love, the perfect tenderness that slept

Within thy bosom, on itself has preyed,
        Till thou wert laid
Within the shelter of earth's quiet breast,
The sinless victim of a love unblest.

Still thou didst glory in that love; thy brow
With deep affection's brightest flush would glow;
And though with bitter tears, when last we met,
        Thy cheek was wet,
Yet thou didst bear a spirit high and proud,
And bid me suffer on with soul unbowed.

Alas! I hoped thou wouldst have heard my name
Linked with the voice of song, the breath of fame:
I fondly deemed that thou wouldst yet behold
        My name enrolled
Amid my country's records, while my lyre
Should wake within all hearts a patriot fire.

But that is past; once I had wept, and raved,
And cursed the fate that, through such perils, saved
Me to lament o'er early-faded dreams;
        Now reason seems
Gifted with life to add new stings to pain;
For frenzy rules my heart, but not my brain.

No outward sign such mortal woe may speak;
No tears, my Catharine, stain my hollow cheek;
For ah! this languid frame, this sinking heart
        Tell me we part
But for a season; soon my toil-worn soul
Shall throw aside this weary life's control.

Then shall death sanctify my lyre ; and then
Shall nations praise " him of the sword and pen ; "
Then shall my grave become a pilgrim shrine ;
   And then too thine,
Thus hallowed by a poet's love, shall be
Sought when forgot are thy proud ancestry.

THE POOL OF BETHESDA.

(St. John v. 2–9.)

RANQUIL Bethesda's waters lay,
 No breeze the surface stirred,
 When sudden through the brightening air
A rustling wing was heard ;
Then loudly rose the joyous cry :
" The angel of the pool is nigh ! "

Well might they shout, the lame, the blind,
 The fevered who had lain
Beside Bethesda's healing wave,
 Through many a day of pain ;
They knew it was the destined hour
When God would show his pitying power.

Then with the selfishness that marks
 Deep misery, they rushed
Towards the holy fount that now
 With heaven-sent freshness gushed ;

For he who first should reach its brink,
New being from its wave might drink.

But there was one who stirless lay
  Upon his weary couch;
Nor sought amid the hurrying crowd
  The troubled waters' touch;
But in his bitter sigh was heard
The agony of "hope deferred."

Almost reproachfully he turned
  His eye upon the stream;
When lo! a gentle voice awoke,
  Like music in a dream,
So soft, so sweet its accents stole, —
"My brother! wilt thou not be whole?"

Slowly he turned his feeble frame,
  And gazed upon a face
Of more than woman's loveliness,
  Of more than kingly grace;
"Alas! in vain my will," he cried,
"I cannot reach Bethesda's tide.

"In more than infant feebleness,
  Through long and changeless years,
I've lain beside this healing pool
  And yet no help appears;
For ere my palsied limbs draw nigh,
The hour of mercy is gone by."

The Saviour bent his noble form,
  A heavenly smile passed o'er
His placid lip : " Arise ! " he cried,
  " Go hence and sin no more ! "
Lo ! touched by those almighty hands,
Once more in manhood's strength he stands.

Surely this deed of wondrous power
  A truth to *us* imparts :
When Heaven's best gifts have not the skill
  To heal our broken hearts,
May we not look through faith to thee
Thou first-born of eternity ?

CHRIST IN THE TEMPEST.

(St. Matthew viii. 24-27.)

MIDNIGHT was on the mighty deep,
    And darkness filled the boundless sky,
    While 'mid the raging wind was heard
  The sea-bird's mournful cry ;
For tempest clouds were mustering wrath
Across the seaman's trackless path.

It came at length ; one fearful gust
  Rent from the mast the shivering sail,
And drove the helpless bark along,
  The plaything of the gale ;
While fearfully the lightning's glare
Fell on the pale brows gathered there.

But there was One o'er whose bright face
  Unmarked the vivid lightnings flashed ;
And on whose stirless, prostrate form
  Unfelt the sea-spray dashed ;
For 'mid the tempest fierce and wild,
He slumbered like a wearied child.

O ! who could look upon that face,
  And feel the sting of coward fear ?
Though hell's fierce demons raged around,
  Yet Heaven itself was here ;
For who that glorious brow could see
Nor own a present Deity?

With hurried fear they press around
  The lowly Saviour's humble bed,
As if his very touch had power
  To shield their souls from dread ;
While, cradled on the raging deep,
He lay in calm and tranquil sleep.

Vainly they struggled with their fears,
  But wilder still the tempest woke,
Till from their full and o'erfraught hearts
  The voice of terror broke :
" Behold ! we sink beneath the wave ;
We perish, Lord ! but thou canst save."

Slowly he rose ; and mild rebuke
  Shone in his soft and heaven-lit eye :
" O ye of little faith," he cried,
  " Is not your master nigh ?

Is not your hope of succor just?
Why know ye not in whom ye trust?"

He turned away, and conscious power
    Dilated his majestic form,
As o'er the boiling sea he bent,
    The ruler of the storm;
Earth to its centre felt the thrill,
As low he murmured: "Peace! Be still!"

Hark to the burst of meeting waves,
    The roaring of the angry sea!
A moment more, and all is hushed
    In deep tranquillity;
While not a breeze is near to break
The mirrored surface of the lake.

Then on the stricken hearts of all,
    Fell anxious doubt and holy awe,
As timidly they gazed on him
    Whose will was nature's law:
"What man is this," they cry, "whose word
E'en by the raging sea is heard?"

THE SURRENDER OF CALAIS.

THE king was in his tent,
    And his lofty heart beat high,
    As he gazed on the city's battered walls
With proud and flashing eye;
But darker grew his brow and stern,
    As slowly onward came
The chiefs who long had dared to spurn
    The terror of his name.

With calm and changeless cheek
    Before the king they stood,
For their native soil to offer up
    The sacrifice of blood.
Like felons were they meanly clad,
    But the lightning of their look,
The marble sternness of their brow,
    E'en the monarch could not brook.

With angry voice he cried:
    "Haste! bear them off to death;
Let the trumpet's joyous shout be blent
    With the traitors' parting breath!"
Then silently they turned away,
    Nor word nor sound awoke,
Till from the monarch's haughty train,
    The voice of horror broke.

4

When hark! a step draws near,
  Not like the heavy clang
Of the warrior's tread, and through the guards
  A female figure sprang:—
"A boon! a boon! my noble king!
  If still thy heart can feel
The love Philippa once could claim,
  Look on me while I kneel!

"'Tis for thyself I pray;
  Let not the dark'ning cloud
Of base-born cruelty arise,
  Thy glory to enshroud!
Nay, nay, I will not rise;
  For never more thy wife
Will hail the victor, till thy soul
  Can conquer passion's strife!

"Turn not away, my king,
  Look not in anger down,
I've lived so long upon thy smile
  I cannot bear thy frown;
O! doom me not, dear lord, to feel
  The pang all pangs above—
To see the light I worship fade,
  And blush for him I love.

"Think how for thee I laid
  My woman's fears aside,
And dared where charging squadrons met,
  With dauntless front to ride;[1]

[1] At the battle of Neville's Cross, in which the Scots were defeated and their king taken prisoner.

Think how, in all the matchless strength
   Of woman's love, I spread
Thy banners, till they proudly waved
   In victory o'er my head.

" Thou saidst that I deserved
   To share thy glorious crown ;
O, force me not to turn away
   In shame from thy renown.
My Edward, thou wert wont to bear
   A kind and gentle heart ;
Then listen to Philippa's prayer,
   And let these men depart."

O, what is all the pride
   Of man's oft boasted power,
Compared with those sweet dreams that wake
   In love's triumphant hour?
Slowly the haughty king unbent
   His stern and vengeful brow,
And the look he turned upon her face
   Was filled with fondness now.

Ne'er yet was woman slow
   To read in tell-tale eyes
Such thoughts as these ; a moment more,
   And on his breast she lies ;
Then while her slender form still clung
   To his supporting arm,
He cried, " Sweet, be it as thou wilt —
   They shall not meet with harm."

Then from the patriot band
    Arose one thrilling cry,
And tears rained down the iron cheek
    That turned unblenched to die;
"Now we indeed are slaves," they cried,
    "Now vain our warlike arts;
Edward has now our shattered walls,
    Philippa wins our hearts."

MARY'S LAMENT.

"The queen ceased not to direct her looks to the shore of France, until the darkness interrupted her wishful eyes. At the dawn of day the coast of France was still in sight, the galleys having made but little progress during the night. While it remained in view she often repeated, 'Farewell, France! farewell! I shall never see you more.'" — CHALMERS' *Life of the Scottish Queen*.

FAREWELL, dear France, my sad heart's chosen
        home,
        Land of my earliest joys, a last farewell.
Still o'er thy shores mine eyes delighted roam,
    But O! the cruel winds the white sails swell,
    And when to-morrow dawns my look shall dwell
Only upon the rushing waves that bear
My bark too swiftly on to reach its port of care.

Alas! alas! till now I never knew
    How sharp might be the thorns that line a crown;
O! woe is mine that thus am doomed to view
    At once the smile of fortune and her frown,
    And find my spirit in the dust cast down,

When pride would bid me think on queenly state,
And spurn mid glory's dreams the humbler ills of fate.

Yet ah ! how can the mournful widow's heart
    Turn to the thoughts ambition might awake !
Doomed from the husband of my youth to part,
    What pleasure now in glory can I take !
    When most I prized it, 'twas for his dear sake ;
My loftiest aim was but to share his throne —
How can my weak hand bear the sceptre's weight alone !

Like you, pale moon, must be my dreary way.
    Lonely she shines, although so pure and bright,
And as she blends not with the sun's rich ray,
    But waits his absence to diffuse her light,
    So only since my day has turned to night
Has so much splendor gathered round my name ;
Alas ! how happier far had I but shared his fame !

But he is gone, and I his heavy loss
    Through many a lonely year am doomed to weep ;
Yet oft my thoughts the dark blue sea will cross
    To seek the spot where all I love doth sleep ;
    For in my husband's grave is buried deep
The all of joy that I could ever taste,
And glory but illumes my lone heart's blighted waste.

FRAGMENT.

THEY knew it was their destiny to sever,
And yet they loved with that intensity,
That deep, devouring passion, which may never
Seek in this selfish world for happiness.
Yet they had learned to suffer, and could see
Their dearest pleasures daily vanishing;
But Fate had yet one arrow left to sting
Their hearts to madness. They could calmly bear
To lose each earthly joy, so they might share
Each other's sorrow, but the hour was nigh
When they must part in life, to linger on
And struggle with a breaking heart alone,
Or yield at once to wretchedness, and die.

She had been beautiful; but now that worst
Most fatal sickness, sorrow, long had preyed
Upon her beauty. Young affection, nurst
In loneliness and tears, 'too soon will fade
The bloom on woman's cheek. Yet she would hide
Her sufferings from him, and whene'er he sighed
In sad foreboding, she would gayly smile,
And with kind, cheerful words his grief beguile.

O! man, ungrateful man can never know
The force of woman's love — how deep, how strong
Is her enduring tenderness in woe.
Still found the firmest friend, when the world's wrong
Weighs on the heart, her hand is ever near
To soothe the pang and wipe the starting tear.

In joy's bright hour her playfulness may gain
A homage that proud man denies in vain;
But 'tis in sorrow, danger, and distress
That woman shines in all her loveliness.
In calm forgetfulness of self she braves
The world's worst storms; one sole reward she craves —
To know that she has turned aside one dart
Meant for his breast, e'en though it rankles in her heart.

THE SISTERS.

HE elder was a small and slender girl,
With sweet low brow, o'erhung by many a curl
Of raven blackness, and soft eyes as blue
As the bright summer sky just trembling through
A silvery cloud; her long dark lashes shaded
A cheek whose roses grief had sadly faded;
But her sweet lips, so statue-like, — O ne'er
Could fancy image loveliness so rare;
Their soft and delicate outline might have seemed
Almost voluptuous,' but that her face beamed
With such soft purity as dwells within
An infant's heart that ne'er has dreamed of sin.

The other sister was more tall and fair,
With lofty forehead, and long dark-brown hair;
Her eyes were bright, but yet they never knew
A beauty of expression or of hue;
At times her cheek wore a slight transient glow,
A trace of earlier days — but her high brow
Was the sole charm that dwelt in Ella's face,
And e'en this was too high for female grace.

And their minds, too, were different. Nina's soul
Was meek and gentle; her soft sweet voice stole
Upon the ear like music heard at night
Across the moonlit waves. Those thousand slight
And nameless kindnesses that to each heart
A feeling of calm tenderness impart,
Like the mild dews that on each flow'ret fall,
Silently shedding freshness upon all;
That unsuspecting innocence which must,
Though oft deceived, to tones of kindness trust;
That purity of heart which never dreams
Man can be other than the thing he seems, —
All these were Nina's charms. But Ella's proud
And haughty spirit never yet had bowed
To such all perfect gentleness; her mind
Was far less feminine. Yet there were kind
And tender feelings hidden in her breast,
But, taught by pride, those feelings she represt;
And oft her heart was crowded by a throng
Of thoughts that the cold world had counted wrong;
Still they were cherished, for she only felt
That none could know the shrine at which she knelt.

It might be wrong that she should thus adore,
But this was nothing, since she calmly bore
The punishment, nor ever sought to be
An idol 'mid the scenes of gayety.

There is a fount of love that ever springs
Unstained and clear in woman's heart, and flings
Its sweetness over all within the sphere
Of her mild kindness ; this made Nina dear
To all that dwelt around her : but 'twas hid
Closely in Ella's bosom, and forbid
To pour its full and perfect tenderness
Where it most wished to flow ; 'twas given to bless
The only being who on her relied
For comfort or affection ; and with pride
She gazed upon her Nina's gentle form,
Whose every slightest movement had a charm
Equally lovely when she gayly smiled
As innocent and playful as a child,
Or when some sudden recollection brought
Back to her heart its dreams of saddened thought.

Nina had suffered sorrow ; her short life
Had been a mournful scene of pain and strife.
Her heart was like a delicate wild flower given
To grow up 'neath the light and dews of heaven,
Unfit to suffer e'en the wind's wild's mirth ;
Yet it had felt the rudest storms of earth,
And when the wintry tempest had passed o'er
It seemed to smile as gayly as before.
Alas ! no sunshine's renovating power
Could give its wonted brightness to that flower,

For withering grief consumed it, and decay
Was slowly wasting all its bloom away.

Months rolled away, but painful thought had lain
With a deep burning weight on Nina's brain,
And maddened her; now 'mid strange fantasies
Her mind was ever dwelling, and her eyes
Roamed o'er the world as o'er a dreary waste
Whose very fruits were bitter to the taste.
Yet was her spirit pure, e'en as the brook,
Though turned aside its course, gives back the look
Of the blue heaven, while meaner things find rest
Only in broken shadows on its breast.
But if there was a solitary trace
Of memory left, 'twas when the mournful face
Of Ella met her view, and still she clung
To that fond bosom while her own was wrung
With agonizing pain; yet Ella's doom
Was one of unmixed suffering, for the bloom
Was quickly fading from young Nina's cheek,
And her frame grew more wasted and more weak, —
Aye, many a lengthened night and weary day
She watched the certain progress of decay
O'er Nina's loveliness, till friendly Death
Gave his last summons. Then, as if the breath
Of some much loved one thrilled her frame, she sighed,
And, smiling tenderly on Ella, died.

EDGAR AND ADA.

"The wretched are the faithful."
BYRON, *Lament of Tasso.*

HE was all manly beauty, and she seemed
As fair a form as ever poet dreamed
'Mid early love's imaginings ; with eyes
Dove-like and beautiful, and lofty brow,
White as the snow on Alpine summits lies ;
Upon her cheek there was a brilliant glow
Like young Aurora's earliest, brightest blush,
Deepening at her sweet lip, till it became
The crimson tint of summer eve ; the flush
Of changeful feeling, hope, or joy, or shame,
Gave sweetness to a face that else had been
Too samely beautiful : none e'er had seen
Her innocent smile but paused to look again,
She seemed so pure, so free from every stain
Of earthly feeling ; and young Edgar's heart
Scarce trusted its own bliss when in her face
He read (what nought save looks can e'er impart)
The love, the tenderness that steals new grace
From maiden bashfulness ; aye, low his proud
And lofty spirit at her shrine was bowed.
The guileless fancies of unsullied youth ;
Its high-souled aspirations after truth ;
The innocent wishes, vague and undefined ;
The brilliant visions of a lofty mind ;
The hope that only on fame's mountain height
His eagle spirit e'er should rest its flight, —

All these were his; and when the traitor Love
Around that spirit's snowy pinions wove
His silken bonds, in vain might he essay
Its heavenward course 'mid myrtle groves to stay;
The soft, light fetters only seemed to bring
Renewed freshness to each radiant wing.

Yet all his soul was hers; and what did she
With such a prize? Did she not joy to see
Its proud upspringing? Did she not aspire
To catch a spark of the ethereal fire?
And did not her less powerful mind reflect
A brightness from his vivid intellect?
No! all too glorious was the dazzling blaze
Of genius placed before her timid gaze;
She shrank before his brilliancy, content
To find in vanity her element.
His love for her was pure as it was deep;
Not like the shallow brook whose wavelets break
When the light breezes o'er its surface sweep,
But like the mighty ocean that can wake
Only to brave the tempest.
But when all thought him happiest, — for the time
When he might claim his promised bride drew near
(Alas! they know not the heart's changeful clime
Who only see its summer flowers), — a shade
Gathered upon his brow; he seemed to wear
Less joyous smiles than he was wont. 'Twas said
That she was faithless; but he breathed not one
Unkind reproach; the soul of life was gone
From him forever; and nought now was left

Save a wide waste of all its bloom bereft.
The idol he had worshipped was o'erthrown;
Its ruined fane was in his heart alone.
Yet he could not believe that she would brook
Another's tenderness — a little while
And she was wedded; he beheld her smile
Upon another with the same sweet look
That once had greeted him: then first he knew
His bosom's hopeless misery; then too
He felt how surely she had withered all
His spirit's high-wrought energies; in vain
He strove his hopes of glory to recall —
Alas! there was no guerdon now to gain.

He deemed hope dead within his heart, and then
Alas! he plunged amid the haunts of men.
Aye, that proud heart, so full of holy feeling,
Was joined unto the world — the stain of earth
So slowly o'er his guileless bosom stealing,
Though hid beneath the sparkling flowers of mirth,
A darker, deeper madness could impart
Than even grief had left within his heart.
His spirit's plumes were sullied; but not long
He paused to hear soft pleasure's syren song;
Not long his noble nature thus could bear
The joys where innocence might find no share.

There was a gentle girl for whom he felt
A brother's tenderness, and she knew well
His wrongs and sufferings; often had she knelt
Beside him when she marked the fearful swell

Of the blue veins upon his brow, which told
That thought again her record had unrolled ;
And she alone his sadness could beguile
With her soft voice, her sweetly pensive smile,
Or soothe with tears she sought not to repress.
She spoke to him of peace (for happiness
She knew he hoped no longer), and she gave
Fresh motive for exertion : day by day
Her gentle kindness won its silent way,
Until he felt that he again could brave
The world's wild storms.   Affection's deepest stream
Was sealed within his bosom ; but the beam
Of kind benevolence across it glowed
Until it seemed as though again it flowed
Unfettered ; but such thought indeed were vain—
Nought now on earth could e'er unloose that chain ;
His lip again a tranquil smile might wear,
But memory's waste was ruled by fell despair.

Yet Ada felt that deep and passionate love
Was in *her* heart ; at first she vainly strove
Against its power ; she knew she ought to fly ;
Yet what kind, gentle one would then be nigh
To watch o'er Edgar's melancholy mood,
And save him from the heart's dread solitude ?
O ! man can never know what treasures lie
Within the quiet depths of woman's soul ;
How strong the fortitude that dares to die
E'en with a broken heart, yet can control
Each painful murmur.   Ada knew she ne'er
Could be aught than his .sister, though so dear

Her innocent heart had held him — a few years
Of mingled joys and sorrows, hopes and fears,
And then they must be parted ; he would wear
Upon his brow the laurel's fadeless bloom,
While her heart, worn by many a secret tear,
Would find its shelter in the silent tomb.

Days passed away, and Ada's bloom had fled.
She felt that soon the city of the dead
Would greet her as its habitant; and yet
Her gentle bosom breathed not one regret :
She feared if she should live and he depart,
Grief might reveal the secret of her heart ;
But now while she could listen to his voice
Whose silver tones bade her sad soul rejoice ;
Now while to her his tenderness was given,
Death was the dearest boon she sought from Heaven.
Yet e'en this consolation was denied ;
For accident revealed what maiden pride
Had closely hidden ; pangs that long had slept
In Edgar's breast were roused : "Have I doomed thee,
Mine innocent child, to hopeless misery?"
He clasped her to his bosom and they wept,
Bitterly wept together ; but she rose
As though the fountains of her weeping froze
E'en in their flow, her arms were round him thrown,
One kiss upon his brow, and she was gone.

Days, weeks passed on ; but from that time he ne'er
Had seen sweet Ada ; many a bitter tear
Had he in secret shed, when he was told

That she was dying; ere that heart was cold
Which had loved him so well, ere she was free
From worldly thoughts, she prayed his face to see.
He came; she sat beside the lattice, where
The jasmine twined its bridal blossoms fair;
A transient blush suffused her cheek; she sighed:
"Think like this flower thine own dear Ada died;
It felt no lightning-stroke, no tempest's strife,
But withered 'neath the sun that gave it life."
She laid her head upon his breast — life's last
And happiest moment — then — her spirit passed!

THE MOTHER.

"To aid thy mind's development; to watch
Thy dawn of little joys; to sit and see
Almost thy very growth; to view thee catch
Knowledge of objects, wonders yet to thee!
To hold thee lightly on a gentle knee,
And print on thy soft cheek a parent's kiss, —
This, it should seem was not reserved for me."

Childe Harold.

HERS was no brilliant beauty; a pale tint,
As if a rose-leaf there had left its print,
Was on her cheek; her brow was high and fair,
Crossed by light waving bands of chestnut hair;
Her eyes were cast down on the lovely boy,
Beside whose couch she knelt; but such calm joy,
Such beautiful tranquillity as dwelt
Upon her features, none have ever felt

Save a fond mother: her tall graceful form
Was bending o'er him, and one round white arm
Supported his fair head, while her hand prest
Her bosom, as she feared that he might start
To feel the quickened pulses of her heart.
Yet still she drew him nearer to her breast
Almost unconsciously.   At length he woke,
And the soft sounds that from his sweet lips broke,
Were like the gentle murmurings of a brook
Along its pebbly channel; but her look
Told joy that lay too deep for smiles or tears:
'Twas a strange happiness where hopes and fears
Were wildly blended, yet *'twas* happiness;
For well she knew that nought on earth could bless
A woman's heart like the deep, deathless love
A mother feels: all other joys may prove
But sin or vanity; this, this alone
With perfect peace and purity is fraught.
On the fair tablet of a mother's thought
There is no stain of passion; 'tis the one
Sole trace of that pure joy man's knowledge cost, —
Sole remnant of the heaven our parents lost.

When first man from his paradise was driven,
Woman's sweet wiles and witcheries were given
To cheer him through life's dreary wilderness;
But what was left *her* erring heart to bless?
She once had loved him as a being sent
From heaven in God's own image, yet he went
Astray e'en at her bidding — loved she less?
No, but her adoration now was o'er;

And earthly passions, sinless now no more,
Absorbed her heart, while every pang or sigh
That burst from him thrilled her with agony.
His stern reproach, too, she endured unmoved
And patient, for she felt how much she loved.
Then, to repay her sufferings, and atone
For man's unkindness, seeds of joy were sown
Within her heart — a mother's love was given,
And this repaid her for the loss of heaven.

O ! but to watch the infant as he lies
Pillowed upon his mother's breast ; his eyes
Fixed on her face, as if his only light
On earth beamed from that face with fondness bright ;
Or to gaze on him sleeping, while his cheek
Moves with her heart's glad throbbings that bespeak
Feeling too full for words ; see him break
The silken chains of slumber and awake
All light and beauty, while he lisps her name —
"Mother, !" — although his childish lips can frame
No other sound. O ! who, with joy like this
Could ask from heaven a dearer, deeper bliss ?

Again I saw the mother bending o'er
The pillow of her babe ; but joy no more
Was pictured in her face : her sunken cheek,
Her faltering accents, tremulous and weak,
Told a sad tale : she had hung o'er that couch
For many a weary night, and every touch
Of his thin, wasted hand seemed to impart
A thrilling sense of pain to her young heart ;

Yet deemed she not that death could now destroy
So bright a blossom as her darling boy.
She feared not that; she felt she could not bring
Aught to relieve him; this to her was death.
But when at last she felt his feverish breath
Pass o'er her brow, the deadly withering
Of early hope that young hearts only know,
First taught her all a youthful mother's woe.
Oft would she check the bursting sob of pain
When, as she marked the evening planets wane,
She thought that though another day had past,
Another came as mournful as the last;
And oftentimes the bright, big tear unbid
Would gather slowly 'neath her long-fringed lid,
As rain-drops mark the coming storm whose shock
Shall blast the wild flower and its sheltering rock
In the same ruin; but each coming day
She saw him wasting. One eve as he lay
Within her arms, the moonbeams shining bright
Gave to his pallid face a ghastly light:
She gazed on him — she bent to hear his breath —
His heart throbbed faintly — then — she gazed on Death!

MINA.

*" Nature is fine in love ; and when 'tis fine
It sends some precious instance of itself
After the thing it loves." — Hamlet.*

T was the place of tombs ; the dark-leaved yew
And bending willow their sad shadows threw
Across the lowly graves ; no sound was heard
Save the soft murmur of a rippling stream,
Or the light carol of the lark that stirred
The balmy air with music : it might seem
That all things slept in some delicious dream.
There was a hillock decked with many a wreath
Of young spring-flowers, but they had faded 'neath
The morning sun, like young hopes pure and bright
Withering beneath the look that gave them light.
And to that grave there came the form of one
Who had been beautiful ; but sickness now,
And sorrow, too, had marked her for their own,
And stolen the joyous beauty from her brow.
On the damp grass she many a night had lain,
The star-gemmed heavens her only canopy ;
And this had dimmed the lustre of her eye,
And faded her young cheek ; she came again
To deck with fresh culled flowers the lonely spot
She loved so well. She sighed : " Sure these are not
The flowers I braided ; ah ! the cruel sun
Has touched them, and their loveliness is gone."
She threw herself beside the grave and wreathed
The dewy flowers, while mournfully she breathed
A low and broken melody : —

Aye, flowers may glow
In new-born beauty, and the rosy spring
To deck the earth her sparkling wreaths may bring;
But where art thou?

The early bloom
Of flowers in freshest infancy I wreathe,
Their transient life of fragrancy to breathe
Upon thy tomb.

And I have sought
The lowly violet, that in shade appears
Shrinking from view, like young love's tender fears,
With sweetness fraught.

And rosebuds, too,
Crimson as young Aurora's blush, 'or white
As woman's cheek when touched by sorrow's blight,
O'er thee I strew.

And flowers that close
Their buds beneath the sun, but pure and pale
Ope their sweet blossoms 'neath the dewy veil
That evening throws.

The fragrant leaves
Of the white lily, too, with these I twine,
The drooping lily that seems born to shine
Where true love grieves.

But what doth this
Half withered bud amid my blooming wreath? ·
Already its young charms have faded 'neath
          The sun's warm kiss.

          Ah! this shall lie
Upon my bosom; it is fit to strew
Such blighted flowers o'er her who only knew
          To love and die!—

          There will be none
To deck thy grave with flowers and chant for thee
These snatches of remembered melody
          When I am gone;

          But thou shalt have
A gift more pure than e'en the buds I fling—
A broken heart—my latest offering
          Upon thy grave.

.   .   .   .   She laid
Upon the verdant flower-wreathed turf her head;
The breeze amid her long, dark ringlets played,
And thus she slept—the dying with the dead.

Hers was no wondrous history; should we seek
The cause that fades the bloom of woman's cheek,
'Twould oft be found a tale like this,—she loved
As woman ever loves—undoubtingly;
His rich-toned voice o'er her young pulses moved

Like the soft breath of summer airs that sigh
Upon the wind-god's harp; his glorious eye
To her was as the sunbeam from on high
Nursing the passion-flowers within her heart,
And teaching them their fragrance to impart.
He knew not all her love; she taught the deep
And strong emotions of her breast to sleep
Beneath mirth's semblance, and whene'er she heard
His footstep, though her feelings wildly stirred,
The trembling of her downcast lid, her cheek
Suffused with blushes — these alone could speak
Her woman's fondness. Ernold toyed awhile
With the fond heart whose every throb was fraught
With tenderness for him; and then the smile
Of one more fair claimed all the truant's thought.
Aye, thus man values woman's heart — a toy
That may amuse his changeful hours of joy,
Or charm his bosom's waywardness, then cast
Aside, or broken when the mood is past.

'Twere vain to tell of Mina's hopes and fears,
Her seeming gayety and secret tears;
Woman too oft is doomed such pangs to prove,
And man — why should he know of woman's love?
Too soon the loved, the faithless one was wed
To one so beautiful she seemed to make
A very heaven about her, and to take
Captive those hearts whence feeling long had fled;
Yet she was cold to him as is the snow
On mountain tops — she should have been as pure —
And silently he bade his heart endure

To see the same cold smiles upon her brow,
Like sunbeams glittering o'er a frozen lake.
At length came one with magic power to wake
The beautiful statue into life, and she
Who should have shared her husband's destiny,
Unchanged through every change, was faithless! gave
Her name, her honor to become the slave
Of sinful passion. From that fatal day
Grief wore the wretched Ernold's life away;
And when pain thus had wrung him, and decay
Had marked him for the grave, remembering nought
Save that he now was wretched, Mina sought
To soothe his misery; and oft she led
His trembling footsteps to the river side,
Upon whose green bank they were wont to tread
When life was brighter, and whene'er he tried
To banish sad remembrance, she would smile
And seek with cheerful words his grief to 'guile.
Death came at length; she lived to dress his tomb
With sweet spring flowers, but pain had stolen her
        bloom.
She knew that she was dying; one bright morn
She went again the green grave to adorn,
But she returned not — she had calmly laid
Her cheek upon the grassy mound, a braid
Of fresh buds in her hand, and thus beside
Her lover's tomb her latest breath was sighed.

THE BRIDE.

"Say, as ye point to my early tomb,
That the lover was dear though the bridegroom had come."
Anon.

"But neither bended knees, pure hands held up,
Sad sighs, deep groans, nor silver-shedding tears,
Could penetrate her uncompassionate sire.'
Shakespeare.

THE lady sat in sadness ; her fair lid
Shrouding her eye's dark beauty ; while soft hands
Were wreathing her thick tresses, and amid
The glossy ringlets twining costly bands
Of snowy pearls ; but oft the deep-drawn sigh
Heaved the rich robe that folded o'er her breast ;
And when she raised her head, within her eye
Sparkled a tear which would not be represt.
She glanced towards the mirror, and a smile
Crossed her sweet lip — it was a woman's feeling
Of mingled pride and pleasure, even while
The blight of sorrow o'er her heart was stealing :
Yet as she gazed she thought of by-past hours,
When she was wont, within the orange bowers,
To sit beneath the moonlight ; and the arm
Of one she loved was folded round her form,
While to his throbbing breast she oft would cling
And playfully her loosen'd tresses fling,
Light fetters, o'er his neck ; then, with bright cheek,
Smile when he strove his tenderness to speak.

Another change came o'er her face ; she turned
And raised a crystal cup that near her stood ;

Upon her cheek a deeper crimson burned,
And to her eye there rushed a fearful flood
Of wild emotion : eagerly she quaffed,
With trembling lip, the strangely blended draught,
And then in low and faltering accents cried :
" Am I not now a gay and happy bride ? "

   .   .   .   .

She stood before the altar ; her pale brow
Uplifted to the holy cross. The sun
Shed through the painted window a deep glow
Upon her cheek ; and he who thus had won
Her hand without her heart, was at her side ;
The dark-robed priest, too ; but as less allied
To earth than heaven, she stood.   When called to speak
The sad response, her voice had grown so weak
She scarce could utter it ; her fragile form
Shook with convulsed emotion ; but the arm
Of her stern sire supported her ; her head
Fell helpless on her breast, and she was wed.
The bridegroom pressed his lip to her pale face ;
She shrunk from him as loathing his embrace ;
Then starting up with fearful calmness said :
" Father, I promised ; have I not obeyed ?
But there is yet another vow unpaid ;
For I am the betrothed of Death, and lo !
The bridegroom waits his promised bride, e'en now.
Our nuptial torch shall be the glow-worm's light ;
Our bridal bed the grave. O ! it is sweet
To think that there no grief can throw its blight
O'er young affection — yes, e'en I can greet

The marriage cup when drugged with aconite."
She trembled — would have fallen ; but again
Her haughty father's arm was near : her breath
Grew fainter ; her breast heaved as with pain ;
Lowly she murmured : " Let my bridal wreath
Lie on my bier — he deems me faithless — now
Let him bend o'er this pale and stony brow,
And learn how well I loved " — one fleeting spot
Of crimson crossed her cheek — and she was not.

L'IMPROVISATRICE.

" As in the sweetest bud
The eating canker dwells, so eating love
Inhabits in the fairest wits of all."
Two Gentlemen of Verona.

ER cheek, white as the snowy couch, was prest
Against her delicate hand ; and her dark eye
Beamed with unearthly light and purity :
A hue like that within the rosebud's breast
Was on her lip, and thus she told the tale
Of sorrow which had made her cheek so pale.

It was in life's young morn ; sixteen short springs
Had scarce yet bloomed for me ; my soul was filled
With vague and wandering hopes ; imaginings
Of some yet unknown bliss my bosom thrilled :
I dreamed of some one loving and beloved,

Though yet unseen, whose gentle whispers moved
Like music o'er my spirit, till my heart
Was all attuned to tenderness and love.
It needed but a master's hand to rove
Amid its chords, and teach them to impart,
A melody of magic power to bless,
Whose very echoes had been happiness.
Then, then 'twas I first saw him ; the dark eye
Where dwelt the pride of intellect, the high
And snowy forehead, the lip full and bright,
The beaming smile like heaven's own sunny light —
These were the charms that met my gaze, yet O !
"Twas not alone the beauty of his brow
That won my heart ; it was the mind that dwelt
Within his form before whose shrine I knelt.
Yet I knew not I loved him ; from the time
When I first saw him, and love's passion-flower
Was budded in my young heart's sunny clime,
Until the sad and well remembered hour
That saw its full and perfect blossoming
In ripened beauty, I knew not how well
My tenderness had nursed the fragile thing.
Alas ! his presence was a mighty spell
'Gainst which I could not strive : his look, his smile
Had ever power my sadness to beguile ;
A glance from his all speaking eye at will
The troubled waves of painful thought could still.
He was unhappy, but I knew not why ;
It was enough for me that the deep sigh
Oft heaved his bosom, and the darkening shade
Oft crost his brow, and bade his sweet smile fade.

Why lengthen out the tale? Months rolled away,
Yet I was happy, and each changing day
Brought me new pleasure; for I still could see
The being dearer than the world to me.
But now we soon must sever; I should be
Forgot, or only claim a passing thought,
Although his every look and tone were fraught
With sad remembrance for my after years
Of pain and sorrow, loneliness and tears.

Once — 'twas in twilight's hour — we sat alone.
Each heart responding to a saddened tone.
I had been weeping bitterly, and now
One hand was prest against my throbbing brow,
The other lay in his; — I had nor power
Nor will to draw it thence: then bending o'er
He spoke in gentlest words, and, with a smile
Full of calm tenderness, he sought to 'guile
My mournful feelings, and I felt his arm
An instant closely clasped around my form;
I felt his lip upon my burning cheek —
The *first, first* kiss! I sprang from his embrace
To hide my tearful and, aye, happy face;
A moment past, and then, O! words were weak
My bosom's thrilling agony to speak:
Then first mine eyes were opened, and I knew
How dearly my heart held him, and then too
Came the conviction that I loved in vain;
I dare not dwell on this — too much of pain
Lies in the thought. On the next night we parted,
But stranger eyes were near, and cold ones stood

Around us, and I stilled the fearful flood
Of wild emotion ; though half broken-hearted,
My voice ne'er faltered, and my clouded eye
Was tearless ; if the deep-drawn, struggling sigh
Burst from my lip, 'twas all unheeded, while
My changeless cheek still wore a careless smile.

We parted ne'er to meet as we had met.
I knew too well he loved me not, and yet
'Twas sweet to hear the music of his voice,
And 'neath his smiles to feel my soul rejoice.
Time passed away, yet did my bosom cherish
Its fond idolatry ; aye, love may perish
When nurst 'mid pleasures, but the love that springs
From sorrow, fed by hopelessness, still clings
To the young heart unchanged through every change ;
No grief can chill it, and no time estrange ;
It lives until it wastes the heart away ;
And such was mine — why do I thus delay ?

There was a young, fair girl, with dove-like, eyes,
And voice as gentle as the south wind's sighs ;
And when long months had passed away, and I
Again beheld him, he was seated nigh
That gentle girl ; methought his bright eye burned
More brightly when upon her face it turned.
'Twas said he sought her for his bride, and she
Returned no answering fondness. Could it be .
That he to one who loved him not had given
The tenderness which would have been my heaven ?
I never met him save when at her side,

And then my heart swelled high with woman's pride,
And hid my woman's love. At length I grew
Reckless of everything in life ; a new
And fearful demon haunted all my hours,
And charged with venom all my path's few flowers.
And then — then — all grew darkness ; ask me not
What cast that shadow o'er my wayward lot —
'Twas my own folly — madness ; but no more
Memory extends a barren wildness there
And life would fail me ere I could tell o'er
My bosom's agony, my heart's despair.
But soon a sudden gleam of light dispelled
The darksome cloud, and then my proud heart swelled
With loftier feelings ; I had sometimes strung
My humble lyre, and in low accents sung
Of love and sorrow ; now they bade me sweep
Its chords with bolder hand, nor let them sleep
In silence ; and some said that on my brow
Ere long the poet's garland might be twined.
From that hour I was changed ; I sought not now
To die and leave no memory behind ;
I bade my sleeping intellect unbind
Its listless pinions, and with lofty flight
Soar 'mid Imagination's realms of light ;
I taught my lyre with Fancy's flame to glow,
And the soft notes in loftier strains to flow ;
While gay ones marveled I could spend my days
In painful study. They knew not how strong
The impulse was ; 'twas not mere love of praise
That bade me seek the highly gifted song.
Ah no ! I hoped the time would come when he

Would listen to my melancholy lays:
I hoped that he, so loved though lost, would see,
Gladly, some future day, my humble name
Placed high upon the glorious lists of fame,
And that "the sweet surprise of sudden joy"
Would fill his generous heart, when he beheld
The reckless girl, whom he so long had held
To be the sport of levity, the toy
Of wayward feeling, teach her soaring soul
To spurn the fetters of the world's control ;
And with the pride of genius bear away
Upon her woman's brow the deathless bay.
Were these hopes blighted ?

Since I first saw him five long years have past,
And I am dying ; yet 'tis not the hand
Of grief that o'er my brow this shade has cast :
I long have ceased to weep; an icy band
Seems drawn about my heart; I *cannot* weep,
But now upon my lone couch I could lie
As calmly as an infant turns to sleep
Upon his gentle mother's breast — and die.

THE SHEPHERD BOY.

" Ma pur si aspre vie, ne si selvagge
Cercar non so ch' Amor non venga sempre
Ragionando con meco ed io con lui."

Petrarca.

HE was a slender boy; his coal black hair
Hung in thick masses o'er his brow so fair.
His cheek was pale and sunken, and the light
Of his dark eye seemed as it *had* been bright,
Though now its flashing glance was quenched in tears,
And grief seemed preying on his· early years.
O'erspent with toil he stood; his native land
Lay far beyond the ken of that low vale
Whose gentle breezes now his hot cheek fanned;
And when he strove to tell his simple tale,
It was in broken accents, but with tone
Sweet as love's whisper : he was all alone
In the wide world, and now he sought a home
Where coldness or unkindness could not come.

Four changeful seasons now had rolled away
Since first Celesto dwelt within that vale,
An humble shepherd boy, and yet no ray
Of joy e'er visited his cheek so pale.
He shunned the crowd of gay ones that were met
Upon the green at summer eve ; nor yet
Did he e'er seek to win a maiden's smile :
It seemed that nought on earth had power to 'guile
His wretchedness. He loved alone to sit
And watch the bright and various clouds that flit

Across the sunset sky, or stretched beneath
The fragrant orange groves, to list the breath
Of Zephyr sweeping o'er the leaves that sigh
In answer and return sweet melody.
Once, and once, only, did the sad boy quit
His lonely haunts and join the festive throng;
And then he seized the light guitar and wove,
In broken strains, a melancholy song,
Breathing of blighted hope and hapless love : —

They called her fair; and she oft had heard
    The voice of song in the moon-lit grove;
But O! how wildly her pulses stirred
    When first she bent to the voice of love!

Like heaven's sweet breath o'er the wind god's lyre,
    It woke its tones in her guileless heart;
But scarcely can heaven itself inspire
    Such joy as dwells in love's witching art.

To him who wakened each sleeping string
    She gave her heart; but be this the token
How well he valued the fragile thing, —
    The music has ceased! the heart is broken!

There was a young, fair girl with sunny brow,
And cheek where smiles were ever wont to glow,
The gayest 'mid the gay ones, but her eye
Lost its bright gladness, and despondency
Marked her once laughing face; her faded cheek
Was pale, save when she heard Celesto's name,

And then quick deepening blushes o'er it came —
Those tell-tales that a maiden's fondness speak.
The boy knew that she loved him, but he felt
That none would love him long; for grief had dwelt
Within his heart until it wore away
His life. Although his eye and cheek grew bright,
Yet 'twas the soul's last effort to give light
And beauty to the wasting frame's decay,
And steal from death part of its agony.
Soon, very soon, the boy knew he must die,
And then he sought the pale girl, and unrolled
The tablets of sad memory; then he told
His mournful tale. From that time, though the trace
Of tears was often left on Annette's face,
Yet was her spirit calm.

                At length, one morn,
In that bright season when earth seems new born,
She sought the spot Celesto loved to tread,
And there she saw the fair boy lying — dead !
They came to robe him in funereal vest,
And then they found a maiden's snowy breast
Beneath the shepherd's coat. The imaged form
Of one whose eye possessed the serpent's charm,
Hung from her neck —a dark-browed cavalier.
They sought from sad Annette the tale to hear,
But she was silent: thus by all unknown
The hapless maiden lies. A solitary stone,
Graved with the name Celesta, marks her tomb,
The only relic of her mournful doom.

CLARA.

" You bear a gentle mind, and heavenly blessings
Follow such creatures."

Henry VIII.

SHE had sprung up like a sweet wild flower, hid
From common eyes, in some lone dell, amid
The light and dews of heaven; and ne'er was
found
A purer bud on earth's unhallowed ground.
Her face was fair, but the admiring eye
Loved less its beauty than its purity;
No cloud e'er darkened o'er that placid brow;
No care e'er dimmed her bright smile's sunny glow;
A gentle heart that ne'er had dreamed of sin
Or suffering, shone her dove-like eyes within;
And the high hope that with such calm joy stirs
The trusting soul — the Christian's hope — was hers:
'Twas this that gave such sweetness to a mien
So softly gay, so peaceful and serene;
Calm without apathy, as woman mild,
Yet innocent and playful as a child.

But in her heart there was one unbreathed thought
With all a woman's holiest fondness fraught.
Here was not wild, fierce passion, such as glows
In untamed hearts, but the calm love that grows
Within the soul like an expanding flower,
Breathing its perfume o'er each passing hour:
From infancy it grew. The graceful boy
To whose embrace she clung with childish joy,

And on whose breast her head had oft reposed
When weariness her infant eyes had closed,
Was still as dear to her young bosom now,
Though time had written man upon his brow.
There was no shame in such a love concealed
In her heart's quiet depths, or but revealed
By the slight tremor or the blush that came
O'er cheek and bosom when she heard his name.

And did not Henry look with loving eyes
On the fair orphan who so tenderly
Cherished his image?   Long he vainly strove
To check the feeling he dared not call love ;
He thought of earlier days when she had smiled
In his encircling arms, a reckless child ;
Could she forget the difference in their years
And listen to a lover's hopes and fears
From one so much her elder?   He might claim
A sister's tenderness ; but the pure flame
Of deep and deathless love could never be
Kindled by him in its intensity.
Thus deemed he in his hopelessness ; but vain
His efforts to repress the thrilling pain
That filled his heart, while thinking of the hour
When he should see his loved and cherished flower
Breathing its fragrance in another's bower.

One balmy summer eve, with him she roved
Through many a greenwood haunt they long had loved ;
When as they gazed upon the glorious west,
Dark clouds obscured the bright sun's glowing crest ;

And through the forest trees the wind's wild cry
Rang as of some strong man in agony.
A storm was coming, and, while pale with fear,
She clung to him, his own proud castle near
Offered them shelter; in his arms he bore
The maiden to those halls oft trod before
In childhood's day; and while the tempest's strife
Blackened the scene so late with gladness rife,
His heart was filled with joy; for maiden pride
Was hushed by fear, and Clara dared to hide
Her face upon his breast, while the red fire
Flashed from dark clouds careering in their ire
Like angry spirits; ere an hour had past,
The storm was spent, and its terrific blast
Hushed into stillness; but before they turned
To leave the spot, the restless thoughts that burned
In Henry's breast were breathed o'er Clara's cheek,
And silence answered more than words could speak.

And they were wed. O, gentle Love, how dear
Is thy sweet influence when thou dost rear
Amid our household gods thy sacred shrine,
And givest thy torch upon our hearths to shine,
Folding in calm repose thy radiant wings,
And gathering round our homes earth's purest, loveliest
        things!

THE LONELY ONE.

" What deep wounds ever closed without a scar?
   The heart bleeds longest, and but heals to wear
   That which disfigures it ; and they who war
   With their own hopes, and have been vanquished, bear
   Silence but not submission."

Childe Harold.

 HERS was not such love as worldings feel ;
But an intense and passionate devotion,
Pure as an infant thought, was in her heart.
Yet she had none of woman's charms ; the low
And gentle voice, the full bright lip, the eye
All light and beauty, — these were not for her.
But on her spirit genius poured its rays,
And in her eye the pride of intellect
Was visibly enthroned ; yet proved she not
Herself a mere, mere woman, when she gave
Her heart to man's control? No, he was one
Whom not to love had almost been a crime :
It seemed that Heaven had formed him to be loved
E'en as itself was worshipped : well did she.
Obey its will ; he was the life, the soul
Of her existence ; and she poured forth all
The richest fullness of her untouched heart
As incense on his shrine, e'en though she knew
Its sweetness would be wasted. Hopelessly
She gave it ; for she knew he looked on her
With kindness, friendship, everything but love.
And yet she murmured not ; could she repine
When she received a brother's tenderness?
She turned from scenes of gayety : for there

She could not think of him ; and gifted ones
Oft sought her love as 'twere a precious thing.
But how could one who worshipped the bright sun,
Pay the same homage to the meaner stars?
She gave herself to loneliness ; a life
Of self-devotion to her hopeless love
Was dearer to her than all earthly joy.

At length the hour she long had looked for came,
And he was wed. She knew the very hour
That gave him to another. It were vain
To paint the fearful conflict of her heart ;
She knew he would be wretched if he dreamed
Of her deep sorrow ; and this gave her strength
To conquer woman's weakness. When she next
Beheld him he was near his youthful bride :
Calmly she met his proffered hand, and looked
With smiles on her bright face, and though her cheek
Was deadly pale, yet her voice faltered not.
Her course through life was marked out by the hand
Of changeless destiny ; her days were past
In painful study ; she explored the paths
Of science with a sad delight ; for one
Faint hope yet lingered, that, in after years,
When men should breathe her name in tones of praise,
He would remember her with thoughts of pride.
Yet she was not unhappy ; she had taught
His wife to love her, and the innocent face
Of his fair child oft rested on her heart,
While its soft arms were twined about her neck
With all an infant's fondness.

Years passed on,
And long ere she had reached life's middle course,
Sorrow amid the lone one's dark brown locks
Had mingled silver, while her sunken cheek
And wasted figure told a mournful tale
Of the heart's struggle. Well had she subdued
Each rebel thought ; her eye no longer quailed
In anguish to behold his tenderness
Bestowed upon another ; for she gave
To his fair child the fullness of that love
She dared not yield to him. Alas ! alas !
And did she think the heart would thus be swayed
E'en as she listed ; that her will could change
The course of its affections ? vain deceit !
E'en as the breath of winter, while it binds
The mountain torrent in its icy chains,
Checks not the current which still rushes on
Beneath its frozen surface, so the strong,
Resistless energy of mind may stay
The outward struggles of the restless soul,
But cannot reach its inmost depths, where still
The waves of passion moan. Too soon she knew
How much she was deceived. Death came, but not
To her who waited him ; the grief-worn frame
Was all too mean a prey for him ; he seized
The gentle wife and mother ; she whose life
Had been a fairy tale.

No selfish thought
Was in the bosom of the lonely one,
As, bending o'er the bed of death, she wept,

Mingling her tears with his; but when she found
That still he sought for comfort in her kindness,
E'en when the smile revisited his lip,
What marvel if within her breast awoke
Again the sweet delusions of young hope.
The passionate feelings of his youth were gone;
And now he turned with tranquil tenderness
To her affection, e'en as one will pause,
Amid the weary vanities of life,
To hear some half-forgotten melody
That charmed his childish hours; but ah! the heart
Which bore so well with sorrow could not brook
The fullness of such joy; and as the flower
May bide the pelting of the storm, to die
Beneath the very sun that gave it life,
Thus did she wither. But how did she shrink
To meet the death she once had sought; how weep
To check again the love but half subdued?
Thus months and weeks passed onward, until he
Who, in her hour of youth and bloom, had turned
In coldness from her love, now sought for it
As 'twere his very being. Who can speak
The anguish of her spirit, as with sick
And swelling heart she gasped: "It is too late!"
As the worn traveller amid the wilds
Of burning Araby, o'erspent with toil,
Falls ere he reach the brink of that pure wave
Which proffers life to his parched lip, thus she
Found joy within her grasp but when she knew
It was her last, her dying hour. She died —

Yet as a day of storms will ofttimes sink
With a rich burst of sunlight at its close,
Thus did the rays of happiness illume
Her parting spirit.

AN HOUR OF SADNESS.

'M weary of this false and hollow world !
Its brightest smile is but the fickle light
That leads the 'wildered traveller astray ;
Its dearest joys are but vain morning dreams ;
Its very mirth is madness ; and the man
Who seems most blest, is only he who best
Can feign, and 'neath a smiling brow conceal
The bosom's secret anguish. There is nought
On earth but sorrow. Where can mortals look
For happiness or peace? Shall we seek fame,
Ambition, knowledge, love?   Alas ! in vain.
The laurel wreath is stained with human blood,
Or blighted by the feverish breath of him
Who won it by the sacrifice of health.
What can ambition give? Vain man may tread
Upon the neck of thousands, and become
A god among the nations, yet his deeds
Will be forgotten. Knowledge, too, is but
The painful guerdon of protracted toil.
And thou, Love ! though thine altar is in heaven,
Thy flame is burning in the hearts of those

That worship thee on earth. O it is sad
That aught so sweet should bring such desolation —
That woman, too, that gentle, timid woman
Should oft'nest be the victim. When success
Has crowned thy votaries, they have found the prize
Scarce worth the pain and anguish that it cost ;
Or, if unkindly early hope is crost,
The end is death or madness.
All, all is sorrow ! Ask the aged man
By his enjoyments to compute his years ;
Will he *then* say that he can count three-score ?
O ! happy they who die ere they awake
From their illusive dream of joy. Men weep
Upon the early tomb which haply saved
Its tenant from a thousand living deaths ;
And happy they whom the first grief can kill —
Who are not doomed to drag the lengthened chain
Of wearisome existence — but to live
Among the selfish beings of this earth,
As one whose thoughts dwell elsewhere — to endure
The secret workings of a restless spirit
That once aspired to higher, nobler things ;
To bear the desolation of a heart
Broken by early suffering, and to feel
That though we would not live, we cannot die !
This, this is sorrow, yet it may be borne.
For many painful years, e'en in life's spring
It may have been endured, and yet the lip
May wear a smile. But 'tis a bitter mirth
That seems to mock itself ; the eye may beam,
The cheek still brightly glow, but on the brow

Are furrows which the hand of Time ne'er planted —
Traces of scathing grief.   And this is life !
This is the life to which fond man will cling
And spend his years in toil, yet vainly strive
'Gainst friendly Death.   O doom me not, sweet
     Heaven,
To waste, Prometheus-like, away, but grant
To me thy kindliest boon — an early grave !

TO FRANCESCA.

WHO thy brow's sweet pensiveness can view,
    Thy blue eye's deep and thrilling tenderness,
Thy witching mouth, thy young cheek's tender
    hue,
Nor feel emotions he may not express.

Thine is not brilliant beauty; there may be
    Forms which can boast of more majestic grace
And brighter cheeks, but none can ever see
    Such pure, pale softness in another face.

It is the mind that in each feature gleams,
    The feeling that each gentle glance displays,
The heart as pure as infancy's young dreams, —
    They are more sweet than beauty's brightest rays.

Yet I have seen that brow with grief o'ercast,
    And those eyes dimmed with sorrow's bitter tears —

Ah! even from thee is pleasure fleeting fast?
  Art thou, too, doomed to sad and lonely years?

O! may the task to soothe thy woes be mine;
  And though the brilliant flowers of joy be dead,
Yet some pale buds of hope I yet may twine,
  Their gentle fragrance o'er thy heart to shed.

LOVE.

O love, what is it? 'Tis to shed
    Fond woman's little all of light
  On rainbow clouds, whose tints are fled
  Ere scarce they meet the raptured sight;
To yield her youthful heart to one,
    To live on earth for him alone,
And feel 'twere almost grief to bear
    E'en bliss unless he, too, might share.

To give to one her every thought,
    And feel that even though bereft
Of every joy on earth, 'twere nought,
    So the wide storm that dear one left;
To know that she to him has given
    The worship which was due to Heaven —
Yet in his love to find such bliss
    She asks no other heaven than this.

Vain man may talk of woman's guile,
  And curse the hour he learned to prize
The magic of her sunny smile,
  And drink the light of her sweet eyes.
But timid woman may not speak
  The wrongs that pale her tender cheek ;
No, deep within her heart they lie —
  What matters it ? she can but die.

Full many a cheek has lost its bloom,
  And many a brilliant eye grown dim ;
Man heeds it not — the silent tomb
  Soon shrouds the heart that broke for him.
When first he was allowed to sip
  The honey-dew from woman's lip,
And knew that it was all his own,
  Its greatest charm for him was gone.

O woman's love is a gentle light,
  That sheds its beams on hope's young bowers,
Man's is the fell sirocco's blight,
  That blasts the fairest, sweetest flowers ;
Yet, though the buds of hope are gone,
  That steady light will still shine on,
Shine on, despite of grief and gloom,
  Like sunbeams o'er a mouldering tomb.

TO THE EVENING·STAR.

> " A single star
> Is rising in the east, and from afar
> Sheds a most tremulous lustre ; silent night
> Doth wear it like a jewel on her brow."
>
> *Barry Cornwall.*
>
> " O what a vision were the stars
> When first I saw them burn on high."
>
> *Moore.*

PALE, melancholy star ! that pourest thy beams
So mildly on my brow, pure as the tear
A pitying angel sheds o'er earthly sorrow,
I love to sit beneath thy light, and yield
My heart to its strange musings, wayward dreams
Of things inscrutable, and searching thoughts
That would aspire to dwell in yon high sphere.
I love to think that thou art a bright world
Where bliss and beauty dwell — where never sin
Has entered to destroy the perfect joys
Of its pure, holy habitants. 'Tis sweet
To fancy such a quiet, peaceful home
Of innocence, and purity, and love.
There the first sire still dwells with all his race,
From his loved eldest-born to the sweet babe
Of yesterday ; there gentle maids are seen,
Fair as the sun, with all that tenderness
So sweet in woman ; and soft eyes that beam
The fondest love, but freed from passion's stain.
There all have high communion with their God,
And though the fruit of knowledge is not plucked,
Yet doth its fragrance breathe on all around.

O ! what can knowledge give, to recompense
The happy ignorance it cost? Man gave
His heaven to gain it; what was his reward?
Deep, lasting misery!

Sweet star ! can those in thy bright sphere behold
Our fallen world? do they not weep to view
Our blighting sorrows? and do they not veil
Their brows in shame, to see Heaven's choicest gifts
Profaned and trampled by our maddening passions?
Surely this world is now as beautiful
As 'twas in earliest prime : the earth still blooms
With flowers and brilliant verdure ; the dark trees
Are thick with foilage, and the mountains tower
In proud sublimity ; the waters glide
All smoothly 'mid the green, enameled mead,
Or dash o'er broken cliffs, flinging their spray
In high fantastic whirls. Surely 'tis fair
As it could be before the wasting flood
Had whelmed it. Let us forth and gaze upon
The face of nature. All is peaceful now,
Yet man will tread there too ; cities will rise
Where now the wild bird sings ; thousands will dwell
Where all is loneliness ; but will it be
More beautiful? No ; where the wild flowers spring,
Where nought but the bird's note is heard, we may
Find friends in every leaf; each simple bud
Speaks to the heart and fills it with the sweet,
Soft tenderness of childhood ; but vain man
Makes it a peopled wilderness : the blight
Of disappointment and distrust is found

7

Wherever man has made his troubled home ;
And the most fearful desert is the spot
Where he best loves to dwell.

O, let me hope, while gazing on thy light,
Sweet star, that yet a peaceful home is left
For those sad spirits who have found this world
All sin and sorrow. Haply in thy sphere
I yet may dwell, when cleansed from all the stains
Of passions that too darkly dwell within
This throbbing heart. O ! had I early died,
I might have been a pure and sinless child
In some sweet planet ; and my only toil,
To light my censer by the sun's bright rays,
And fling its fire forever towards the throne
Of the Eternal One.

TO FANCY.

" Fancy, my internal sight."
Milton.

SWEET Fancy ! I have been thy favored child
From earliest infancy ; and thou wert wont
To show me thy bright imagery, ere yet
My young lips could frame language to describe
The fair but fleeting shadows: thou hast nursed
Those warm and ardent feelings nature gave ;
And though 'tis true that thou hast taught my heart
To heave the quickened throb of deeper anguish

Than cold ones e'er can feel, yet thou hast given
Joys they can never know. I love to see
The setting sun resting his broad bright rim
Upon the golden wave, as lingering there
To bid the world farewell; and when he sinks,
To watch the thousand summer clouds he leaves
Of strange fantastic shape and varied hue.
Then is thine hour, bright Fancy—then is felt
Thy softest, sweetest influence o'er the heart.
O! when I gaze upon th' unclouded heaven
Studded with gems of brilliancy, my soul
Forgets the lapse of time, and doth recall
The fantasies so proud and beautiful
Of ancient times : the stars were then in truth
"The poetry of heaven," and had high power
O'er mortal fate. 'Tis sad that those sweet dreams
Are now denied us. O, how much more bliss
Lies in the legend of our infant years,
Than in the sad reality we learn!

Many would deem me weak; but I have gazed
Upon the fairy clouds and pictured there
Familiar forms and faces; and have felt
That I could almost weep to see them fade,
So like a presage of the transient date
Of all life's changeful joys. It may be vain
To yield to these impressions; but what heart
Could scorn such gentle dreams in early youth.

I love to look upon the clouded sky,
When the fierce forked lightning flashes bright,

And the deep roar of heaven's artillery
Sounds fearfully; and I can calmly view
The strife of elements, and fancy then
I hear the shouts of proud rebellious spirits
Storming the towers and battlements of heaven.
O, what a depth of feeling lies within
The full, the o'erfraught heart in such an hour!
And this, too, is thine hour, bright Fancy, this
Thy proudest, mightiest power. In the sweet calm
Of evening, thou dost come with whispers bland,
And all its gentleness; but when the storm·
Is raging thou dost speak in majesty,
And the full heart is lifted to the heavens,
While we can feel there yet is high communion
Between fallen man and pure angelic natures.

Could but the skeptic feel the thrilling power
Of chastened Fancy at a time like this,
Surely the blush of shame would tinge his cheek.
Would not the deep emotions of his soul
Prove that high soul immortal? Can it be
That we should have such glimpses of a light
Not of this world, if we are ne'er to see
The fullness·of its glory? Can the man
Who feels the restless workings of a mind
Aspiring after knowledge, think that earth
Can limit the expansion of his soul?
No; he must deem that there will come a time
When all shall be unfolded. 'Tis a proud,
An elevating thought. O, who would doubt?

MIDNIGHT.

THE moon is riding high in the blue heavens,
  And like a delicate drapery the clouds
  Hang o'er the vast expanse; the air is calm;
No voice, no sound is heard, save the soft note,
Far distant, of a solitary lute;
All things are hushed in that tranquillity
Which speaks e'en to the worn and troubled heart
And bids its passions rest. How beautiful
Is this fair world! There's not a leaf that falls
Within the forest, not a flower that springs
Beneath our footsteps, not a twinkling star
That gems the brow of night, but gives the heart
A lesson it should ne'er forget, of peace
And innocence. Surely this world was made
For pure, angelic habitants; the breath
Of heaven, that passes o'er the spangled earth
And fills with fragrance every flower, was meant
To fan the golden hair of such as those
Who throng around the eternal throne with harps
Of thrilling melody. Earth is too fair
To be the scene of turbulence — the abode
Of pain and misery. O! why will man
Transform thy gentle paradise of sweets
To a dark waste of sorrow and of sin!

LOVE SLEEPING.

OVE sleeps! O do not strive to break
His slumbers, he too soon will wake.
But now all tranquilly he lies,
And the fair lid that shrouds his eyes
Is like the silvery cloud when driven
Across the deep blue summer heaven,
That bids the sunbeams shine less bright,
But cannot hide their glorious light.

He dreams of some ecstatic bliss,
His full, red lip pouts forth to kiss,
His brightly mantling blushes speak
Like those upon the maiden's cheek,
When, clasped to her fond lover's breast,
The first. kiss on her lip is prest.

And on his gentle brow the while
Is that sweet look, half frown, half smile,
Like virgin coyness that reproves
The very tenderness it loves ;
Now o'er his face a calmness steals —
O! nothing such deep bliss reveals ;
Joy's ecstasy nought else can tell,
A smile, a sigh would break the spell.

But Love's bright visions cannot last ;
E'en now they are already past ;
See, ere his eyelids yet unclose,
Down his fair cheek the tear-drop flows.

Nay, hush thee, foolish boy, and sleep,
Since thou dost only wake to weep ;
Alas ! thou seekest for rest in vain —
Once waked, Love cannot dream again.

TO ———.

WHERE'S a cloud on the mountain, a mist on the
            lake, —
    Is not this a warning the storm soon will break?
Though the sun on the meadows is still shining clear,
Yet the wild winds are sighing, the tempest is near.

There's a shade on thy brow, and a tear in thine eye,
Seen through the long lashes that over it lie ;
And though on thy lip is the bright beaming smile,
Yet sad thoughts are hid in thy bosom the while.

The sun's brilliant beams have dispersed the dark cloud,
And no longer the mist the lake's bosom doth shroud ;
O, thus let the smile on thy lip ever glow,
Till its brightness has driven the shade from thy brow.

Aye, changes may pass over nature's sweet face,
And smiles may the gloom of the countenance chase ;
But when sorrow has long made its home in the heart,
O, where is the light that can bid it depart ?

STANZAS.

" The early grave
Which men weep over, may be meant to save."
Byron.

EEP not for those
    Who sink within the arms of death,
    Ere yet the chilling wintry breath
  Of sorrow o'er them blows ;
But weep for them who here remain
The mournful heritors of pain,
Condemned to see each bright joy fade,
And mark grief's melancholy shade
    Flung o'er hope's fairest rose.

    Nay, shed no tear
For those who soundly, sweetly sleep ;
They heed not the cold blasts that sweep
    Across their lowly bier ;
But weep for those who see the cloud
Of misery youth's bright heaven enshroud,
And view the flowers that deck life's path
    Fall dry and sear.

    Dread not the tomb ;
To those who feel that youth survives
The joys that youthful fancy gives,
    It wears no face of gloom.
It is a quiet, peaceful home
For those who through life's desert roam —

A place for wearied ones to rest,
Where o'er the painful, care-worn breast
  Spring flowers may bloom.

LIFE.

WHEN Hope's fairy fingers are straying
    O'er the chords of the youthful heart,
    And fancy in prospect displaying
The bliss that new years may impart ;
When sweet feelings are ever up-springing,
  And the pulses all joyously beat ;
When each day a new pleasure is bringing,
  O ! then indeed life is most sweet.

When the torch of affection just lighted,
  Burns bright on the altar of truth,
Ere the cold, selfish world yet has blighted
  One innocent feeling of youth ;
When earth seems a garden unfading,
  Where flowers spring round our glad feet ;
When no cloud our bright heaven is shading,
  O ! then indeed life is most sweet.

When the cold breath of sorrow is sweeping
  O'er the chords of the youthful heart,
And the youthful eye, dimmed with strange weeping,
  Sees the visions of fancy depart ;

When the bloom of young feeling is dying,
  And the heart throbs with passion's fierce strife ;
When our sad days are wasted in sighing, —
  Who then can find sweetness in life ?

When unkindness or coldness has faded
  The pure, hallowed light of true love,
And the mists of the dark earth have shaded
  The dreams that o'er young spirits move ;
When earth seems a wide waste of sorrow
  No longer with bright blessings rife ;
When we look but for clouds on each morrow, —
  Who then can find sweetness in life ?

SONG OF THE FAIRIES.

 HASTE ye, haste to the Avis grove,
The home that the fairies so dearly love ;
There a leaf never dies save when others
    are springing,
More beautiful far, on each slender spray ;
There bright-plumaged birds, ever joyously singing,
Are glancing like sunbeams — away, haste away !

Since last we met we have wandered far
Beneath the light of each dewy star ;
Borne on the wings of the viewless air,
We have basked in the smile of maidens fair ;
And sad ones have blessed the soothing touch
Of our odorous wings o'er their sleepless couch.

But still the farther away we roam,
The dearer we love our own sweet home;
The eye of beauty is not as bright
As the stars in our queen's fair crown of light,
And 'tis dearer far — O no! there is nought
In our own sweet shadowy world so fraught
With exquisite joy, as 'tis thus to stray
Doing good to all; then away, away!

FRAGMENT.

HERE is a something in my heart that speaks
Of death! E'en in my wildest bursts of joy
That thought is ever present, but not then
In fearfulest array; e'en as the man
Who dwells beside a gushing rivulet,
Will seem to hear, when far away, the sound
Of rippling waters, so 'tis blended with
My every thought. In hours of tranquilness,
Fancy displays the green grass and wild flowers
Growing in rich luxuriance o'er my grave,
And I, a blessed spirit, hovering near
The gentle ones I love, unheeding then
The grosser air of earth; for well I know
That yon bright heaven would be too sad a home
Were I bereft of them.
And yet I sometimes sigh for length of days:
I scarce know why, but when I see the crowds
Of gifted ones that throng around the shrine
Of Liberty, and bring their blooming bays

To form a garland for Columbia's brow,
Which there may live for ages, I could wish
I too might add a wild flower. This is vain,
Nay, more than vain ; such thoughts should never dwell
Within the quiet depths of woman's heart.
While Halleck wreathes the laughing vine amid
The verdant oak leaves and the myrtle bough,
And Bryant culls the lily and the rose
To twine with the rich autumn leaves, 'tis vain
To dream a pale half-budded violet
Could mingle with their sweets.

TO ———.

AS the bright beacon still will glow
   When summer billows gently flow,
   And smile on the tumultuous wave
When winds are loud and tempests rave,
So such enduring love as mine
Through years of joy would calmly shine ;
But should the world's rude storms arise,
Then will it glad thy weary eyes —
The one bright star amid the gloom,
The one lone spot where hopes still bloom.

WILLIAM TELL ON THE MOUNTAINS.

" Yet, Freedom ! yet thy banner, torn but flying,
Streams like a thunder-storm against the wind."
Childe Harold.

ONCE more I breathe the mountain air, once more
I tread my own free hills ; e'en as the child
Clings to its mother's breast, so do I turn
To thee my glorious home. My lofty soul
Throws all its fetters off: in its proud flight,
'Tis like the new-fledged eaglet, whose strong wing
Soars to the sun it long has gazed upon
With eye undazzled. O ! ye mighty race,
That stand like frowning giants, fixed to guard
My own proud land, why did ye not hurl down
The thundering avalanche, when at your feet
The base usurper stood? A touch, a breath,
Nay, e'en the breath of prayer, ere now has brought
Destruction on the hunter's head, and yet
The tyrant passed in safety. God of Heaven !
Where slept thy thunderbolt ?

                              O ! Liberty,
Thou choicest gift of Heaven, and wanting which
Life is as nothing, hast thou then forgot
Thy native home ; and must the feet of slaves
Pollute this glorious scene? It cannot be !
E'en as the smile of Heaven can pierce the depths
Of these dark caves, and bid the wild flowers bloom

In spots where man has never dared to tread,
So thy sweet influence still is seen amid
These beetling cliffs: some hearts yet beat for thee
And bow alone to Heaven: thy spirit lives,
Aye, and shall, when e'en the very name
Of tyrant is forgot. Lo! while I gaze
Upon the mist that wreathes yon mountain's brow,
The sunbeam touches it, and it becomes
A crown of glory on his hoary head.
O! is not this a presage of the dawn
Of freedom o'er the world? Hear me, thou bright
And beaming Heaven! while kneeling thus, I swear
To live for Freedom, or with her to die.

WILLIAM TELL IN CHAINS.[1]

WHAT! does he think that bonds can chain the
mind?
That dungeon air can taint the spotless soul?
Fond fool! let Gesler wear his princely pomp
If he would know the weight of real chains;
And learn that to the base and crouching slave
All earth is one wide prison house. In vain
They shut me from the blessed light of heaven;
They cannot dim the inward ray that sheds
Such brightness on my spirit. I have dwelt

[1] The first of these two pieces was written after seeing Macready's personation of William Tell: and the second after seeing Inman's admirable picture of that distinguished actor as William Tell in chains.

Upon the lofty mountain tops, and held
High converse with the elements, and gazed
Upon the sun, until his very beams
Became as 'twere a language; shall I seek
To win the smile of princes? I have watched
The storm-clouds gather round the snow-capped cliff,
And, in the rolling thunder, heard the threat
Of an offended God; shall I bow down
Before the wrath of tyrants?   Never, never!
When thou canst tame the eagle down to wear
The jesses of the falcon, or canst yoke
The lion to the humble steer, then hope,
Proud Gesler, to behold the brow of Tell
Bending before thy footstool.

LINES

ON HEARING OF THE DEATH OF A VERY BEAUTIFUL
WOMAN THREE WEEKS AFTER HAVING MET HER AT A
BALL.

HER dark, bright glances seemed to fall
With equal tenderness on all,
And shed such lustre o'er her cheek
As when the setting sunbeams break
An instant from the evening cloud
That seeks its crimson light to shroud,
And sheds upon the mountain snow
A bright and rosy tinted glow.

Her high, white forehead gave to view
Its branching veins of deepest blue;
The gentle touch of sickness there
Gave sweetness to a brow so fair;
Her form so exquisitely frail,
Her face so softly, purely pale,
Seemed as if to her soul was given
Already less of earth than heaven.

And yet amid the festive throng
She paused to hear the mirthful song
And listened to the voice of mirth
As though she felt the joys of earth
Had yet some power left to impart
A sense of pleasure to her heart.

But though in all life's early bloom
She seemed soon destined for the tomb,
And it was this that bade each ray
Of beauty more serenely play;
'Twas this that gave a softened light
To eyes else too intensely bright;
'Twas this that threw a charm around
Her every movement; the sweet sound
Of her low voice the feelings stirred
Like tones of music faintly heard.

Three little weeks — the funeral vest
Was folded o'er that gentle breast,
For Death had set his seal on all
So loved, so lovely; the dark pall,

Forever must that form enshroud
So late the idol of the crowd.

Forgot by many, yet with me
Thy form shall live in memory,
Like half-traced shadows of a dream
Where all things fair and lovely seem —
Such shadows as the moonbeam makes
When half through silvery clouds it breaks.

SWEET REMEMBRANCE.

LOVELY is yon sunset sky
As fades the dying day,
And tranquil are the rippling waves
That in its glory play;
A woodland odor fills the breeze,
And bloom is on the bough,
But where, 'mid all this outward joy,
Are the hopes of childhood now?

The voice of song is breathing round
When summer zephyrs sigh,
And rippling waves in music wake
Upon the shore to die!
A thousand symphonies are heard
Amid spring's rosy bowers,
But we miss the music of the heart
That charmed our early hours.

SYMPATHY.

" Or sai tu dove e quando questi amori
Furon creati e come."
Dante.

 LOVED thee, not because thy brow
　　Was bright and beautiful as day,
　　Not that on thy sweet lip the glow
　Was joyous as the morning ray ;
No, though I saw thee fairest far,
The sun that hid each meaner star,
Yet 'twas not beauty taught me first
The love that silent tears have nurst.

Nor was it that thine every word
　With stores of mental wealth was fraught,
With eloquence each heart that stirred,
　With deepest feeling, holiest thought ;
Nor thy rich voice, whose 'witching spell
Like music on my spirit fell,
Sweet as the notes the bugle-horn
Breathes when o'er moonlit waters borne.

But I beheld the darkening stain
　Of sorrow cloud thy beaming eye,
I heard thy bosom's secret pain
　Find utterance in the struggling sigh ;
And, like some lone, neglected lute,
My young heart's sweetest chords were mute :
No hand had ever touched its strings,
To wake its blissful murmurings,
And silent still its chords would be
But for the touch of sympathy.

A DAY DREAM.

E'LL have a cot
Upon the banks of some wandering stream,
Whose ripple, like the murmur of a dream,
Shall be our music; roses there shall twine
Around the casement, with the jessamine,
Whose starry blossoms shine out from beneath
Their veiling leaves like hope, and whose faint breath
Is sweet as memory's perfume. All the flowers
That Nature in her richest beauty showers,
Shall deck our home; fresh violets that, like light
And love and hope, dwell everywhere; the bright
And fragrant honeysuckle, too; our feet
Shall press the daisy's bloom. O! 'twill be sweet
To sit within the porch at even-tide,
And drink the breath of heaven at thy dear side.
The sky will wear a smile unseen before,
The sun for me more genial light will pour,
Earth will give out its treasures rich and rare,
New health will come in every balmy air.
Then thou wilt ope to me great Nature's book,
And nightly on the star-gemmed heavens we'll look;
Thou, with the pride of knowledge, wilt unfold
The mighty chart where science is enrolled,
And gayly smile when I recount to thee
My wild and wayward flights of fantasy;
For the frail beings of my dreamy heaven
Shrink from the light by scholiast wisdom given.

Wilt thou not joy to see the vivid glow
Of my expanded mind, when I shall owe
Its treasures all to thee?
Methinks it would be grief for me to bear
E'en bliss, beloved, unless thou, too, might share ;
But O ! were joy poured forth in such excess,
My heart would break from very happiness.

THE MOTHER'S FAREWELL TO HER WEDDED DAUGHTER.

NO, dearest one, my selfish love shall never pale
        thy cheek —
    Not e'en a mother's fears for thee will I in sad-
        ness speak ;
Yet how can I with coldness check the burning tears
        that start ?
Hast thou not turned from me to dwell within a stranger
        heart ?

I think on earlier, brighter days, when first my lip was
        prest
Upon thy baby brow while thou lay helpless on my
        breast :
In fancy still I see thine eye uplifted to my face,
I hear thy lisping tones, and mark with joy thy childish
        grace.

E'en then I knew it would be thus; I thought e'en in
    that hour,
Another would its perfume steal when I had reared the
    flower;
And yet I will not breathe a sigh — how may I dare
    repine?
The sorrow that *thy* mother feels was suffered once by
    mine.

A mother's love! O, thou knowest not how much of
    feeling lies
In those sweet words; the hopes, the fears, the daily
    strength'ning ties:
It wakes ere yet the infant draws its earliest vital breath,
And fails but when the mother's heart chills in the grasp
    of death.

Will he, in whose fond arms thou seek'st thine all of
    earthly bliss,
E'er feel a love, untiring, deep, and free from self, like
    this?
O, no! man's deepest tenderness thy gentle heart may
    prove,
But only in a mother's breast dwells such unselfish love.

My thoughts to thee must ever turn as in the years
    gone by,
While to thy heart I shall be like a dream of memory;
Go, dearest one, may angel hosts their vigils o'er thee
    keep —
How can I breath love's sad farewell, and yet forbear
    to weep?

THE DYING YEAR.

HE dying year! How are those few words fraught
    With images of fading loveliness!
How do they fill with dreams of saddened
        thought
The heart that sighs o'er all that once could bless!
They fall with mournful sound upon the ear,
The knell of something we have long held dear.

Thou frail and dying year! ah! where are now
    The charms that have in turn been all thine own?
The spring's young bloom, the summer's ripened glow,
    The autumn's mournful splendor, all are gone,
And thou art sinking in oblivion's wave:
Would that the griefs thou gavest might there, too, find
        a grave!

Aye, years may pass; but yet time's rapid flight
    Would be unheeded, were it not he flings
A cloud o'er all youth's hopes and fancies bright:
    Alas! he bears upon his shadowy wings
Darkness, distrust, and sorrow; while the mind
Pines 'mid the gloom to which it is consigned.

Thou dying year! hast thou not swept away
    Joys dearer far than any thou hast left?
Have we not seen our hopes with thee decay —
    Felt ourselves almost desolate and reft
Of all the fairest, brightest things of earth?
Have we not turned away sick of the world's vain mirth?

Have we not prayed that thou wouldst quickly fleet,
　When we were sunk in sorrow's deepest gloom?
Have we not learned each coming day to greet,
　Because it brought us nearer to the tomb?
And thou *hast* fleeted, and with thee has past
The strong, deep misery that could not last.

Sorrow treads heavily, and leaves behind
　A deep impression e'en when she departs;
While joy trips by with steps light as the wind,
　And scarcely leaves a trace upon our hearts
Of her faint footfalls: only this is sure, —
In this world nought save suffering can endure.

Yet thou art a kind monitor; and we
　In thee may trace the progress of our lives:
My spring-time is yet new; I ne'er may see
　The summer; and the fruits that autumn gives
For me may never ripen — o'er my brow
Ere then the grass may rustle.　Be it so!

SUNSET.

FAREWELL, farewell, thou setting sun!
　　I love thy gentle ray,
　　Thus brightening, when thy task is done,
　The dying day's decay;
It seems the pardoning smile of Heaven
O'er errors past and sins forgiven.

'Twas 'neath such glowing skies as this,
  In fancy's high-wrought hour,
That first the living soul of song
  O'erwhelmed me with its power;
Aye, from thy ray was drawn the fire
That lit my heart's funereal pyre.

O, many a change since then has past
  Across this wayward heart;
Then I could almost weep to see
  Thy gentle light depart;
But now I love thy fading ray,
For with it sinks another day.

Farewell, farewell, thou setting sun!
  Thy last faint smile is gone;
Thou goest to make another clime
  A bright and smiling dawn.
But ah! too soon thy morning beam
Will wake me from soft slumber's dream.

Farewell, farewell, thou setting sun!
  I will not thus complain,
What though thy dawning light will wake
  My heart to thoughts of pain?
Will it not wake my spirit, too?
Are there no duties left to do?

Farewell, farewell, thou setting sun!
  I love thy gentle ray,

When thus calm feelings can look back
  Upon a well-spent day,
And bid me seek new strength from Him
Before whose brow thy light is dim.

SABBATH MORNING.

HERE is a quiet beauty on the sky,
  A balmy freshness in the tranquil air,
  That fills my mind with holiest thoughts, my
    heart
With gentlest feelings; e'en the glorious sun
With softer splendor seems to usher in
The peaceful Sabbath. Well may it be called
A day of rest, when it thus sweetly stills
Not merely the wide city's busy hum,
But the fierce warfare of the human heart.
O, how could passion wake in this calm hour?
E'en my proud soul is humbled, and I lift
Mine eye to Heaven, not now in wild reproof,
Murmuring at its decrees, but with the deep
And calm submission of a wounded spirit,
Praying for strength to suffer. Well I know
My lot is sorrow; pain, and sickness, aye,
The sickness of the heart, and early death,
These fill the measure of my destiny.
And O, how often do my feelings rise
In vain rebellion, when with weary limb
I press the couch of sickness! or when pain,
The worst of pain, wrings my lone heart, how oft

Does my worn spirit pray that soon may come
The rest too long delayed! but when I feel
The fragrant breath of heaven, e'en though as now
It fans a feverish brow, or stirs across
A cheek that tears have faded, it awakes
My slumbering energies. The Power that stills
The raging of the swelling seas, can stay
The wild tempestuous waves of earthly feeling,
And teach me calm endurance.

DEVOTION.

MINE eyes are pained with watching, for the brow
Of heaven has lost its crown of starry light,
And soon upon my dim and dazzled sight
The gladdening morn will come with all its glow
Of new-born loveliness; then let me bow
The knee to Heaven, and lift my heart in prayer,
Ere earth with all its vain and troublous care
Comes back upon my spirit, ere the flow
Of holy thought be stayed: yet 'tis for thee
That I would pray, beloved one, for thy lot
I dare to question God's untold decree,
And ask the bliss my own heart knoweth not;
Be thy path marked with light! enough for me
If in thy glory's hour I be not quite forgot.

LINES

ON READING, IN A SHORT POEM BY F. G. HALLECK, THE FOLLOWING STANZAS :—

> " Bid thy thougnts hover o'er that spot,
>   Boy-minstrel, in thy dreaming hour,
> And know, however low his lot,
>   A poet's pride and power.
>
> " And if despondency weigh down
>   Thy spirit's fluttering pinions then,
> Despair — thy name is written on
>   The roll of common men."

MINSTREL, full oft thy varied song
    Has waked the echoes of my heart,
And gloomy fancies cherished long
    Have fled before thy art,
And now thou comest with holier power
    To nerve the spirit's wearied wing,
And o'er its path, where tempests lower,
    Reflected light to fling.

Though heaven-born inspiration ne'er
    Breathe o'er my melancholy strain,
Yet with a poet's heart I bear
    A poet's lot of pain ;
And hard it is to bring the soul
    Back to the low pursuits of earth,
When where the stars in beauty roll
    It seeks its place of birth.

While all on earth grew dark beside,
  I've lived but on the hope that fame,
Since happiness was now denied,
  In death would bless my name;
Vain hope! when men upon whose brow
  The hand of Heaven has set his seal,
Whose souls with God's own spirit glow,
  The world's neglect must feel.

Yet is it cherished, — I would lie
  This moment on the bed of death,
Calm as a wearied child, nor sigh
  To yield my failing breath;
And dear as are affection's ties,
  Strong as is friendship's holier charm,
Gladly I'd grasp the richer prize,
  And barter life for fame.

FILIAL LOVE.

MY father, weep not that my cheek
    Has lost health's roseate glow,
    And look not thus with mournful gaze
  Upon my wasted brow.
Tis hard to die in early youth,
  When hope fills every breath;
But only when I look on thee,
  I feel the sting of death.

Long since I knew it would be thus:
  Upon my sleeping ear
Came the stern voice of death, in words
  Of anguish and of fear ;
And 'mid my waking visions, too,
  Within my silent heart,
There dwelt the secret consciousness
  That I must soon depart.

How lovely seemed the world around,
  Whene'er I thought of this !
The very air and light of heaven
  Seemed redolent of bliss ;
And O, how fondly have I gazed
  Upon earth's flower-decked face,
When I remembered it would soon
  Smile o'er my burial-place !

All those sweet feelings that within
  A woman's bosom dwell,
And throw o'er life's most desert scene
  Love's soft bewitching spell,
Were in my heart. How could I turn
  From all this light and bloom,
To think upon the dark things hid
  Within the silent tomb ?

Nay, weep not, father ; I have learned
  To bow my stubborn will :
The Power that calms the swelling seas,
  The rebel heart can still ;

Now I can look with fearless eye
    On mine approaching fate ;
But O how can I bear to die,
    And leave thee desolate ?

THE EXCUSE.

HE tribute of a passing lay,
    The song that stranger eyes may see,
    Not such the homage I would pay,
My own dear love, to thee ;
No ! poesy's less fragile flowers,
    The riches of affection's mine,
And all the spirit's loftier powers
    Are offered on thy shrine.

When on the wing of fancy borne,
    My spirit soars to realms of bliss,
And seeks those joys which ne'er adorn
    A world of pain like this,
'Tis only that I would illume
    The temple where mine idol dwells
With heaven's own light, and chase the gloom
    Of earth's bewildering spells.

Though oft I feel that could I bind
    Around my brow fame's fadeless wreath,
Filled with the power and pride of mind
    My soul would smile at death ;

Yet 'tis but for thy sake I claim
  The honors of the poet's lot ;
For why should glory be my aim
  If thou couldst share it not?

TO MY HARP.

IN vain ! in vain ! my hand no more
    Thy charm of silence now can break ;
  No longer wilt thou deign to pour
  The music I was wont to make.
In vain with wooing touch I fling
My fingers o'er each radiant string ;
Still all are hushed, or but reply
In strains of broken melody.

Have I, then, lost the power to sway
  Thy magic chords with former skill?
Or art thou wearied to obey
  The impulse of a wayward will?
This feeble hand has now new power
In painful study's toilsome hour,
This wayward will no longer strays
'Mid passion's wild and devious ways.
Where, then, my lonely harp, has gone
The sweetness of thy early tone?

Ah ! well I know ; thou wert not made
  'Neath pleasure's sunny light to dwell,
'Tis only in dark sorrow's shade
  Thy song can wake its powerful spell ;

Thou wast but formed with gentle art
To charm the desolated heart.

And now that o'er my wearied soul
  The light of happiness is shed,
No more thou yield'st to my control,
  Thy soul of melody is fled.
Well be it so — I will not seek
That thou in tones of joy shouldst speak ;
But ah ! too soon the clouds of woe
Their darkness o'er my soul will throw,
Then will I woo thy soothing strain
To cheer my saddened hours again ;
And when despair's fell demons throng
I will invoke thy gentle song
The fearful shadows to dispel :
Till then, loved harp, farewell, farewell.

THE FAREWELL.

" It was a peasant girl's, whose soul was given
  To one as far above her as the pine
  Towers o'er the lowly violet."

L. E. L.

O, dearest one ; nor think my heart will ever
    breathe a sigh
  Because it never now can share thy glorious
    destiny.
My love has never sought reward ; 'twas joy enough for
    me
To pass my life in loneliness, and cherish thoughts of
    thee.

While yet a child, I freely gave affection's untold wealth ;
Since then I've known the swift decay of hope, and joy,
        and health,
And murmured not at Heaven's decree, though thus of
        all bereft ;
How could I mourn ? whilst *thou* wert mine a world of
        bliss was left.

Though other ties may bind thee, dear, though we are
        doomed to part,
Yet still it is not sin to hide thine image in my heart ;
So pure, so holy was the spell which love around us cast,
That even now I would not wake, although the charm
        be past.

And in thy memory by-past days will leave their gentle
        grace ;
Not all the fondness of a wife those bright tints can
        efface.
Her lot may be of happiness beyond stern fate's control ;
But *I* have known a purer joy — *the union of the soul.*

Farewell, beloved one ; when thy brow the laurel crown
        shall bind,
And when adoring crowds shall own the sovereignty of
        mind,
Then think of one who looks on thee with more than
        woman's pride,
And glories in the thought that she has been *thy spirit's*
        bride.

9

SONNET.

PASS on, stern Time ! I know thy shadowy wing
  Is bearing youth, and health, and hope away ;
  Then swiftly fleet, and bring th' appointed day
When this worn spirit may no longer cling
To earth-born vanities, but gladly fling
Its weight of clay aside. My wearied soul
Pines 'neath the fetters of the world's control,
Sick of the thousand petty cares that sting
The heart almost to madness. I have sought
My joy in dreams ; alas ! its end was pain,
And hope's unreal fancies and deep thoughts
Cherished in solitude have been my bane ;
But now upon my lone couch I could lie,
Calm as a wayward, wearied child, and die !

SPRING BREEZES.

YE joyous breezes, I trace your way
  O'er the meadows decked in their bright array ;
  The flow'rets are bending your steps to greet,
New blossoms are springing beneath your feet,
While the rosebud her freshest fragrance flings,
And woos ye to rest your wearied wings.

But on ye pass ; for no charm ye stay ;
Still onward ye hold your gladdening way.

Your breath has rippled the mountain stream,
And a thousand suns from its surface gleam ;
Your voice has wakened the wild bird's note,
And fragrance and melody round you float.

Ye joyous breezes, still on ye go ;
Your breath is passing o'er Beauty's brow ;
Your wings are stirring her radiant hair ;
Your kiss is brightening her cheeks so fair ;
And the innocent thoughts of her heart rejoice
With the mirthful tones of your wild sweet voice.

" Though flowers may gladden our path to-day,
When to-morrow we come, they are passed away ;
And the cheerful smile and the rosy hue,
From the cheek of beauty have faded too ;
And our gentle whispers no more impart
A feeling of joy to her youthful heart.

" Is our path then marked by so much of mirth ?
Alas for the folly and blindness of earth !
Is there not mingled a voice of wail
With the sweetest tones of the young spring gale ?
If like infancy's joyous laugh we rise,
Pass we not onward like manhood's sighs ?

" We but do the will of our Master here,
Our joy is found in a holier sphere :
We are born in heaven ; can our purer breath
Pass mirthfully over the fields of death ?
And what is earth with its transient bloom
And fading charms, but a flower-decked tomb ? "

SONNET.

NAY, spring is not now fair; I cannot now
Greet its glad wakening, though I oft have loved
To watch its coming when its breezes moved
Like music o'er my spirit, and my brow
Was bright with hope and health. The joyous glow
Of nature's new-born loveliness to me
Is fraught with pain; for ere the budding tree
Shall put forth all its beauty, ere the snow
Melts from the mountain summits, we must part,
Mine own dear friend! Thou o'er the trackless sea,
Borne by spring's earliest gales, wilt leave my heart
To mourn in loneliness, bereft of thee,
While to thy memory I shall only seem
The half-traced image of a pleasant dream.

CONFIDENCE IN HEAVEN.

IT is in vain the weary spirit strives
With that which doth consume it: there is
        born
A strength from suffering which can laugh to scorn
The stroke of sorrow, even though it rives
Our very heart-strings; but the grief that lives
Forever in the heart, and day by day
Wastes the soul's high-wrought energies away,
And wears the lofty spirit down, and gives

Its own dark hue to life, O! who can bear?
Yet, as the black and threatening tempests bring
New fragrance to earth's flowers and tints more fair,
So beneath sorrow's nurture virtues spring.
Youth, health, and hope may fade, but there is left
A soul that trusts in Heaven, though thus of all bereft.

THE TRANSPLANTED FLOWERS.

NAY, hold, sweet lady, thy cruel hand,
   O! sever not thus our kindred band,
   And look not upon us with pitiless eye,
As on flow'rets born but to blossom and die.

Together we drank the morning dew,
And basked in the glances the sunbeams threw,
And together our sweets we were wont to fling,
When Zephyr swept by on his radiant wing.

When the purple shadows of evening fell,
'Twas sweet to murmur our low farewell,
And together with fragrant sighs to close
Our perfumed blossoms in calm repose.

But now with none to respond our sigh,
In a foreign home we must droop and die;
The bonds of kindred we once have known,
And how can we live in the world alone?

O, lady, list to·the voice of mirth
By childhood wakened around thy hearth,
And think how lonely thy heart would pine
Should fortune the ties of affection untwine.

E'en now, in the midst of that circle blest,
There are lonely thoughts in thine aching breast,
And how wouldst thou weep if, bereft of all,
Thou shouldst sit alone in thy empty hall!

SONG.

THOU art amid the festive halls
    Where beauty wakes her spell for thee;
Where music on thy spirit falls
    Like moonlight on the sea;
But now while fairer brows are smiling,
And brighter lips thy heart beguiling,
    Thinkest thou of me?

Fair forms and faces pass thee by
    Like bright creations of a dream;
And love-lit eyes, when thou art nigh,
    With softer splendors beam:
Life's gayest witcheries are round thee;
But now while mirth and joy surround thee,
    Thinkest thou of me?

LOVE UNSOUGHT.

THEY tell me that I must not love,
    That thou wilt spurn the free
    And unbought tenderness that gives
Its hidden wealth to thee.
It may be so; I heed it not,
Nor would I change my blissful lot,
When thus I am allowed to make
My heart a bankrupt for thy sake.

They tell me when the fleeting charm
    Of novelty is o'er,
Thou'lt turn away with careless brow
    And think of me no more.
It may be so! enough for me
If sunny skies still smile o'er thee,
Or I can trace, when thou art far,
Thy pathway like a distant star.

SONNET.

AYE! they may talk of conquerors, and tell
    Of trophies that adorned a Cæsar's car,
    And spread his glory to the world afar,
Until his name becomes ·as 'twere a spell
To wake the hearts of nations. It is well
That men should be thus roused; but are there not

Far nobler triumphs in the humble lot
Of him who turns, when passion's hosts rebel,
Undaunted to the conflict? when the heart
Against itself in warfare must arise,
Till, one by one, the joys of life depart,
And e'en the hope that nerved the spirit dies !
Yet not to him are earthly honors given ;
Enough if conquest win th' approving smile of Heaven.

THE MAIDEN TO HER REJECTED LOVER.

MY heart is with its early dream ; it cannot turn
        away
    To seek again the joys of earth, and mingle with the gay :
The dew-nursed flower that lifts its brow beneath the
        shades of night,
Must wither when the sunbeam sheds its too resplen-
        dent light.

My heart is with its early dream ; and vainly love's soft
        power
Would seek to charm that heart anew, in some unguarded
        hour.
I would not that some gentle one should hear my fre-
        quent sigh :
The deer that bears its death-wound turns in *loneliness*
        to die.

My heart is with its early dream; I cannot now forget
The fantasy whose faded light illumes my spirit yet:
The summer sun may sink at once beneath the western
    main,
But long upon heaven's dark'ning brow the clouds his
    light retain.

My heart is with its early dream; yet there are mo-
    ments still
When, like a pulse within my soul, I feel joy's transient
    thrill;
For never can I hear unmoved the words of friendship
    spoken:
The blast that rends the wind-god's harp may leave
    one string unbroken.

THE REMEMBRANCE OF YOUTH IS A SIGH.

YES, we may weep over moments departed,
    And look on the past with a sorrowful eye,
For who, roving on through the world weary
    hearted,
But feels "The remembrance of youth is a sigh?"

Though earth still may wear all its verdure and flowers,
    Though our pathway may smile 'neath a bright sum-
    mer sky,
Yet the serpent lies hid in life's sunniest bowers,
    And still "The remembrance of youth is a sigh."

Then surely the heart whose best pleasures have van-
    ished,
 As spring birds depart when cold winter draws nigh,
The bosom whence hope's sweet illusions are banished,
    Must know " The remembrance of youth is a sigh."

Too early have faded my moments of gladness,
    Ere the bloom and the spring-time of youth are gone
        by ;
Too early my days have been shrouded by sadness,
    And to me " The remembrance of youth is a sigh."

GRATITUDE.

BELOVED one, beloved one,
    When in thine eye I see
    Thy look of placid tenderness
So fondly turned on me,
My heart rebounds with sudden joy,
    Its sorrows are forgot ;
And all unmarked the clouds that now
    Have gathered o'er my lot.

Beloved one, beloved one,
    When on thy glowing cheek
I see a pleasant smile again,
    Of cheerful fancies speak,
Methinks I hear Hope's siren voice ;
    She whispers that the hour

Will come at length when peace may shed
  O'er both her pitying power.

Beloved one, beloved one,
  Whene'er thy soft caress
Is proffered in the gentle hour
  Of tranquil tenderness,
My heart o'erflows with grateful joy ;
  Love's pent-up streams once more
O'er all my life's swift fading flowers,
  Their dews of freshness pour.

SONNET.

ALAS ! alas, for those fresh feelings now
  That shed such sweetness o'er my early days !
  Alas for that bright fancy whose rich rays
E'en o'er earth's darkest moments threw a glow
Like heaven's own light, and tinged all things below
With hues of paradise. My spirit's gaze,
Like the young eaglet's, hung upon the blaze,
Of glory's sun undazzled, and my brow
Brightened with fame's proud hope ; the poet's crown
Was all I sought, and thou, beloved, wert nigh
To cheer my heart when pained by fortune's frown.
O ! hearken to my melancholy cry ;
Behold my spirit in the dust cast down,
And let me once more drink new being from thine
  eye.

THE WEARY DAY.

HE weary day, the weary day,
    Its endless round I trace,
And vainly seek with tale and song
  The heavy hours to chase;
But in thy absence, idle all
  Such arts, beloved, must be,
The hours but fly on eagles' wings
  When I am near to thee.

Unwaked by thy sweet voice, my lute
  Has lost its wonted tone,
Or if perchance I touch its strings,
  It breathes of pain alone!
Unlighted by thy sun's bright smile,
  My wild flower wreath is dead;
Too worthless now its faded bloom
  To deck thy gentle head.

But when the lengthened shadows fall
  To close the drooping flowers,
No longer do I vainly chide
  The slowly lagging hours.
For ere the dews of evening shed
  On earth their fragrance sweet,
I know that my impatient heart
  Thy beauty, love, shall greet.

THE DYING POET.

'TIS over! life's bewildering dream is fading from
    my sight,
And soon my weary heart shall rest in death's
    untroubled night ;
To-morrow's setting sun will gleam upon the icy brow
Of him who turns with failing eyes to watch its glories
    now.

Thou setting sun! how oft on thee I've gazed in early
    years,
Until my infant eyes have filled with soft delicious tears !
Alas ! I little knew such tears from those deep fountains
    sprung,
That since o'er all the flowers of life their venomed
    sweets have flung.

My thoughts were not as others' thoughts, for Nature
    ever spoke
A deeper language to my heart, and sweeter feelings
    woke ;
The glorious sun, the flower-decked earth, the moun-
    tain's rushing stream,
Each filled my wild and restless thought with some en-
    rapturing dream.

O! ne'er can I forget the hour, the blissful hour when
    first
O'er Castaly's pure fount I bent to quench my spirit's
    thirst ;

When dazzled by my glorious dreams, o'ermastered by
　　　a throng
Of thoughts too beautiful for speech, I poured them forth
　　. in song.

And then, too, came the voice of praise, whose all-resist-
　　　less spell
Upon my burning fancy sweet as dews of evening fell.
Alas ! as night-dews fall alike to freshen weeds and
　　　flowers,
Thus, while it wakened loftier thoughts, it roused dark
　　　passion's powers.

With fearless foot I dared to climb ambition's dizzy way,
For by its own resplendent light my soul was led astray.
I lived but on the breath of fame ; the gentler hopes
　　　of life
Were all unheeded while I gave myself to envious strife.

Yet there was one, a gentle girl, whose look had power
　　　to still
The busy demon in my heart and mould me to her will ;
But ah ! she feared to share with me a poet's wayward
　　　fate,
She could not prize a minstrel's love, and I am desolate.

Yet not unblest has been my lot ; my song has had
　　　high power
To cheer the heavy thoughts of woe in many a weary
　　　hour ;

And many a gentle heart has ceased to feel its own
    distress,
While bending o'er the page that told the poet's wretch-
    edness.

My lot has been a lonely one, and now unwept I die,
Strangers will close my glazing eyes, and bear my latest
    sigh ;
Yet they will write upon the stone that marks my lonely
    grave,—
" Joyless and lone he passed his life, but joy to others
    gave." [1]

THE FADED PASSION-FLOWER.

AYE, keep the flower ; 'tis faded now,
    And all unmeet to deck thy brow ;
    But though of beauty thus bereft,
How much of sweetness still is left !

Aye, keep the flower ; and if it grieves
Thy heart to see its faded leaves,
Forget it ever was more fair,
And think its fragrance still is there.

Aye, keep the flower ; another eye
Might heedless pass the blossom by ;

[1] " Joyless I lived but joy to others gave." — *Delille.*

But will it not far dearer be
When wakes its perfume but for thee?

Aye, keep the flower; and shouldst thou seek,
An emblem of my faded cheek,
Thou'lt find it there — from Heaven's own light
Came both its beauty and its blight.

Aye, keep the flower; and it may seem
An emblem of my bosom's dream;
Joy's brilliant hue not long could last;
But when, O! when shall love be past?

LOVE'S VIGIL.

HE slumbered, and unseen I gazed
    Upon her gentle brow;
The eye, where so much brightness blazed
Was closed in darkness now;
And yet its glories scarce were hid
Beneath that soft and shadowy lid.

She slumbered, and her velvet lip
    Was like the folded rose,
Ere yet the bee its sweets could sip,
    Or mar its calm repose;
O! language were too cold and weak,
Its silent eloquence to speak.

She slumbered; o'er her placid face
  A gleam of softness came,
And while I watched its winning grace,
  I heard her breathe my name;
Blest be the heart that thus could keep
Love's vivid memories e'en in sleep.

TO ——.

THY glorious smile, thy glorious smile
    Beams as 'twas wont to do,
    When o'er my youthful feelings first
Love's summer light it threw:
Then it was worshipped from afar,
But still it was my guiding star.

Thy gentle voice, thy gentle voice,
  O, still it has high power
To rouse joy's echoes in my soul,
  As in the blessed hour
When first I heard the low-breathed tone
That made my childish heart its own.

Thy sunbright eye, thy sunbright eye,
  Once more it turns on me
The sweetness of its early look,
  And mingles tenderly
Affection's moonbeams, pure and bright,
With intellect's refulgent light.

10

STANZAS.

" I did love once
As youth, as woman, genius loves."

L. E. L.

KNOWEST thou, dear one, the love of youth,
With its wayward fancies, its untried truth;
Yet cloudless and warm as the sunny ray
That opens the flowers of a summer's day,
Unfolding the passionate thoughts that lie
'Mid feelings pure as an angel's sigh,
Till the loftiest strength of our nature wakes
As an infant giant from slumber breaks —
O, knowest thou, dear, what this love may be?
In earlier days such was mine for thee.

O, knowest thou, dear one, of woman's love,
With its faith that woes but more deeply prove;
Its fondness wide as the limitless wave,
And chainless by aught than the silent grave;
With devotion as humble as that which brings
To his idol the Indian's offerings;
Yet proud as that which the priestess feels,
When she nurses the flame of the shrine while she
　　　　kneels —
O, knowest thou, dear, what this love may be?
Such ever has been in my heart for thee.

O, knowest thou the love of a poet's soul,
Of the mind that from heaven its brightness stole;

When the gush of song, like the life-blood, springs
Unchecked from the heart, and the spirit's wings
Are nerved anew in a loftier flight
To seek for its idol a crown of light;
When the visions that wake beneath fancy's beam,
But serve to brighten an earthly dream —
O, knowest thou, dear, what this love may be?
Such long has been in my heart for thee.

O, tell me, dear, can such love decay
Like the sapless weed in the morning ray?
Can the love of earlier, brighter years
Be chased away like an infant's tears?
Can the long-tried faith of a woman's heart
Like a summer bird from its nest depart?
Can affection nursed within fancy's bowers,
Find deadly herbs 'mid those fragrant flowers?
O! no, beloved one, it cannot be:
Such end awaits not my love for thee.

Youth's pure fresh feelings have faded now,
But not less warm is love's summer glow;
Dark frowns may wither, unkindness blight
The heart where thou art the only light;
And coldness may freeze the wild gush of song,
Or chill the spirit once tameless and strong;
And the pangs of neglected love may prey
Too fatally, dear, on this fragile clay:
But never, O never, beloved, can it be
That my heart should forget its deep fondness for thee.

LOVE RETURNED.

NE arm around her silent harp was flung;
Her brow was bending o'er it, and its chords
Were twined with her dark tresses. Wrapt in
thought,
She stirless sat; and when the soft breeze fanned
The ringlets from her cheeks, a glow was there,
Like the rich hue that decks the Florence rose,
While the sweet smile that hovered round her lip
Was bright as April sunlight; in her eye
Was hope with sadness blended, as if joy
Had been so long a stranger to her heart
That now she scarce dared welcome it.

                                        She spoke;
And the low accents of her voice were sweet,
Yet melancholy as the moaning wave:—

"'Love must win love'—O, were not these the words,
The blessed words he uttered? While my heart
With life and feeling throbs, I must remember
How like the freshening dews of heaven they came,
Waking new hopes, renewing faded dreams,
And thrilling all my frame with sudden joy."

She paused; and her light fingers touched the harp,
Calling out low and plaintive symphonies;
Then, as with bolder touch she swept the strings,
Her voice broke forth responsive, and she sung:—

" Love must win love : " believest thou aught of this ?
O ! then no more
My heart o'er early faded dreams of bliss,
Its wail shall pour.

Give me this hope, though only from afar
It sheds its light,
And like yon dewy, melancholy star,
With tears is bright.

Let me but hope a heart with fondness fraught,
That could not sin
Against its worshipped idol e'en in thought,
Thy love may win.

Let me but hope the changeless love of years,
The tender care
That fain would die to save thine eye from tears,
Thy heart may share.

Or let me dream, at least, that when no more,
My voice shall meet
The ear that listens only to think o'er
Tones far more sweet —

When never more my weary steps of pain
Around thee move,
When loosed forever is thy heavy chain —
" Love will win love."

SONG OF MORNING.

COME, I come from the fields of light;
My herald-star chases the shadows of night;
The dew of the evening lies thick on the grass
Still gemming the pathway my footstep must pass;
While the wild flower joyously raises its head,
And breathes its rich sweets 'neath my echoless tread.

O'er gardens just waking from slumber I fling
The perfumes of heaven from my noiseless wing;
My breath is crisping the silent lake,
Till its gentle wavelets in brightness break;
And the soft air is mingled with music and glee,
By the song of the lark and the voice of the bee.

But man, who alone of all creatures may raise
To the glories of heaven his uplifted gaze —
Is joy in *his* heart? does delight fill *his* eye
When he sees my glad footsteps in brightness pass by?
Like the song of the bird and the bee, does his voice
In the pride of new life and new vigor rejoice?

O, no; for too often my earliest glance
But rouses his soul from sleep's bright-visioned trance;
And coldly he turns from the sweet dreams of night
To the splendors that waken with morning's glad light;
And the sunbeam small pleasure to him can impart,
When it wakes to new sorrows his slumbering heart.

How often has burst forth the weariful sigh,
As the bloom and the freshness of morning came by,
Outshining the light of the student's pale lamp,
But chilling the ardor no darkness could damp;
While with loathing he looks on the glorious ray
That calls him from intellect's treasures away.

How oft have the sweets of my perfumed breath
Fanned the clustering locks on the forehead of death,
And played in the folds of the snow-white vest
That encircled the form for the earth-worm dressed,
Till it seemed to the mourner's bewildered eye
As if moved by the life-pulse again strong and high!

And they who in dreams see the gentle smile
That never their waking thoughts more shall beguile;
The broken in health, and the wearied in heart —
O, joy they not rather to see me depart?
And smile they not more at night's gathering gloom,
Since another day brings them more nigh to the tomb?

THE MORAVIAN BURIAL-GROUND.

The following lines are an attempt to convey an idea of the simple beauty of the
Moravian Burial-ground at Bethlehem, Penn. The feelings described suggested
themselves on the spot, and the incident alluded to actually occurred.

'TWAS one of those sweet days when spring awakes
Her gentlest zephyrs and her softest light,
Wooing the wild flowers in the sunny brakes,
And winning the young bird to joyous flight;

While rose the lulling murmur of the bee
'Mid the sweet sounds of Nature's jubilee.

Our loitering feet unconsciously we turned
  Towards a green and solitary lane ;
A pure, calm spirit in our bosoms burned,
  And feelings saddened, though unmixed with pain :
O ! surely we were then in fitting mood
To ponder on the grave's dread solitude.

Through a low gate our quiet steps we bent ;
  Was this sweet, lonely spot a burial-place ?
Here was no urn, no sculptured monument,
  But o'er it spring had shed her loveliest trace ;
For the bright verdure and the fragrant bloom
Of the wild violet, decked each smiling tomb.

A lowly mound of earth, an humble stone,
  Traced with the name of him who lay beneath,
A name still dear to love, though never known
  To fame, were all that spoke of dreaded death ;
Fresh grass, and flowers, and scented herbs were
        there,
Filling with brightness earth, with odors air.

High swelled my heart as 'mid those graves I trod ;
  I felt life's nothingness in that calm hour ;
My spirit knew the presence of its God,
  And bowed submissive to Almighty power ;
While humbly now I deemed I ne'er should shrink
To drain the cup that earthly love must drink.

I had been an idolater — aye, still
  My heart was vowed upon an earthly shrine;
Though checked a moment by that holy thrill,
  I knew my bosom never could resign
Its deep idolatry till life was past;
Had I not cause to fear Heaven's frown at last?

Filled with these thoughts, I turned e'en from the brow
  That most I loved, to hide my gushing tears,
And gazing on the humble graves where low
  Lay buried many a love of other years,
I threw myself beside a grassy mound
With reverence, for I felt 'twas holy ground.

For there, with eyelids closed in changeless night,
  The mother and her sinless infant lay;
In the same hour death breathed o'er both his blight,
  And in one pang their spirits passed away:
The all of mother's feelings she had known
Were the keen throe, the agony alone.

Alas for earthly joy, and hope, and love,
  Thus stricken down e'en in their holiest hour!
What deep, heart-wringing anguish must they prove
  Who live to weep the blasted tree and flower!
O, woe, deep woe, to earthly love's fond trust,
When all it once has worshipped lies in dust!

There was one hillock decked beyond the rest,
  Where rue, and thyme, and violets were sighing;
No trace of earth defaced its verdant breast;
  The wild bee o'er the sunny flowers was flying,

Or hiding, 'mid the odorous buds and leaves,
Beneath the dewy veil the evening weaves.

There slept the patriarch of fourscore years,
　Whose long life like an April day had closed
In smiles and sunshine after clouds and tears;
　Now calm in death his aged form reposed;
While oft affection's pearly tears bedewed
The flowers that decked his peaceful solitude.

Lo! while we gazed, with slow and noiseless tread
　A female form drew nigh; her right hand bore
A water-urn; and o'er th' unconscious dead
　Lowly she bent, its freshening dews to pour,
Till the flowers brightly 'neath the sun gleamed up,
Each bearing a rich gem within its cup.

Ten years had passed since he who slumbered there
　Had cast aside the weight of clay, and yet
His grave still fondly claimed a daughter's care;
　Still was it visited with deep regret:
Such was the love of hearts o'er which no trace
Of earth had passed affection to efface.

Then with tumultuous feelings all subdued
　By death's undreaded presence, I awoke
My song's low murmurs in that solitude,
　And thus my half-breathed whispers softly broke:—

　　When in the shadow of the tomb,
　　　This heart shall rest,

O, lay me where spring-flowerets bloom
    On earth's green breast.

But ne'er in vaulted chambers lay
    My lifeless form;
Seek not of such poor, worthless prey
    To cheat the worm.

In some sweet city of the dead
    I fain would sleep,
Where flowers may deck my narrow bed,
    And night-dews weep.

And raise not the sepulchral urn
    To mark the spot;
Enough if but by love alone
    'Tis ne'er forgot.

THE MINSTREL'S LAST SONG.

SINCE childhood's hour
Song was the natural language of my heart;
O let me pour forth all its thrilling power
    Once more ere I depart.

    To that far land
Which gave my spirit birth it hastens now;
How doth it long its pinions to expand,
    And soar to Heaven's high brow.

How doth it strive
To burst from all its earthly bonds away,
Unheeding all the fearful pangs that rive
　　Its tenement of clay.

　　Alas, alas,
Why comes thy gentle image, my sweet wife,
Slaying my spirit in the darksome pass
　　That lies 'twixt death and life.

　　Those accents dear
Awoke too much of earthly tenderness ;
Life has too many charms when thou art near,
　　My lonely heart to bless.

　　Much hast thou borne
Of sorrow and deep suffering since thy lot
Was joined with mine, yet meekly hast thou worn
　　Thy chain, and murmured not.

　　The smile that shone
On thy sweet lip is faded, and the light
That sparkled in thy star-like eyes is gone :
　　My love has been thy blight.

　　I would have poured
My life-blood forth like water but to gain
One hour of joy for thee, my own adored,
　　Or spare thy heart one pain.

Yet my hand fixed
Within thy gentle breast grief's deathless sting,
And for thy lip affliction's chalice mixed,
　　Drawn from my life's dark spring.

Mine eyes are dim;
The dews of death are chill upon my brow,
The frosts of death are stealing o'er each limb,
　　And the grave calls me now.

Aye, this is death;
For never yet my heart so faintly stirred
When on my cheek I felt thy balmy breath,
　　Or thy sweet accents heard.

When I am laid
Within the earth, to the dark worm a prey,
Let not my image from thy memory fade,
　　Like April clouds, away.

The strain is done;
My swan-like song is ended; let me dwell
Amid thy kindliest thoughts, my gentle one;
　　One kiss, — sweet love, farewell.

"PRAY FOR YOUR QUEEN."

" Endue her plenteously with heavenly gifts: grant her, in health and wealth, long to live, ... And, finally, after this life, may she attain everlasting joy and felicity, through Jesus Christ our Lord.   Amen."— *Liturgy*.

RAY for your Queen ; upon your sovereign's brow
  Youth lingers still ; nor has experience there
  Written her duties in the lines of care.
The hand that holds fair England's sceptre now
  Is but a gentle maiden's ; can it clasp
  That mighty symbol with a steady grasp?
Dark clouds are lowering o'er our sunny sky ;
  If they should gather, could that fragile form
  " Ride on the whirlwind, and direct the storm?"
Wisdom, strength, energy are from on high ;
  Wouldst thou enrich her with these blessings? Pray!
  One reigns above, whom heaven and earth obey.

Pray for your Queen: hers is a woman's heart,
  And woman's perils lurk around her way ;
  Pleasure may lead her heedless steps astray,
Or flattery soothe when conscience wings its dart.
  Love, that sweet well-spring of domestic joy,
  Scarce rises in a court without alloy,
And woman's sorrows may be hers to share ;
  Sunshine has beamed upon her path thus far,
  But this bright scene one sudden storm would mar,
And England's rose might droop, though now so fair.
  Say, wouldst thou shield her from these perils ? Pray!
  Strength shall be granted equal to her day.

CHARADE.

(Mocking-Bird.)

THE boldest heart that ever yet
  Was cased in mortal clay,
  Rather than hear my first would face
An armèd host's array;
For by brute sufferance alone
  The body's pains are borne,
But e'en the mind's unbending strength
  Quails 'neath the sting of scorn.

My second comes with all things fair,
  Spring sunshine, dews, and flowers,
And though it shuns the leafless bough,
  Loves well the summer bowers.
Full many love its matin song,
  But more its vesper hymn,
When twilight's gentle breezes wake
  And the sunset's light grows dim.

My whole is born in southern clime,
  Where summer rules the year;
Oft in the wilderness its strains
  Delight the traveller's ear.
But like a patriot, stern and true,
  It brooks no foreign shore,
And ere it reach a stranger land
  Its life and song are o'er.

BALLAD.

" La rose cueillie et le coeur gagné ne plaisent qu'un jour."

THE maiden sat at her busy wheel,
  Her heart was light and free,
And ever in cheerful song broke forth
Her bosom's harmless glee.
Her song was in mockery of love,
  And oft I heard her say,
" The gathered rose and the stolen heart
  Can charm but for a day."

I looked on the maiden's rosy cheek,
  And her lip so full and bright,
And I sighed to think that the traitor love,
  Should conquer a heart so light:
But she thought not of future days of woe,
  While she caroled in tones so gay,
"The gathered rose and the stolen heart
  Can charm but for a day."

A year passed on, and again I stood
  By the humble cottage-door ;
The maid sat at her busy wheel,
  But her look was blithe no more ;
The big tear stood in her down-cast eye,
  And with sighs I heard her say,
" The gathered rose and the stolen heart
  Can charm but for a day."

O! well I knew what had dimmed her eye,
  And made her cheek so pale;
The maid had forgotten her early song,
  While she listened to love's soft tale.
She had tasted the sweets of his poisoned cup,
  It had wasted her life away:
And the stolen heart, like the gathered rose,
  Had charmed but for a day.

TIME.

"We take no note of time but by its loss."

ROLL on, roll on, unfathomable Ocean!
  On whose dark surface years are but as waves,
  Bearing us onward with resistless motion,
Till in some deep abyss we find our graves;
While scarce a bubble breaks to mark the spot
Where sunk the bark that bore a mortal's lot.

What myriad heaps of countless wealth have lain
  Entombed for centuries beneath thy tide!
Ruins of empires, kingdoms reared in vain,
  Temples and palaces,— man's faith and pride;
Trophies of times when things of mortal birth
Amid their fellows walked like gods on earth.

What is the lore of ages? Wrecks upthrown,
  Torn fragments of the wealth thou hast despoiled,

11

Records of nations to our race unknown—
　Men who, like us, once lived, and joyed, and toiled,
Yet whom as men we know not, for their kings
Alone flit by us—dim and shadowy things.

And what is science but a beacon light,
　Revolving ever in the same small round,
Shedding upon the wave a lustre bright,
　Yet scarcely seen beyond its narrow bound?
'While o'er the trackless waste its shifting ray
Too often leads the voyager astray.

What is philosophy?　A chart ill traced,
　An antique map drawn by Conjecture's skill;
There many a fair Utopia has graced
　The vacant canvas which truth could not fill:
Like vain researches for the fount of youth
Must be man's quest for speculative truth.

Vainly, O Time, we seek thy mystic source,
　We hope, believe, but nothing can we know;
And still more vainly would we trace thy course,
　And learn what shore receives thy ebbs and flow.
We know it is Eternity—what then?
What is Eternity to finite men?

Our faculties all " cabined, cribbed, confined,"
　We bear earth's soil upon our spirit's wings,
And but by sensual images the mind
　Such abstract fancies to its vision brings;
Not all a Newton's energy could teach
Our fettered souls infinite to reach.

Years multiplied by years, till feeble thought
  Grows dizzy — lost in calculation, maze,
Such are our vague imaginings ; we've sought
  Eternity, and found but length of days.
Not till we lay aside this weight of clay,
Can our dim sight bear truth's refulgent ray.

Ocean of Time ! thy tiniest wavelet bears
  To fatal wreck some richly laden bark :
O ! but for that bright star in heaven which wears
  A brighter glory when the storm grows dark,
But for the Star of Bethlehem, how should we
Direct our course o'er thy tempestuous sea ?

NAPOLEON AT SAINT HELENA.[1]

    FOR thy wings,
Monarch of air ! that I might mount on high,
And find no meaner barrier than the sky ;
    My spirit springs
Beyond the ties that bind it down to earth,
And fain, like thee, would soar, to seek its place of birth.

    Away, away
To the high goal where all my wishes lead,
Thought rushes onward with a whirlwind's speed ;
    Curse on the clay

[1] Suggested by an engraving, which represented him alone on the sea-shore, watch-
ng the flight of an eagle.

That, like a fetter, cumbers my soul's flight,
And chains me at the foot of fame's cloud-compassed
    height !

    Bound to the rock
While vulture passions all my being waste,
Forbidden e'en the stirring joy to taste,
    Of danger's shock ;
So I am doomed the Titan's pain to know,
Without the conscious pride that banished half his woe.

    How have I toiled
To blend my country's glory with my fame,
Till both should be eternal ! Shame, deep shame,
    To be thus foiled !
Thus doomed to see the robe of purple torn
From off her giant limbs, and trampled on in scorn.

    Am I not he
Whose strong right arm the bolt of vengeance hurled ?
Whose name like thunder shook the echoing world ?
    How can it be
That like a mean and slave-born hind I lie
Thus manacled and spurned, forbidden e'en to die !

    O God of heaven !
Let me not perish thus beneath thine ire ;
Where sleep thy lightnings ? — strike ! — by thine own fire
    Be my heart riven !
But leave me not thus piecemeal to decay,
'Reft of the power to drive the earthworms from their
    prey.

LAMENT OF THE EMPRESS JOSEPHINE.

THE fearful strife of feeling now is o'er,
The bitter pang can rend my heart no more;
A martyr's spirit now within me burns,
And love, that spurns
All thought of self, is waking, till its power
Can conquer e'en the anguish of this hour.

Yes; for thy sake I can resign e'en thee,
My noble husband! though there still may be
Enough of woman's weakness in my heart
To bid tears start,
Yet not one murmur of reproach shall swell
Amid the accents of my last farewell.

I loved thee in thy lowliness, ere fame
Had shed a halo round Napoleon's name;
In the veiled lightnings of that falcon eye
I read the high
And godlike aspirations of a mind,
Whose loftiest aim was power to bless mankind.

And when thy name through all the world was known,
When monarchs quailed before thy triple crown,
When queens beheld me in mine hour of pride,
Thy glorious bride,
No selfish vanity my heart could swell —
I shared a throne, but would have shared a cell.

Like thine, my soul was formed for lofty fate;
I loved thee as the eagle loves its mate;
Nor did I seek with borrowed strength to climb
    The height sublime
Where thou hadst built thine eyrie; 'twas for me
Enough that thou wert there — I followed thee.

And in thy toils, too, have I borne a part;
In scenes where might have quailed man's sterner heart,
When dark Rebellion reared his hydra crest,
    My heart carest
And soothed the dreaded monster till he smiled,
And bowed him down submissive as a child.

Though all unskilled the warrior's brand to wield,
Yet went my spirit with thee to the field
Where charging squadrons met in fierce array;
    Nor 'mid the fray
Awoke one terror for a husband's life —
Such fear were idle in Napoleon's wife.

Alas! how has my pride become my shame!
I saw thee mount the rugged steep of fame,
And joyed to think how soon thy mighty soul
    Would reach its goal;
But never dreamed, ambitious though thou art,
That thy last step would be upon my heart.

Vain sacrifice! no second of thy race
Shall wield the world's dread sceptre in thy place;
Rude Nature might have taught how vain must be
    Such hope to thee:

For lofty minds but with like minds should wed ;
Not in the dove's soft nest are eaglets bred.

Ours was the soul's high union; and the pain
That wears my spirit down, breaks not its chain ;
No earthly power such bonds can e'er untwine;
    And I am thine,
As fondly, proudly thine in exile now,
As when thy diadem begirt my brow.

STANZAS

ON THE DEATH OF THE DUKE OF REICHSTADT.

HEIR of that name
  Which shook with sudden terror the far earth,
  Child of strange destinies e'en from thy birth,
When kings and princes round thy cradle came,
And gave their crowns, as playthings, to thine hand —
Thine heritage the spoils of many a land !

  How were the schemes
Of human foresight baffled in thy fate,
Thou victim of a parent's lofty state !
  What glorious visions filled thy father's dreams,
When first he gazed upon thy infant face,
And deemed himself the Rodolph of his race !

 Scarce had thine eyes
Beheld the light of day, when thou wert bound
With power's vain symbols, and thy young brow crowned
 With Rome's imperial diadem — the prize
From priestly princes by thy proud sire won,
To deck the pillow of his cradled son.

 Yet where is now
The sword that flashed as with a meteor light,
And led on half the world to stirring fight,
 Bidding whole seas of blood and carnage flow?
Alas! when foiled on his last battle plain,
Its shattered fragments forged thy father's chain.

 Far worse thy fate
Than that which doomed him to the barren rock;
Through half the universe was felt the shock
 When down he toppled from his high estate;
And the proud thought of still acknowledged power,
Could cheer him e'en in that disastrous hour.

 But thou, poor boy,
Hadst no such dreams to cheat the lagging hours;
Thy chains still galled, though wreathed with fairest
  flowers;
 Thou hadst no images of by-past joy,
No visions of anticipated fame,
To bear thee through a life of sloth and shame.

 And where was she
Whose proudest title was Napoleon's wife?

She who first gave, and should have watched thy life,
  Trebling a mother's tenderness for thee.
Despoiled heir of empire ! on her breast
Did thy young head repose in its unrest?

  No ! round her heart
Children of humbler, happier lineage twined ;
Thou couldst but bring dark memories to mind,
  Of pageants where she bore a heartless part :
She who shared not her monarch-husband's doom,
Cared little for her first-born's living tomb.

  Thou art at rest,
Child of Ambition's martyr ! Life had been
To thee no blessing, but a dreary scene
  Of doubt and dread and suffering at the best ;
For thou wert one whose path in these dark times,
Must lead to sorrows — it might be to crimes.

  Thou art at rest !
The idle sword has worn its sheath away,
The spirit has consumed its bonds of clay ;
  And they who with vain tyranny comprest
Thy soul's high yearnings, now forget their fear,
And fling Ambition's purple o'er thy bier !

MADAME DE STAËL.

HERE was no beauty on thy brow,
   No softness in thine eye,
    Thy cheek wore not the rose's glow,
  Thy lip the ruby's dye;
The charms that make a woman's pride
  Have never been thine own;
Heaven had to thee these gifts denied,
  In which earth's bright ones shone.

Far higher, holier gifts were thine —
  Mind, intellect were given,
Till thou wert as a holy shrine,
  Where men might worship Heaven.
Yes; woman as thou wert, thy word
  Could make the strong man start,
And thy lip's magic power has stirred
  Ambition's iron heart.

The charm of eloquence; the skill
  To wake each secret string,
And from the bosom's chords at will
  Life's mournful music bring;
The o'ermastering strength of mind, which sways
  The haughty and the free,
Whose might earth's mightiest one obeys, —
  These — these were given to thee.

Thou hadst a prophet's eye to pierce
  The depths of man's dark soul,

And bring back tales of passions fierce,
  O'er which its dim waves roll;
And all too deeply hadst thou learned
  The lore of woman's heart;
The thoughts in thine own breast that burned,
  Taught thee that mournful part.

Thine never was a woman's dower
  Of tenderness and love;
Thou couldst tame down the eagle's power,
  But couldst not chain the dove.
O! love is not for such as thee;
  The gentle and the mild,
The beautiful thus blest may be,
  But never Fame's proud child.

When 'mid the halls of state alone,
  In queenly "pride of place,"
The majesty of mind thy throne,
  Thy sceptre, mental grace, —
Then was thy glory felt; and thou
  Didst triumph in that hour,
When men could turn from Beauty's brow
  In tribute to thy power.

And yet a woman's heart was thine;
  No dream of fame can fill
The bosom which must vainly pine
  For sweet Affection's thrill;
And O! what pangs thy spirit wrung
  E'en in thine hour of pride,

When all could list Love's wooing tongue
  Save thee, bright Glory's bride.

Corinna ! thine own hand has traced
  Thy melancholy fate ;
Though by earth's noblest triumphs graced,
  Bliss waits not on the great ;
Only in lowly places sleep
  Life's flowers of sweet perfume,
And they who climb Fame's mountain steep
  Must mourn their own high doom.

THE ANNIVERSARY.

ADDRESSED TO A FRIEND ON HIS BIRTHDAY.

SUFFER not a cloud thy brow to darken,
  Nor let thy spirit in deep sadness hearken
    To the low knell of thy departing hours ;
Thou shouldst not grieve that Time still onward fleeteth,
For when thy steps the kindly gray-beard meeteth,
  He pauses there to fling his freshest flowers.
Measured by thought, thou art of patriarch age,
  Measured by feeling, thou art yet a boy :
And as thou ponderest on life's o'erpast page,
  Thou seest each sorrow mated by a joy.
Why shouldst thou, then, at Time's swift flight repine,
When youth, and age, and hope, to bless thy years com-
      bine ?

Wouldst thou recall thy dreams of early thought,
The wild pulsation of a heart o'erwrought
  With its vain yearnings for a vague ideal?
Wouldst thou, again, crowd years into a day?
Again resign thy soul to passion's sway,
  And grasp at rainbow joys, bright but unreal?
Rather rejoice that Time could thus accord
  His soothing power to still each fierce emotion,
And bless the Heaven-directed hand that poured
  The oil of peace on youth's tempestuous ocean,
And pointed out a beacon light to guide
Thy richly-freighted bark safe o'er the treacherous tide.

THE CONSUMPTIVE.

BRING flowers, fresh flowers, the fairest spring
          can yield —
    The poetry of earth, o'er every field
  Scattered in rich display ;
Bring flowers, fresh flowers, around my dying bed,
The sweetness of the sunny south to shed,
    Ere I am called away.

Bring flowers, fresh flowers, from every sheltered glade ;
I know their brilliant beauties soon will fade
    Beneath my feverish breath,
But their bright hues seem to my wondering thought
With promises of bliss and beauty fraught,
    Winning my heart from death.

Bring flowers, fresh flowers ; ere they again shall bloom
I shall be lying in the narrow tomb,
  Mouldering in cold decay.
Bring flowers, fresh flowers, that I may cheer my heart
With pleasant images, ere I depart
  To tread the grave's dark way.

Bring fruits, rich fruits, that blush on every bough
Bending above the traveller's weary brow,
  And wooing him to taste ;
Bring fruits ; methinks I never knew how sweet
The joys that every day our senses greet,
  Till now, in life's swift waste.

Bring fruits, rich fruits ; earth's fairest gifts are vain
To minister relief to the dull pain
  That steals upon my heart.
Yet bring me fruits and flowers ; they still have power
To cheer, if not prolong life's little hour ;
  Bring flowers ere I depart.

THE WIDOW'S WOOER.

HE woos me in the honeyed words
  Which women love to hear,
Those gentle flatteries, that fall
  So sweet on every ear ;
He tells me that my face is fair,
  Too fair for grief to shade,

My cheek, he says, was never meant
  In sorrow's gloom to fade.

He stands beside me when I sing
  The songs of other days,
And whispers in love's thrilling tones,
  The words of heartfelt praise ;
And often in my eyes he looks
  Some answering love to see ;
In vain — he only there can read
  The faith of memory.

He little knows what thoughts awake
  With every gentle word,
How by his every tone the founts
  Of tenderness are stirred ;
The visions of my youth return,
  Joys far too bright to last,
And while he speaks of future bliss,
  I think but of the past.

Like lamps in Eastern sepulchres,
  Amid my heart's deep gloom
Affection sheds its only light
  Upon my husband's tomb ;
And, as those lamps, if brought once more
  To upper air, grow dim,
So my heart's love is cold and dead
  Unless it glow for him.

LINES

ADDRESSED TO A FRIEND ON HER DEPARTURE FOR ENGLAND.

AFAR, afar o'er the dark blue tide,
  To a distant home thou art borne, fair bride;
  We miss thy voice 'mid the tones of mirth
That waken around our cheerful hearth;
There's a void in our social circle now,
We have lost the smile of thy sunny brow;
Thou art gone from us, and we vainly sigh
For the pleasant light of thy loving eye.

Thou art gone from us, on the mighty sea,
Where the billows are rolling all tameless and free,
Thou art gazing now with unquailing eye
And unblenching cheek, for thy lover is nigh:
E'en the quickened pulses of fear are stilled
When with deep devotion the heart is filled;
And this has nerved thee, fair bride, to part
From the matchless love of a mother's heart.

A father with quivering lip may press
On thy snowy forehead his fond caress;
A brother in sadness may say farewell
To the gentle being long loved so well;
And a sister's eye may be dimmed with tears
To lose the friend of her early years;
Yet time will the course of their feelings stem,
But a mother's feelings!—O, search not them.

Thou art gone from us, and though love will keep
His vigils o'er thee, we yet must weep :
We know that a blissful lot is thine,
Yet bereft of thy presence our hearts must pine.
Farewell, beloved one ; when far away
Through England's green valleys thy footsteps stray,
O, think of the friends who are praying for thee,
In thy native home o'er the dark blue sea.

STANZAS.

"How have you thought of me?"

OW have I thought of thee? As flies
　　The dove to seek her mate,
　　Trembling lest some rude hand has made
Her sweet home desolate ;
Thus doth my bosom seek in thine
The only heart that throbs with mine.

How have I thought of thee? As turns
　　The flower to meet the sun,
E'en though, when clouds and storms arise,
　　It be not shone upon ;
Thus, dear one, in thine eye I see
The only light that beams for me.

How have I thought of thee? As thinks
　　The mariner of home,

When doomed o'er many a weary waste
   Of waters yet to roam ;
Thus doth my spirit turn to thee,
My guiding star o'er life's wild sea.

How have I thought of thee ? As bends
   The Persian at the shrine
Of his resplendent god to see
   His earliest glories shine ;
Thus doth my spirit bow to thee,
My heart's own radiant deity.

STANZAS.

LOOKED on the face of the summer-decked
    earth,
   With its gorgeous herbage, its bright-hued
    flowers,
And it smiled as fair as when first its birth
   Marked young creation's hours :
But a cloud passed over the sunny sky,
And the wind arose with a wailing cry,
Like a feeble infant's half-uttered moan,
Yet gathering strength as it speeded on,
Till the trees that lifted their trunks so high,
Like columns supporting the vaulted sky,
Were borne like gossamer threads on the blast,
And earth was laid bare as the storm swept past.

I looked on the ocean ; each little wave
  Leaped gladly up 'neath the sunny ray,
And the music hid in each secret cave
  Awoke with its magic lay :
But the tempest arose with its voice of might
And summoned the waves to a fearful fight ;
Like evil spirits each dark cloud came,
Each hurling its red bolt of living flame.
Then wildly to combat the elements rushed,
Till, spent with its fury, the tempest was hushed ;
Nor left one trace of its madness behind,
Save the throb of the ocean, the wail of the wind.

I turned to look on a nobler sight —
  The glorious tablet of manhood's brow,
Still marked with the impress of Heaven's own light,
  Though earth-stained and faded now.
That brow was writhed with its thoughts of pain,
And passion had swollen each starting vein ;
More fearful the light of that lurid eye
Than the flashing of swords as they gleam on high, —
Till passion, tamed by itself, grew mild,
And the strong man wept like a wayward child.

O what is the madness of earth and seas,
To the fearful fury of storms like these?
The tempests of nature at length find rest,
But when sleep the storms of the human breast?

ELEGIAC STANZAS.

THOU hast left us, and forever !
  The light of those sweet eyes
Will beam upon us never,
  Till we meet above the skies.
Life's sunshine was around thee,
  The world looked glad and bright,
And the ties of love that bound thee
  Might have stayed thy spirit's flight ;
But the bonds that earth entwineth
  Are all too weak to stay,
When the far-off heaven shineth,
  The spirit's upward way.

Thou hast left us, and forever !
  Thy smile of quiet mirth,
Thy low, sweet voice shall never
  Soothe our aching hearts on earth.
The joys thy presence cherished,
  Like morning dreams have fled,
And many a fair hope perished
  Upon thy narrow bed.
For the love that we have borne thee
  Thy loss we needs must weep,
Yet, even while we mourn thee,
  We envy thee thy sleep.

THE LAST VIOLET.

'M weary of biding the pitiless blast,
I'm weary of lingering the lonely, the last;
Too long I have pined for the soft summer
  shower,
And the sunbeam to waken each slumbering flower;
Too long I have drooped o'er the leaf-covered bed,
Where my kindred so early lay withered and dead.

In vain my rich treasures of fragrance I fling,
They mingle not now with the breezes of spring;
Too rude are the rough blasts of winter to bear
Such perfume as gladdens the mild summer air;
And the violet, the pride of the spring-time, soon dies
Unknown and unwept, 'neath December's dark skies.

O! better, far better 'twould be could I fade
'Mid the clustering locks of some pitying maid;
But I listen in vain for the echoing tread
Of the young and the gay round my verdureless bed,
And too long I have waited the hand that might save
My tempest-bowed form from a snow-hidden grave.

Thou art come, thou art come; aye, I know thee now,
By the silent step and the thoughtful brow,
By the calm, sweet smile on the lip which tells
Of a soul that in peace and purity dwells:
By the tenderness glassed in the depths of thine eye,
I know thou wilt not pass the last violet by.

SONG.

WHEN 'mid the festive scene we meet,
　To joyous bosoms dear,
　Though other voices fall more sweet
Upon thy listening ear,
Yet scorn not thou my ruder tone ;
O ! think my heart is all thine own,
　And love me still.

When o'er young Beauty's cheek of rose
　Thine eye delighted strays,
Half proud to watch the blush that glows
　Beneath thine ardent gaze ;
O ! think that but for sorrow's blight
My pallid cheek had yet been bright,
　And love me still.

LINES ON AN OLD PICTURE OF A MONKISH STUDENT OF THE MIDDLE AGES.

GRAVE old Student ! oft ere now
　I've gazed upon thy placid brow,
　And little thought thou wouldst have power
To cheer full many a languid hour ;
But now, while on my couch I rest,
With pain and weariness opprest,
Thy calm, still brow above me bends,
And seems like some familiar friend's.

Grave old Student, time has laid
A gentle hand upon thy head;
That brow and form still wear the trace
Of manly beauty, early grace:
Thy hand is marked by time's dark stain,
And swoln is each blue starting vein,
Yet still a touch of beauty lingers
Upon those well-turned, slender fingers;
That face just lifted from the page,
Though marked by the deep lines of age,
And furrowed, it may be, with cares,
Still intellect's high beauty wears.

Grave old Student, has thy mind
New and precious truths divined?
Or art thou still pondering o'er
Knowledge ofttimes conned before?
Pure and hallowed thought lies hid
'Neath thy dark eye's down-cast lid;
Thou art one whom time has found
No mere cumberer of the ground.

Grave old Student, while I gaze
Fancy brings back other days,
When learning, hid in cloistered nook,
Beneath the stole concealed her book;
But in thy time, although she wore
The trappings still of monkish lore,
She dared to throw the cowl aside,
And show unveiled her brow of pride.

Grave old Student, when the trace
Of years is left upon my face,
When round my furrowed temples wave
The snowy blossoms of the grave,
Fain would I hope my changeful brow
May then be calm as thine is now.
But vain such hope; life's wintry years
Seal not the source of woman's tears.

STANZAS TO A FRIEND AFTER A LONG SEPARATION.

THEY tell me thou art cold and changed, they
　　　say thou hast forgot
The friendship that once bound our hearts, ere
　　　sorrow crossed thy lot;
But when on thy familiar face I fix my saddened gaze,
And listen to thy well-known voice, the echo of past
　　　days,
The pleasant memories of youth come thronging round
　　　my heart, —
I think but of the friend thou wert, and heed not what
　　　thou art.

And yet I cannot deem thou art from friendship quite
　　　estranged,
Not always are the feelings chilled when most the mien
　　　is changed;

There is a sadness in thine eye, a shadow on thy brow,
Which tells me that the hand of care has done its work
    ere now :
And who by common laws would judge the heart that
    deeply grieves ?
What - eye may penetrate the veil that silent sorrow
    weaves ?

O ! when in after life the heart from hollow friendship
    turns,
How often o'er its early dreams in bitterness it yearns !
How oft it pines with vain regret o'er memories of the
    past,
When all the gloom that dimmed its sky by April clouds
    were cast ;
And then, when all too late, it learns how much more
    holy truth
Than e'er again can bless our lot, was in the love of
    youth.

THE REFUSAL.

NO, dearest one, not mine the hand
    To bind thy free and tameless heart
In fetters which thou canst not break
When changeful fancy bids us part.
Be it my task alone to bear
    The daily strengthening chain,
And thou mayst wreathe its links with flowers,
    But never share its pain.

The slender fibre which unites
  The young peach blossom to the bough,
Is not more fragile than the tie
  That binds our hearts together now;
Yet better to be thus, for when
  The tempest comes, — as come it will, —
It can but rend the fading flower,
  The branch may flourish still.

HAPPINESS.

NOT in wealth's gorgeous hall,
  Decked out in all art's costliest arraying,
  Where, 'mid tall columns, silvery fountains play-
      ing ·
Upon the ear like music's echoes fall;
The home of pomp, the daily haunt of pride —
Not there — not there, doth Happiness abide.

  Not in the humble cot
Whose walls no ray of fortune's sunshine blesses,
Where the dull weight of penury oppresses
  The hearts that wither 'neath their heavy lot;
The home of want, too oft the den of guilt —
Not there has Happiness her mansion built.

  Not in the quiet nook
Where the pale student his lone watch is keeping,
While his high thoughts, the bounds of time o'erleaping,
  Forgetting earth, on things immortal look;

The home of genius, wisdom's calm retreat —
Not even there has Happiness her seat.

O! seek her not on earth,
Where all the brightest hopes our hearts can cherish,
Like flowers in desert isles, are doomed to perish,
    Unknown beyond the spot that gave them birth:
O! ne'er on earth can aught so fair find rest;
Not here shall Happiness reward thy quest. .

THE FORSAKEN.

"The cure is bitterer still."

FOR one hour, one blissful hour
    Like those my young heart knew,
    When all my dreams of future joy
From love their coloring drew;
I deemed affection then might be
The very life of life to me:
Alas! 'twas source of every ill,
But yet, "The cure is bitterer still."

I loved! O, fearful is the strength
    Of woman's love, combined
With all the spirit's high-wrought powers,
    The energies of mind:
Such deep devotedness as feels
The Indian when he humbly kneels
Before his idol's car to meet
A death of rapture at his feet —

Such love was mine; though fraught with ill ;
"The cure — the cure is bitterer still."

O grief beyond all other griefs !
  To feel the slow decay
Of love and hope within the heart,
  Ere youth be past away :
To know that life must henceforth be
A voyage o'er a tideless sea,
No ebb or flow of hopes and fears
To vary the dull waste of years ;
O ! love may be life's chiefest ill,
But ah ! "The cure is bitterer still."

SONNET.

 CHASE that dusky shadow from thy brow,
    My own beloved one ! though a threatening
        cloud
  May seem the future scenes of life to shroud,
Though, like a way-benighted traveller, now
Thou wanderest on with painful steps and slow,
  Yet thou dost bear a soul too high and proud
  To be by earthly suffering crushed and bowed.
Bear up awhile ! E'en as from every blow
That felled the fabled Titan to the earth,
  He rose with strength redoubled to the strife,

So shall thou find thy very griefs give birth
  To strength sufficient for the ills of life ;
Thou'st stood unblenched 'mid passion's fearful war,
Then let not sorrow now thy soul's bright sunshine mar.

STANZAS.

'TWAS but for thy sake I taught
    My harp a louder tone,
  And checked its low-breathed murmurs fraught
With love for thee alone ;
Thou badest me with a bolder hand
  Awake a lofty strain,
And when, dear love, did thy command
  Fall on my ear in vain?

Yet hard the task ; each trembling string
  Was formed but to express
The gentle thoughts from love that spring,
  The dreams of tenderness ;
They cannot breathe of dark remorse,
  Of souls untamed and wild,
Of passions to whose fearful force
  The tempest's wrath is mild.

But of the pure and stainless soul
  That keeps its onward way,
Though storms and clouds before it roll,
  And lightnings round it play,

The soul that with an eagle's wing
Soars up to truth's bright beam
Of such, beloved one, I may sing
For thou art then my theme.

NIGHT.

NIGHT, queenly Night approaches, her dark robe
  Gemmed thick with stars; and, while her gen-
    tle touch
Opens the sun-sealed fountains of the dew,
Her fragrant breath is passing o'er the earth,
Closing the flowers in slumber. Beautiful,
And strong as beautiful art thou. The child
Who lifts his tiny hands in joy to see
The crescent on thy brow, is not more fair;
And the stern king at whose dread name men shrink,
Is scarce more powerful. Thy soft whisper lulls
Whole cities to forgetfulness, and sheds
The sweets of slumber o'er the armèd host
No less than o'er the busy insect tribes
That hum their hour away; till silence reigns
Unmoved, save by the melancholy song
Old Ocean wakes within his hollow caves.

Night, queenly Night, like woman's holy love,
Thy blessed influence breathes on all around,

And fills the earth with gentleness and peace.
O ! who, while gazing on thy placid brow,
Thou first-born of eternity ! can feel
The weight of earthly vanities ? 'Tis thine
To loose the fetters which the world has twined
Around the spirit's eagle wings, and give
Free flight to daring thought, till the proud soul
O'erleaps the narrow bounds of time and sense
To pierce the glorious mysteries of Heaven.

BYRON IN THE CERTOSA CEMETERY.

"I found such a pretty epitaph, or rather two; one was, — 'Martini Luigi, implora pace.' The other ' Lucrezia Picini, implora eterna quiete.' That was all, but it appeared to me that these two or three words comprise and compress all that can be said on the subject. They contain doubt, hope, and humility. Let me have the ' Implora pace,' and nothing else, for my epitaph."

Letter of Byron to Mr. Hoppner in 1819.

"IMPLORA PACE !" 'tis the cry
　　Of some meek child of want and care
　　Whose life has been a long, long sigh,
A weary struggle with despair.
"Implora Pace !" 'tis the prayer
　　Low breathed from out a contrite heart,
When, turning from the things that are,
　　Through death's dark shadows to depart.

"Implora Pace !" hark ! the groan
　　Bursts from the quivering lip of one

Who proudly stands on earth alone,
  'Mid many stars the only sun.
He bends above the lonely tomb;
  Dark thoughts have dimmed his flashing eye,
His brow wears sorrow's heaviest gloom;
  Then list his agonizing cry:—

"'Implora Pace!' I have quaffed
  From pleasure's wine-cup mantling high,
But never in the maddening draught
  Was found the peace for which I sigh.
In love, earth's best deceit, I sought
  The rest for which my bosom pined;
With bliss, deep bliss, the dream was fraught,
  Its madness still remains behind.

"'Implora Pace!' I have run
  With speed unslackened glory's race;
In the world's wondering sight have won
  Its bays my boyish brow to grace;
My name is heard from every tongue,
  My words on every heart imprest,
My strains in every clime are sung,
  Yet fame brings not my spirit rest.

"'Implora Pace!' I have tried
  All that earth knows of joy or pain,
Its bliss, its woe, its hopes, its pride,
  All, all alike, are worse than vain.
Withered and old in heart I stand
  Upon the brink of death's dark wave,

And hope, aye hope no better land
  Awaits the soul beyond the grave.

" ' Implora Pace ! ' all I seek
  Is rest — the soul's eternal rest.
Thou mouldering clay beneath me, speak !
  Say, will death satisfy my quest ?
Thou canst not tell — I dare not think —
  Child-like at phantom forms I quake ;
Yet fain of death's dark stream would drink,
  My feverish spirit's thirst to slake."

STANZAS

WRITTEN AFTER THE SECOND READING OF " CORINNA."

CHILDHOOD'S glad smile was on my lip, life's
    sunshine on my brow,
  When first I looked upon the page that lies
    before me now ;
'Twas mystery all — I had not learned the love of
    woman's heart,
No meaning to my spirit could its thrilling words im-
    part.

Years fleeted on ; the sunny smile had faded from
    my face,
Upon my brow was graved the sign which pain alone
    can trace ;

13

Youth still was mine, but not the youth of childhood's
    laughing day,
Youth still was mine, but early hope and joy had passed
    away.

O, then no mystery was the page that told Corinna's
    woe,
Too deeply had my spirit learned such bitter truth to
    know ;
Mine own wild heart ! did I not read thy secret sorrow
    there,
Thy lofty dreams, thy fervent love, thy bliss, and thy
    despair ?

Feelings that long had wrestled on within my inmost
    soul,
Thoughts that had ne'er found voice, and dreams that
    spurned at truth's control,
Love far too pure and deep to pour on aught of mor-
    tal mould,
All that my heart so long had hid, Corinna's passion
    told.

O ! none but woman's tongue such tales of woman's
    heart could tell,
Its varied perils when the tides of passion wildly swell,
Its hopes, its fears, its visions wild, its weakness, and
    its power —
The reed when wooed by zephyr's breath, the oak when
    tempests lower.

TO MY SISTER.

" Her lot is on you, silent tears to weep,
    And patient smiles to wear in suffering's hour,
And sumless riches from affection's deep,
    To pour on broken reeds — a wasted shower,
To make them idols and to find them clay,
And to bewail that worship — therefore pray ! "
                                        Mrs. Hemans.

AYE, mark the strain, sweet sister — watch and
        pray,
    Wean thy young, stainless heart from earthly
        things ;
O, wait not thou, till life's bright morning ray
    Only o'er blighted hopes its radiance flings,
But give to Heaven thy sinless spirit now,
Ere sorrow's tracery mar that placid brow.

Sinless and pure thou art, yet is thy soul
    Filled with a maiden's vague and pleasant dreams ;
Sweet fantasies that mock at thought's control,
    Like atoms round thee float in fancy's beam ;
But trust them not, young dreamer, bid them flee ;
They have deceived all others, and will thee.

Well can I read thy dreams ; thy gentle heart
    (Already woman's in its wish to bless)
Now longs for one to whom it may impart
    Its untold wealth of hidden tenderness,
And pants to know the meaning of the thrill
That wakes when fancy stirs affection's rill.

Thou dreamest, too, of happiness — the deep
　And placid joy which poets paint so well:
Alas! man's passions, even when they sleep,
　Like ocean's waves are heaved with secrct swell,
And they who hear the frequent, low-breathed sigh,
Know 'tis the wailing of the storm gone by.

Vain, vain are all such visions! couldst thou know
　The secrets of a woman's weary lot —
O! couldst thou read upon her pride-veiled brow,
　Her wasted tenderness, her love forgot,
In humbleness of heart thou wouldst kneel down,
And pray for strength to wear her martyr crown.

But thou wilt do as all have done before,
　And make thy heart for earthly gods a shrine,
There all affection's priceless treasures pour,
　There hope's best flowers in votive garlands twine;
And thou wilt meet the recompense all must
Who place in earthly love their faith and trust.

TO MY FIRST-BORN.

MY own, my child, with strange delight I look
　　　upon thy face,
　And press thee to my throbbing heart in a
　　　mother's fond embrace;
Each breath that stirs thy little frame can a thrill of joy
　　　impart,

And the clasp of thy tiny hand is felt like a pulse
    within my heart.
Thy little life lies but within the compass of a dream,
And yet how changed does every scene of my existence
    seem !
For over e'en its dreariest path in freshening gushes roll
Feelings that long, like hidden springs, slept darkly in
    my soul.

My own, my child, what magic power is in that simple
    word !
The very depths of tenderness by its sweet sound are
    stirred,
And, like Bethesda's heaven-blessed pool, give out a
    healing power ;
For how can sorrow dwell with thee, fair creature of an
    hour ?
Though from my breast had died away each spark of
    hope's pure flame,
Though pain and anguish wrung my heart as erst they
    racked my frame,
Yet would each pang seem light compared with the
    deep rapturous glow
That thrilled each nerve when first I gazed upon thy
    baby brow.

My own, my child, fain would I draw the shadowy veil
    that shrouds
The future from my view, with all its sunshine and its
    clouds,
To learn what storms must gather yet around thy sin-
    less head,

And gaze upon the varied path which thou through life
     must tread.
It may not be! no human skill these mysteries may
     divine,
The God who led my erring steps will surely watch
     o'er thine;
Enough if to thy mother's hand the blessed power be
     given,
To shield thy heart from passion's strife and fix its
     hope on Heaven.

STANZAS.

" Je serai enchanté, si ma chère amie me présente de nouveaux vers."

IF it be true, as some have said,
     That they who court the muses' smile
     Must ne'er allow the joys of earth
  Their feelings to beguile;
If it be true that love ne'er blooms
  For those who to such gifts aspire,
That they must joy but in the song,
  Must live but for the lyre, —
Then surely, dear one, I may not
E'er hope to share a poet's lot.

If it be true, as some have said,
     That they who rove in fancy's bowers,
Must never turn their steps aside
     To pluck earth's fragile flowers;

If it be true that they must yield
  The treasures of affection's mine,
And all the spirit's high-wrought powers
  To deck the muses' shrine, —
Then surely ne'er for me can glow
The wreath that binds the poet's brow.

If it be true, as some have said,
  That love is all a woman's power,
That tenderness and truth alone
  Are woman's richest dower;
If it be true that though she ne'er
  May win the meed of deathless fame,
She yet may teach some gentle heart
  To treasure up her name, —
Then tell me, dear one, may I not
Contented share a woman's lot?

If it be true, as some have said,
  That woman's heart alone can teach
The way to that pure happiness
  Which genius scarce may reach, —
If this be true, O! ask me not
  To seek a poet's lofty name;
I would not give my cherished love
  To win undying fame,
And dearer far one smile from thee
Than hopes of immortality.

STANZAS ON THE DEATH OF A SISTER.

WEEP for the dead! 'tis meet that tears should
　　consecrate the spot
　　Where sleep the loves of better years, the hopes
　　that cheered our lot;
When the once peopled heart is left all desolate and
　　lone,
'Tis meet that tears should gem the trace of each de-
　　parted one;
Yet not in hopeless grief we mourn, — we know that
　　they are blest,
" Where the wicked cease from troubling, and the weary
　　are at rest."

Weep for the dead! a vacant place is left beside our
　　hearth,
We miss a low and gentle voice with its tones of quiet
　　mirth;
The meek and placid face that seemed a moonlight ray
　　to shed,
Now, veiled forever from our view, rests with the dream-
　　less dead;
Yet not in hopeless grief we mourn — that spotless
　　soul is blest,
" Where the wicked cease from troubling, and the weary
　　are at rest."

Weep for the dead! as summer showers refresh the
thirsting earth,
So on the scathed heart fall the tears that mourn departed worth ;
And virtues, all unseen before, 'neath their pure influence rise,
As summer's fairest flowers are nursed by April's weeping skies.
Surely the dead may claim our tears, e'en though we
know them blest,
" Where the wicked cease from troubling, and the weary
are at rest."

Weep for the dead ! the bounteous God who gave us
hearts to feel,
Meant not that we their hidden founts of tenderness
should seal ;
How could we learn our mighty debt of gratitude to
pay
For blessings left, if nought we recked of blessings
snatched away ?
Yes! we may weep the sainted dead, e'en though we
know them blest,
" Where the wicked cease from troubling, and the weary
are at rest."

THE WIFE'S SONG.

THEY told me that, when time had sped on rapid wing away,
Such fervent tenderness as mine must sink by slow decay;
That, springing thus 'mid earth-born cares, love's precious buds would fade;
Such passion flowers were all too frail to bear the world's cold shade.
It may be so with some; my love is like that northern flower[1]
Which blooms in beauty though unnursed by sun, or earth, or shower;
The breath of heaven is all it needs to call it into life,
As heedless of the summer sky as of the tempest's strife.

They told me that when days had passed, and found my task the same,
On the Penates' lowly shrine to trim the sacred flame,
And to that humble service bend the spirit that of yore
Within the muses' glorious fane was wont its gifts to pour —
They told me I would spurn the toil, and grieve that I had turned
From the high dreams of fame with which my youthful fancy burned;
They little know that pleasant toil has given my soul new power
To realize the dreams it formed in youth's enchanted hour.

[1] The Air Plant.

They told me that when time had made my bosom's
      idol seem
Familiar to my daily sight as to my nightly dream,
That charm by charm would be dispelled, and my sick
      heart would pine
For those high attributes which once it fondly fancied
      thine ;
It may be so with some, but I could tell another tale ;
I would but point to thee, and show how fancy's tints
      may fail,
And teach them that full many a year of wedded love
      may be
Still marked by all the fervent faith of youth's idolatry.

ADIEU OF THE EMPRESS AMELIA OF BRAZIL TO THE INFANT EMPEROR.

The following stanzas are little more than a poetical version of the farewell which
the Empress is said to have uttered by the couch of her adopted son, the infant Emperor, who was lying asleep when the ex-Imperial family embarked to place themselves under the protection of an English ship of war.

FAREWELL, farewell, child of my love — joy of
      mine eyes, farewell !
  Thou canst not know the bitter pangs that in
      my bosom swell ;
Thou sleepest, while above thy couch my deep lament
      I pour,
Thou sleepest — ah ! my lip shall greet thy wakening
      smile no more !

Calmly thou liest, my beautiful — how strangely doth
    Heaven show
Its power by such weak instruments to work our weal
    or woe ;
Thou liest in infant helplessness, yet on that baby brow
Ere long the splendors of a crown, earth's deadliest
    gift, must glow.

A throne is thine, and yet how sweet thy cradled rest,
    my boy !
A crown is thine — yet in thy hand is grasped a sim-
    ple toy ;
The robe of royalty is but an infant's mantle now,
The ruler of a mighty realm — a helpless babe art thou !

O ! wert thou mine by nature's right as well as love's
    strong claim,
Couldst thou but lisp, in holy truth, a mother's sacred
    name,
No power on earth should turn my feet, beloved one,
    from thy side,
Still would I live thy menial slave if all else were de-
    nied.

Alas ! alas ! Heaven never gave so rich a boon to me ;
My duty to my lord is vowed — how can he turn from
    thee ?
I go, his lone and weary life of exiled grief to share,
To find a home in foreign climes — a home ! — and
    thou not there !

Brazilian mothers! ye who bend o'er your fair boys
    with love,
As o'er her tender nursling broods the patient turtle-
    dove,
O! bless the Power that gave you sons of humbler,
    happier birth,
And take the crownèd orphan boy home to your hearts
    and hearth.

Strew o'er his couch the fadeless leaves of Freedom's
    stately tree,
And, when the crown upon his brow a weary weight
    shall be,
Then twine the sweet vanilla bud, the rose, the jas-
    mine fair, —
A diadem of nature's gems best suits that golden hair.

Far from his cradled slumbers chase the dark-winged
    bird of prey,
The viper, and, more poisonous still, the courtier chase
    away ;
And should foul treason rear its crest, then rouse all
    to the field,
Valor's strong arm his sure defense, woman's soft breast
    his shield.

Teach his young lips the voice of love, of mercy, and
    of truth,
Teach him on Freedom's holy shrine to consecrate his
    youth ;

Teach him to love his own fair land, and let his boy-
    ish glee
Be sometimes saddened by a thought, a yearning thought
    of me.

Pure, beautiful as Eve's first-born, I give him to your
    care ;
The germ of future bliss or woe, a nation's hope is
    there.
He slumbers still ; O ! wake him not ! his look would
    rend my heart ;
His lips are bright with sunny smiles — he smiles, and
    I depart !

Farewell, young victim ! thou wert born too noble to be
    blest ;
A peasant boy might still repose upon his mother's
    breast,
But thou, poor orphaned Emperor ! — O words are vain
    to tell
Thy mother's mortal agony ! — one kiss — beloved, fare-
    well !

FAREWELL TO THE SUMMER FRIENDS WHOM I MET AT WEST POINT.

WE shall meet no more on the green hill-side,
    We shall gaze no more on the wild cascade,
    Nor e'er shall our feet range far and wide
The rugged cliff and the sunny glade ;

We shall look not again on the glorious sun,
  As he wends his way to the glowing west,
And pauses to smile, ere his task is done,
  On a scene so fair, as he sinks to rest.

We shall roam not again by the mountain stream,
  As it dashes down on its rocky way,
Through the deep, dark glen where the sun's glad beam
  Scarce touches its wave with a noontide ray;
We shall meet no more on the mountain height
  Where the mouldering fort in its ruin stands,
While our hearts are thrilling with proud delight
  As we think on the deeds of our patriot bands.

We shall wander no more amid nature's wealth,
  The gold-'broidered field and the silver rill;
We shall meet not again as we woo sweet health
  In the shady dell, on the breezy hill;
Like the passing shade on the mountain's brow,
  Which fleets with the cloud that gave it birth,
Are the joys that in this world around us glow,
  And the transient friendships of changing earth.

LINES ON HEARING MY CHILDREN SING.

HOSE clear, ringing voices ! how simple the spell
     That sends my sad thoughts, prisoned, back to
       their cell !
Dark phantoms of ill cease around me to throng
While I list to the tones of my children's sweet song.

Not an impulse to-day in my chilled heart had stirred,
Yet how wildly it bounds to each innocent word !
The stream of affection seemed frozen for aye,
But already the ice chains are melting away.

Those clear, ringing voices ! my lone bosom feels
New hopes spring to life as the melody steals
On the calm evening breeze, and I hail it a token
Of joys yet to come, of sweet ties all unbroken.

Alas ! for the heart with its fond, foolish trust,
And its hopes that are born but to crumble to dust !
Full many a joy that my young heart once cherished,
Like violets in winter, have budded and perished.

Those clear, ringing voices ! I could not live on
'Mid the discords of earth if those voices were gone,
Yet I tremble when listening to echoes so glad,
For life's music must ever be dirge-like and sad.

A LAMENT.

'ER the wide waters of the swelling sea,
   Whose mystic music once I loved to hear,
  But whose low moaning now must ever be
The voice of death and sorrow to mine ear,
Echoed by many a wild and restless wave,
I pour my wail above a brother's grave.

Not on the lap of gentle mother earth,
   Whose worn and wearied children come to lay
Their aching heads on her who gave them birth,
   Glad to forget life's long and toilsome day —
Not on her quiet bosom didst thou close
Thine eyes, my brother, in their last repose.

Thine was a death of agony — a brief
   And mortal struggle with the foaming deep;
Yet, while we mourn with unavailing grief,
   Thou, pillowed on the shifting surge, dost sleep
As tranquilly as if spring's earliest bloom
Was showered in roses on thy early tomb.

I weep for thee; but wherefore? Thou didst drink
   One draught of bitterness, then put aside
The cup forever; better thus to sink
   Beneath the raging ocean's whelming tide,
Than live till cares had gnawed thy heart away,
And left thee nought to hope for but decay.

14

What is our life ?   I know not — but I feel
    That 'tis a scene of suffering at the best ;
Nor know I what is death — yet when I kneel
    In prayer to Heaven, I hope that death is rest ;
O ! then how selfish are the tears we shed
Upon the grave of the untimely dead !

And yet thou wert so full of hope, so young,
    Thy visions of the future were so bright,
Joy's mirthful accents ever on thy tongue,
    And pleasure lending to thine eye its light —
O ! why wert thou thus snatched away, ere truth
Had blent its bitter with the sweet of youth ?

It may have been in mercy — it may be
    That thou wert taken from the ill to come ;
The hollow murmur of the moaning sea
    I fain would deem thy welcome to a home ;
And though my heart may inly bleed, no more
My wild repinings would I idly pour.

Thou art at rest ! the peace for which all pine
    Through many an hour of weariness and woe,
Too soon, perhaps, for thy young hopes, is thine :
    And, though my selfish tears for thee may flow,
The Power that stays the mighty deep can still
The restless murmurs of my wayward will.

STANZAS

ADDRESSED TO A FRIEND ON HER MARRIAGE.

NO voice but that of gladness
   Should meet thine ear to-day,
  Yet only in deep sadness
   Can I love's tribute pay;
Unbidden tears are springing,
   Their source thy heart can tell:
Of joy I should be singing,
   I can but sigh — Farewell!

When from life's fairy garland
   Has fallen a precious gem,
Can I smile to see it glisten
   In another's diadem?
Could I hear thy deep vow spoken
   Without a thought of pain,
When I felt the best link broken
   In friendship's golden chain?

Yet mine is selfish sorrow,
   Which love should hush to rest,
And my heart should solace borrow
   From the thought that thou art blest;
Where hope once claimed dominion,
   Joy holds his revel bright,
And thy spirit's drooping pinion
   Waxes strong in love's pure light.

I know that thou art happy!
  O may affection's glass
With its diamond sparkles measure
  Life's changes as they pass.
Could friendship's gentle magic
  Rule thy horoscope of doom,
Not a moment e'er should meet thee
  In sadness or in gloom.

Farewell, farewell, beloved one,
  Though destined far to roam,
When thoughts come crowding on thee
  Of thy distant native home —
The home from whence has vanished
  One dear familiar face,
And the hearth whence joy was banished
  When thou left a vacant place —

When memory's mournful music
  Awakes thy pleasant tears,
O! let one chord still vibrate
  To the friend of early years.
I've loved thee in thy sorrow,
  I'll love thee still in joy:
Time could not change our friendship, —
  Shall absence it destroy?

TO MY PARENTS.

AS he who, travelling through a lengthened day,
　　Reaches at summer eve some green hill-side,
　　And, looking back, sees veiled in twilight gray
The dreary path through which he lately hied,
While o'er his onward path the setting sun
　Sheds its sweet light on every wilding flower,
Till he forgets the weary labors done
　And his heart tastes the quiet of the hour, —
Father and mother! be it thus with you!
　While memory's pleasant twilight shades the past,
May hope illume the path you still pursue,
　And each new scene seem brighter than the last;
Thus wending on t'wards sunset ye may find
Life's lengthening shadows ever cast behind.

STANZAS

ADDRESSED TO MY FATHER ON NEW YEAR'S DAY.

WEAR not, dear father, looks of gloom upon this
　　　festal day,
　　Nor yield thy soul to pensive thoughts when
　　　all around are gay;
Why shouldst thou pause and sadly gaze through time's
　　　dim vista back,
When so much sunshine gathers yet above thine on-
　　　ward track?

What though the sun of life declines from its meridian
    height,
Since thus it sheds upon thy path a softer, mellower
    light ?
Across its morning beam full oft the tempest cloud was
    driven,
But all undimmed is now the ray that lights thy even-
    ing heaven.

O, look not on these festive hours as monitors unkind,
That mark how much of life's short road thy steps
    have left behind ;
Rather, like green and shady spots along our weary
    way,
They offer rest to those who bear the burden of the
    day.

PEACE.

"The Lord will bless his people with peace."

SEEK her not in marble halls of pride,
Where gushing fountains fling their silver tide,
  Their wealth of freshness toward the summer
    sky ;
The echoes of a palace are too loud, —
They but give back the footsteps of the crowd,
  Who throng about some idol throned on high,
Whose ermined robe and pomp of rich array,
But serve to hide the false one's feet of clay.

Nor seek her form in poverty's low vale,
Where, touched by want, the bright cheek waxes pale,
  And the heart faints with sordid cares opprest;
Where pining discontent has left its trace
Deep and abiding in each haggard face.
  Not there, not there Peace builds her halcyon nest:
Wild revel scares her from wealth's towering dome,
And misery frights her from a lowly home.

Nor dwells she in the cloister, where the sage
Ponders the mystery of some time-stained page,
  Delving with feeble hand the classic mine;
O, who can tell the restless hope of fame,
The bitter yearnings for a deathless name,
  That round the student's heart like serpents twine!
Ambition's fever burns within his breast;
Can Peace, sweet Peace, abide with such a guest?

Search not within the city's crowded mart,
Where the low, whispered music of the heart
  Is all unheard amid the clang of gold;
O! never yet did Peace her chaplet twine
To lay upon base mammon's sordid shrine,
  Where earth's most precious things are bought and
     sold;
Thrown on that pile, the "pearl of price" would be
Despised, because unfit for merchantry.

Go! hie thee to God's altar; kneeling there,
List to the mingled voice of fervent prayer
  That swells around thee in the sacred fane,
Or catch the solemn organ's pealing note

When grateful praises on the still air float,
  And the freed soul forgets earth's heavy chain;
And learn that Peace, sweet Peace, is always found
In her eternal home on holy ground.

THE FAREWELL.

WE met as strangers, lady, not as strangers do
        we part;
      Long will thy memory remain enshrined within
        my heart;
Else would not these unbidden tears beneath mine eye-
        lids swell,
As standing on the pebbly shore, I breathe my sad
        farewell.

We met as strangers, but that heart must be as winter
        cold,
Which asks revolving years before love's blossoms can
        unfold;
A look, a word, a simple tone, oft wakes the spirit's
        strings,
And calls forth all the melody from sympathy that
        springs.

The chambers of mine imagery an added treasure show;
Thy graceful form is pictured there, thy calm and cloud-
        less brow;

Traced by affection's skillful hand, illumed by memory's
　　light,
Fadeless those tints will still be found when years
　　have sped their flight.

O! dark indeed would be this world, did we not some-
　　times find
That best of all earth's fairy gifts, a gentle kindred
　　mind;
And though we only meet to part, yet pleasant thoughts
　　remain
To cheer our onward path when time has strewed that
　　path with pain.

Farewell, sweet friend; I speak the word with vain but
　　fond regret;
It may be long ere we shall meet again as we have
　　met;
But at the quiet evening hour, O! let my memory seem
The half traced image of a past and not unpleasing
　　dream.

THE THOUGHTLESS WORD.

" Why should you weep at a thoughtless word? "

WHEN like a fairy scene in youth
　　The untried world is spread before　us,
　　When fancy wears the garb of truth,
And sunny skies are smiling o'er us,

When never yet one thought of woe
  The heart's deep tenderness has stirred,
How little then our spirits know
  The evils of a thoughtless word.

When one by one our joys depart,
  When hope no more each bright hour measures,
When like a Niobe the heart
  Sits lonely 'mid its perished treasures,
When far from human aid we turn,
  The voice of comfort rarely heard,
O then how bitterly we learn
  The anguish of a thoughtless word.

STANZAS

ON BEING ASKED TO WRITE SOME VERSES, AT A BRIDAL
PARTY.

NEVER 'mid the lighted halls
    Where glad and gay ones throng,
Upon my wayward spirit falls
  The gentle power of song ;
For there too much of brightness dwells,
  Too much of reckless mirth,
And fancy will not weave her spells
  Amid the scenes of earth.

The voice of pleasure in my heart
  Awakes an answering tone,

But, when those joyous sounds depart,
   The echo, too, is gone ;
'Tis only o'er my lonely hours
   Bright dreams of beauty come ;
Then doth my harp awake its powers,
   To cheer my quiet home.

STANZAS

WRITTEN ON THE BLANK LEAF OF A BIBLE PRESENTED
TO A BRIDE.

NOT mine the gift
   Of glittering gem or gold, by sordid hands
   Dug from the dirty mine. I would not be
Remembered only in thy festal hours,
Recalled to mind by some bright jewel's flash,
As, decked in fashion's costliest array,
Thou threadest the mazes of the giddy dance —
I would be linked with holier memories. .
When, in reflection's lonely hour, thy heart
Turns from the turmoil of the busy world
To commune with itself, then let my gift
Be thy companion. Earthly friends may fail,
The voice of sympathy may cease to pour
Its music in the leaden ear of sorrow,
Yet in this casket wilt thou find a balm
For every suffering. As thou ponderest o'er
The precious ·truths of God's most holy book,

O may they be upon thy soul imprest,
Teaching thee grateful love in hours of joy,
Giving sweet solace in thine hour of sorrow,
Offering the only hope that can outlast
The things of time and sense, till thou hast learned
Above all other earthly good to prize
My humble marriage gift.

VIOLETS.

DEARLY I love those simple flowers,
   Half hidden in their dark green nest,
   Yet decked in more than regal pride,
With purple robe and golden vest.

Dearly I love them ; they to me
   With cherished memories are fraught,
And borne upon their perfumed breath
   Comes many a sweet and pleasant thought.

Within our garden's quiet bounds
   Those flowers in wild profusion grew,
And wandered over walk and bed,
   As if their privilege they knew.

Uprooted was each noxious weed,
   Well trained the lily and the rose,
The violets alone were left
   To wander wheresoe'er they chose.

My little one — a dark-eyed child,
  Whose cheek the rose of health had fled,
Learned well to love the purple gems,
  And cull them from their lowly bed.

Her little hands with graceful skill
  A simple garland would entwine,
And then she laughed in childish glee,
  To see them in her dark locks shine.

At morn when dew-drops decked the grass,
  At sunset's bright and gorgeous hours,
Still 'mid the violets was she seen,
  And so we named them " Anna's flowers."

Yet O! how oft my heart was wrung
  While watching o'er her fading bloom ;
Alas ! I feared another spring
  Might strew those flowers upon her tomb.

But, Heaven be thanked ! my fears were vain ;
  Again the rose bedecks her cheek,
Again her light and bounding step
  The garden's vagrant child can seek.

And when beside me oft she sits
  With apron full of those sweet flowers,
Singing some mirthful melody,
  Or picturing scenes of future hours —

I look on her, and inly pray
  That violet-like her life may prove ;
The fragrance of a gentle heart
  Her undisputed claim to love.

TO EMMA, THREE YEARS OLD.

MY youngest and my loveliest, my darling little
      one,
    E'en to a stranger's eye thy face is fair to
      look upon ;
With thy bright locks, thy snowy brow, thine eyes so
    clearly blue,
And thy soft velvet lip that seems a rosebud moist
    with dew.

But to a mother's heart how dear is every childish
    grace ;
How do I love each opening germ of loveliness to
    trace ;
To hear thee lisp each new-found word, or gaze with
    sweet surprise
On all the wonders that each day discovers to thine
    eyes.

Yet sweeter to a mother's hope, my little one, to see
That look of gentle gravity steal o'er thy face of glee ;

It tells the hidden wealth o'er which thy young glad
    thoughts now flow,
As quiet streams reveal how deep their current runs
    below.

THE AUTUMN WALK.

WRITTEN TO ILLUSTRATE A PICTURE IN A JUVENILE ANNUAL.

COME, sister Clara, let me take
    Your skipping rope away ;
    I'm tired of marbles, top, and ball,
I want a walk to-day.

Go, get your hat, the autumn sun
    Shines out so warm and bright,
That you might almost think it spring
    But for the swallow's flight.

In the old woods I found, this morn,
    A drawing-room complete :
A Persian carpet made of leaves,
    A mossy sofa's seat ;

And through the many-colored boughs
    The cheerful sunlight beams,
More beautiful, by far, than when
    Through silken blinds it gleams.

In the twined branches overhead
　　The squirrel gambols free,
Dropping his empty nutshells down
　　Beneath the chestnut tree.

And now and then the rustling leaves
　　Are scattered far and wide,
As the scared rabbit hurries past,
　　In deeper shades to hide.

Among the leafless brushwood, too,
　　You sometimes may espy,
Peering so cautiously about
　　The wood-rat's bright black eye.

Come, let us to that sunny nook, —
　　I love to wander so,
Among the quiet autumn woods;
　　Dear sister, shall we go?

STANZAS.

THE time has been when in the wildest dreams
　　Of gay romance my soul could find delight,
When, till the stars grew pale in the morn's
　　　　glad beams,
I reveled oft in tales of wondrous knight,
And rude misshapen dwarf, and peerless ladye bright.

But then my harp was voiceless; my young hand
  No music from its tuneless chords awoke,
The soul of song breathed not at my command,
  Thought had not yet its early trammels broke,
And fancy but in tones of lisping childhood spoke.

Yet ah ! when but a child in years, my heart
  Grew woman's in its tenderness — it yearned
Its deep and restless feelings to impart ;
  And then my harp its earliest language learned,
Taught by affection's power to breathe the words that
        burned.

Then were the dreams of chivalry forgot,
  No more could knight or dame my feelings move ;
My heart but brooded o'er its lonely lot,
  And my harp mocked the moanings of the dove,
For but one tone it knew, and that it learned of love.

Long years since then have past ; a deeper tone
  Now murmurs from its strings, and as it caught
Its inspiration from the heart alone,
  So to my many dreams of painful thought
My harp responsive breathes in tones with sadness
        fraught.

And whether now I pour the fancied lay,
  Or weave the old world tales of ages past,
Still does my soul its fancies dark display,
  Still o'er my song the spell of sorrow cast,
And the strain dies away in cadence sad at last.

15

STANZAS

WRITTEN FOR A CHARACTER IN A TALE.

I HAVE no heart! I know not where
   The wild and restless thing has fled;
It lives not in a mortal breast,
   Nor is it with the dead.

I have no heart! love, hope, and joy;
   Stir not the current of my life,
Nor know I aught of rapture's thrill,
   Nor passion's fearful strife.

I have no heart! too early chilled
   It slumbered ne'er to wake again,
E'en as the frozen traveller sleeps
   Through all life's parting pain.

I have no heart! no power can wake
   My spirit from its heavy trance;
Alike to me are love's sweet looks,
   Or hatred's withering glance.

I have no heart! nor would I call
   The restless thing to life once more,
E'en if a wish could give me all
   I sought in days of yore.

STANZAS

ON THE DEATH OF MISS CLINCH, BETTER KNOWN AS
"THYRZA."

NEVER looked upon thy face,
  I know not whether it was fair,
Or whether mind alone had set
  glorious impress there ;
Thy form has never met mine eye
  Amid the passing crowd,
Yet few can feel as I do now
  To know thee in thy shroud.

No tone from thy young lip that came
  Has ever dwelt upon mine ear,
And yet how oft my heart has thrilled
  Thy spirit's voice to hear ;
For thou wert one to whom was given
  The minstrel's holy power,
The power to commune with our thoughts
  E'en in the lonely hour.

I knew that thou wert young, for ne'er
  The worn and world-seared soul may know
Such visitings of fancy's light
  As in thy sweet strains glow;
And well I knew the priceless gift
  Of intellect was thine,
E'en though mine eyes ne'er gazed upon
  Thy spirit's earthly shrine.

Surely it is no marvel then
  That I should mourn thy early doom,
And pour a passing stranger's wail
  Above thy lowly tomb ;
Thou wert of those high-gifted ones
  Who to the world belong,
For not alone the social hearth
  May claim the child of song.

Farewell, young minstrel, thou hast shunned
  Perchance a darker, sterner fate,
For rarely does a thornless path
  The steps of genius wait ;
The finer faculties of mind
  That to the bard are given,
Forbid his heart to find its rest
  Beneath its native heaven.

Farewell, though thou wert snatched away
  Too soon to win undying fame,
Yet many a gentle thought shall wait,
  Young minstrel, on thy name ;
And while beloved ones weep thy doom
  With many a fruitless tear,
A stranger's hand would fling its wreath
  Of wild flowers on thy bier.

SONG.

WHEN the summer sunlight closes,
And each weary flower reposes,
When the evening breezes move,
Like whispers of a spirit's love, —
Then to Heaven your voices raise,
'Tis the hour of prayer and praise.

When the tempest cloud is breaking,
And the thunder's voice is waking,
When across the brow of night
Lurid lightning flashes bright, —
Then to Heaven in heart draw near,
'Tis the hour of holy fear.

Offer not your vows in sadness,
Raise the exulting song of gladness;
To the world God's works are shown,
To the world his praise be known;
Sound with harp and timbrel free,
The glories of the Deity.

FRAGMENT.

WHENCE come this painful heaviness of soul,
  These dark presentiments of coming ill,
  These dreams that spurn at reason's sage con-
    trol,
And these thick-gathering fantasies, that thrill
The spirit with deep fearfulness, and chill
  The heart with sudden terror? Are they sent
As portents of the future to fulfill
  The dark decrees of fate? or only meant
To sap the strength of mind, man's noblest battlement?

We know not whence they come, nor can we tell
  Whither they flee; we only feel their power
Withering our hearts by some mysterious spell,
  And stealing o'er us even in the hour
When hope and joy are brightest, till we cower
  Before these shadows, as the warrior steed
Undaunted braves the battle's iron shower,
  And yet will quiver like a shaken reed,
If through a moonlit wood his onward pathway lead.

O, man ! how strange a mystery thou art,
  The noblest yet the weakest of creation ;
Unable to subdue thine own proud heart,
  Yet swaying oft the fortunes of a nation.

God-like in thy high attributes and station,
  Worm-like in each groveling desire,
Yet even in thy lowliest degradation,
  Showing forth glimpses of that heavenly fire
Which, though earth-stained and dim, can never quite
      expire.

SONNET.

ORROW has changed all nature to my view,
    The woods are still as green, the fields as
        gay,
The stars are still as bright, the sky as blue,
  As when they charmed me in my childhood's day;
But now in all their beauty I can see
  Something that ever 'minds me of decay, —
Some leafless branch deforms the stately tree,
  Some blight still lingers on the buds of May,
The starry watchers wear a softened light
  As if I gazed on them through gathering tears;
But when I turn to yon pure sky, a bright
  And glorious vision to my mind appears,
Making this earth seem dull beyond compare,
Since only heaven above is changeless as 'tis fair.

  POEMS.

THE HYMN IN THE TEMPEST.

Mr. Wesley, in his Journal, speaks in terms of the highest commendation respecting twenty-six Germans, members of the Moravian Church, who came to America in the same ship with himself. He continues, " There was now an opportunity of trying whether they were delivered from the spirit of fear as well as from that of pride, anger, and revenge. In the midst of the psalm wherewith their service began, the sea broke over, split the mainsail in pieces, covered the ship, and poured in between the decks as if the great deep had already swallowed us up. A terrible screaming began among the English. The Germans calmly sung on. I asked one of them afterwards, ' Were you not afraid?' He answered, ' I thank God, no.' I asked, ' But were not your women and children afraid?' He replied mildly, ' No, our women and children are not afraid to die.'"—WATSON's *Life of Wesley*.

STRANGE forms and stranger minds and hearts were met
  In the frail bark which bore a precious freight
To the new land of promise. Men had left
The scenes of childhood and the marts of wealth
To seek a home in the dim forest's shades,
Where, all unchecked by man's misguided power,
Their prayers might rise unfettered to their God.
'Twas one of those bright days when nature seems
To hold her quiet sabbath, when the earth
And sea are hushed in silence. The dark waves
Scarce laved the sides of the tall ship, and played
Around the keel in sportiveness. There stood
Within the humble cabin a small band
Of Hernhuth's lowly children ; and thus rose
Their hymn of pure thanksgiving :—

Ancient of Days !
With meek and lowly hearts we come
To pour the exulting hymn of praise

To thee, who led'st us from the home
Where our feet were wont to roam,
O'er the wild untrodden deep
Where the scaly monsters sleep.

Thy mighty will
Thy children in their peril saves,
    The rushing winds are hushed and still,
And slumber bound the tumbling waves
Whose deep abysses yawn like graves.
To an infant world we bring
Tidings of a Heavenly King,
Wonders of thy power and grace,
Saviour of a fallen race !

Glory to God !
For within the trackless wild
    Where foot of man has never trod,
Where never heaven-sent peace has smiled
On scenes by pagan rites defiled,
Soon our hymns with grateful note
On the fragrant breeze shall float,
And upon the air shall swell
That sweetest sound — the sabbath bell.

Hark ! a loud crash,
A sudden wrenching of the lofty masts,
A burst of mighty winds and mountain waves.
On came the sea : gathering new strength it came,
Till on the reeling vessel full it broke,
Rending its very seams. Between the decks

It rushed in fury, pouring its full tide,
Sweeping all things before it; then arose
The shriek of woman's terror, and the groan
That told man's sterner agony. Unmoved
The meek Hernhuthers stood: woman was there
With her calm placid brow; and childhood, too,
With sunny smiles yet lurking on its lip,
Though softened to that pleasant gravity
Which speaks the reverence of an unstained heart. —
A vague and indistinct, but holy fear:
Yet not an eyelid trembled, not a cheek
Blanched at this sight of terror; mothers prest
Their infants to their bosoms, as the wave
Curled foaming round their feet; and sires, too, raised
Their bright-haired boys above the briny stream;
But not a murmur rose. The hymn went on;
A moment it had paused, then rose again
The low, sweet voice, the deep, full tone — but changed
The spirit of the hymn: —

    Maker of heaven and earth!
In peril's fearful hour we call on thee;
  From thee the mighty elements have birth,
Thou mad'st, and thou canst still the raging sea.

    Father, which art in heaven!
We are thy children, fashioned by thy hand, —
  This fleeting breath of life by thee was given, —
As suppliants now before thy face we stand.

    Son of the Father God!
Thou who didst walk unharmed upon the wave,

Thou who, for us, didst kiss the avenging rod,
Hear now thy children's prayer, O! hear and save!

Redeemer of the world!
If thou hast doomed us to this bitter death,
If in the boiling strife of waters hurled,
We must resign to thee our struggling breath —

Grant us thy holy power
To turn unmoved from all that binds the heart,
To give ourselves to thee in peril's hour,
And as in faith we live, in faith depart!

The tempest-cloud had passed; the sudden burst
Of elemental fury had gone by;
And the waves leaped against the vessel's side
With a low moaning, like the murmured sounds
That mar the quiet slumbers of a child
Wearied with its waywardness. The hour
Of peril was forgotten; but one heart
Was troubled with its many doubts and fears,
And to the humble pastor of the flock
That looked so fearless on the face of death,
He came with anxious air: "Had you no fear
That thus your song was poured upon the winds,
When its wild rush was like the knell of death?"
"God rides the tempest; wherefore should we fear?"
Was the meek answer. — "But your wives, your babes,
Have they no terrors?" — "Surely not: they know
That God their Father rules the winds and waves;
They know that death but points the way to Him;
And who would shrink to meet a parent's face?"

LINES

SUGGESTED BY ACCIDENTALLY MEETING WITH AN OLD
COPY OF THE "MYSTERIES OF UDOLPHO."

FULL twenty years have past since last my look
Was left upon thy page, bewitching book!
Aye, twenty years; how very strange it seems
Through such a vista to behold youth's dreams,
To wander so far back o'er life's past ways,
And see what shadows charmed our childish days.

Scarce nine short summers had I seen, when first
Radcliffe's deep horrors on my vision burst;
How well do I remember the lone room
Where first I reveled in her awful gloom;
'Twas a deserted chamber, which o'erhung
A wild neglected garden, where flowers sprung,
Wasting their perfumed beauty on the air —
No eye save mine to heed that they were fair.
Old cherry-trees with dark green foliage, made
Across the casement there a pleasant shade,
While at the sunset hour the gorgeous beams
Pierced the thick branches with their golden gleams.
There till the sunset deepened into gray,
And twilight into night, oft would I stay,
Pondering o'er many a tale of wild romance,
And tasting all the bliss of youth's first trance.
In that sweet solitude I learned the wild,
Mysterious fortunes of St. Hubert's child,

Rapt 'mid Udolpho's horrors until night
Shut all its fearful pictures from my sight;
Then sat in trembling silence, half afraid
To look within the chamber's deepening shade.
The very leaves of the tall trees then stirred
With music such as spirits might have heard,
While in each darkened corner seemed to stand
Spectres with mournful look and beckoning hand;
Filling my inmost soul with pleasant fear,
Till some familiar voice fell on my ear,
Breaking the spell that held me in its chain,
And bringing me to common life again.

O many an hour I spent in that lone spot,
All else on earth for those wild tales forgot,
While wise ones shook their heads and said in scorn,
" From such weak dreams is hopeless madness born."
Had their blood flowed less sluggish in each vein
They had not murmured thus at fancy's reign;
Her gentle rule is felt in every heart
Till passion bids the vanquished queen depart,
And oft we deeply rue the fatal day
That broke her sceptre for his iron sway.

STANZAS.

'TIS done! my pleasant home of happy years
    Has now become the stranger's heritage;
    The home endeared to me by hopes and fears,
Where first I studied life's eventful page,

And, pondering o'er another's heart, was shown
The unsuspected mystery of my own.

Home of my changeful and my brightest days!
    How can I coldly look my last on thee,
When thus, where'er I turn, my saddened gaze
    Beholds some object dear to memory?
The wife's sweet ministry, the mother's care,
Love's costliest gifts,—have all been offered there.

Within this room how oft have I carest
    The playful children sporting at my knee;
In this, ah! here my trembling lip first prest
    The little one who fills our halls with glee:
Through brighter scenes perchance my steps may roam,
But none will be like this—the wife's first home.

My passionate existence has gone by,
    Imagination now has lost its power,
The feelings that within my bosom lie
    Are colored only by the present hour,
For gentle fancy can no more impart
To life's frail flowers the freshness of the heart.

And, therefore, do I feel that never more
    Another home like this to me will seem,
Association's magic spell is o'er,
    Truth has destroyed each wild romantic dream;
I hear no angel voices in the breeze—
Houses are now but houses, trees but trees.

Yet am I happier far than when in youth,
  I gave my heart to fantasies unreal,
My lot has been to find the world of truth
  Brighter and lovelier than the world ideal ;
Nor would I give for fancy's brightest glow
The joys that now my waking senses know.

To thee, my pleasant home, were linked my last
  And sweetest memories ; no more I bind
My thoughts to things inanimate, or cast
  My tenderness abroad upon the wind ;
Wherever Love erects his shrine shall be
Henceforth the dearest, happiest home to me.

THE MOTHER'S SOLACE.

When the Stoic philosopher was informed of the death of his beloved son, he calmly replied, " I always knew that he was mortal ; " but how much more reason has a Christian parent to be resigned under such an affliction, when she can look on the lifeless form of her child, and in the language of undoubting faith, exclaim, " I know that this mortal shall put on immortality."

KNEW that thou wert mortal ! aye, my heart
      Thrilled with vague terror, even while the
          beams
  Of thy soft, loving eyes could still impart
A joy as sinless as thine own pure dreams ;
Thou wert too like a thing of heavenly birth
To tarry long upon this darkened earth.

I knew that thou wert mortal; the blue vein
  Whose delicate tracery adorned thy brow,
I knew might bear the rushing tide of pain,
  Instead of life's pure current, in its flow,
I knew disease thy rosy cheek might pale,
And the hour come when flesh and heart should fail.

I knew that thou wert mortal; yet my tears
  Have flowed in rivers o'er thy lowly bed;
The joys of life, the hopes of coming years,
  Were crushed when thou wert numbered with the
      dead,
And life itself must cease ere I forget
The bitter yearnings of my vain regret.

I knew that thou wert mortal; but the God
  Who filled with deathless love a mother's heart,
Meant not that she should kiss the chastening rod
  Without one feeling of its anguished smart.
Can it be sin to bow the mourning head
When even Jesus wept o'er Lazarus dead?

I knew that thou wert mortal; but can naught
  Bring solace to the soul in sorrow's hour?
Is there not consolation in the thought
  That Christ has robbed the grave of half its power?
Not without hope, beloved one, do I weep,
Thou yet shalt waken from thy dreamless sleep.

I knew that thou wert mortal; but the bright
  And glorious beauty of thine earthly face

Would seem all dim beside the radiant light
 Which crowns thy spirit now with cherub grace:
I know thee now immortal, — and I trust
To meet thee yet again, though dust return to dust.

AUTUMN EVENING.

"And Isaac went out to meditate in the field at the even-tide."

GO forth at morning's birth,
 When the glad sun, exulting in his might,
 Comes from the dusky, curtained tents of
 night,
 Shedding his gifts of beauty o'er the earth;
When sounds of busy life are on the air,
And man awakes to labor and to care,
Then hie thee forth; go out amid thy kind,
Thy daily task to do, thy harvest sheaves to bind.

 Go forth at noontide hour,
Beneath the heat and burden of the day
Pursue the labors of thine onward way,
 Nor murmur if thou miss life's morning flower;
Where'er the footsteps of mankind are found
Thou still mayst find some spot of hallowed ground,
Where duty blossoms even as the rose,
Though sharp and stinging thorns the beauteous bud
 inclose.

Go forth at even-tide,
When sounds of toil no more the soft air fill,
When e'en the hum of insect life is still,
    And the bird's song on evening's breeze has died;
Go forth, as did the patriarch of old,
And commune with thy heart's deep thoughts untold,
Fathom thy spirit's hidden depths, and learn
The mysteries of life, the fires that inly burn.

Go forth. at even-tide,
The even-tide of summer, when the trees
Yield their frail honors to the passing breeze,
    And woodland paths with autumn tints are dyed;
When the mild sun his paling lustre shrouds
In gorgeous draperies of golden clouds,
Then wander forth 'mid beauty and decay,
To meditate alone, — alone to watch and pray.

Go forth at even-tide,
Commune with thine own bosom and be still,
Check the wild impulses of wayward will,
    And learn the nothingness of human pride;
Morn is the time to act, noon to endure,
But O, if thou wouldst keep thy spirit pure,
Turn from the beaten path by worldlings trod;
Go forth at even-tide, in heart to walk with God.

BALLAD.[1]

NEVER shall I forget the song
   I heard in the north countrie,
Crooned forth by an old and withered crone
   As she sat 'neath a blasted tree.

Her back was bowed with the weight of years,
   Her locks were silvery white,
And the ghastly glare of her light-blue eye
   Seemed a church-yard's ominous light.

Slowly she rocked to and fro,
   With hands clasped over her knee,
And sang, "The world is passing away,
   But God has forgotten me!

"Twice fifty years have these dim eyes seen,
   And a weary lot I dree,
The days of man are threescore and ten,
   But God has forgotten me!

"'Tis a fearful thing to behold the graves
   Where our bosom's treasures lie,
To feel alone in this weary world,
   And know that we cannot die.

---

1 Founded on a story, which appeared in a newspaper, of a woman in Hungary, who, at the age of one hundred years, committed suicide from the fear that God had forgotten her.

"O, dark and evil my life has been,
    And lonely it still must be,
But the heaviest thought in my heavy heart
    Is that God has forgotten me!

"O, many and many a year agone
    This foul visage was passing fair,
And the fisherman's child felt a queenly pride
    As she braided her raven hair.

"But youth and beauty have withered away,
    Like flowers on a blasted lea;
Men turn in scorn from my wrinkled brow,
    And God has forgotten me!

"Full fifty years 'neath the cold grave-stone
    Lies he who once called me bride;
And O! how oft have I made my moan,
    And prayed to lie by his side!

"Four boys, four brave and stately boys,
    Once cheered my lonely hearth,
But none are left to weep o'er their graves
    Save her who gave them birth.

"Alone, alone in this weary world,
    I look on man's grief or glee,
Alike unheeding their smiles or tears,
    For God has forgotten me!

"Death garners up the golden sheaves
    For heaven's rich granary,

But I am left like a worthless weed ;
  O ! God has forgotten me ! ”

On the blast was borne that fearful cry,
  As onward in haste I sped ;
I came again — the old crone was there,
  But no longer she envied the dead.

From a knotted branch, in mid air she hung
  (For such fruit a fitting tree),
And her life's last deed, like her latest word,
  Said, “ God has forgotten me ! ”

STANZAS.

“ Life's enchanted cup but sparkles near the brim.” — *Byron.*

ALAS ! for the bard, who thus murmured, while
      tasting
    The sweetest draught fame e'er gave mortal
      to sip,
Who thus his regrets o'er the bubble was wasting,
  Though the bright wine beneath it was wooing his
    lip.

Alas ! for the bard, whose green laurels, distilling
  A poison so deadly, embittered life's draught ;
Far happier the few for whom love's hand is filling
  A cup which in age, as in youth, may be quaffed.

For me life has been, as years onward have glided,
  A beaker o'erflowing with brilliant champagne;
The first effervescence has long since subsided,
  But the sparkle and flavor, I know, yet remain.

LINES.

COME to the vintage feast!
  The west wind sighs 'mid the stately flowers
  That deck so brightly our garden bowers,
Flowers which awoke as the summer died,
To rival her many-colored pride,
Flowers whose rich tint and gorgeous dye
An eastern monarch's pomp outvie.

  Come to the vintage feast!
The sun shines out, but a soft mist lies
Like a gossamer veil o'er the autumn skies,
The air has stolen its sweet perfume
From the crimson clover's rich beds of bloom,
And the insect hum is as musical still
As if summer yet ruled over valley and hill.

  Come to the vintage feast!
The vine bends down with its purple fruit,
The foliage lies thick round its gnarled root,
For the leaves are dropping as if to show
The purple clusters that lie below,

And the tendrils close round the lattice twine,
As if asking support for the burdened vine.

Come to the vintage feast!
In Hebe's temple is spread the board
With the golden treasures of autumn stored ;
The sun of our native skies has shed
O'er the ripened fruitage its glowing red ;
But the grapes that grow 'neath a warmer heaven
The sparkling wine to our feast has given ;
Then come and awaken the choral hymn,
While the bead-drop foams on the beaker's brim.

THE WIFE'S OFFERING ON THE NEW YEAR.

" Aye, years may pass, but yet Time's rapid flight
    Would be unheeded, were it not he flings
A cloud o'er all youth's hopes and fancies bright ;
    Alas ! he bears upon his shadowy wings
Darkness, distrust, and sorrow ; and the mind
Pines 'mid the gloom to which it is consigned." [1]

UCH was my song when my young heart was
        like an untried lute,
    Full of earth's sweetest melodies, but all un-
        touched and mute ;
And, like the lute when swept at eve by zephyr's weary
        wings,
Sometimes a broken melody would murmur from its
        strings.

[1] See page 118.

I knew my heart had richer tones; I felt it had the
    power
To pour a deep and thrilling note in love's impassioned
    hour;
I longed, yet feared, to wake such strains, for ah! full
    well I knew
The hand that called its music forth might rend its
    frail chords too.

Heaven's blessings on thee, dear one; thou first touched
    my silent heart,
And bade it strains of hope and joy, as well as love
    impart;
Like Memnon's harp, it could not wake beneath a
    meaner light,
Its perfect tones were only poured to greet the sun-
    beam bright.

Years have passed by since first I gave my youthful
    heart to thee,
Yet still it breathes its early song in love's sweet mel-
    ody;
But deeper is its music now — the mother and the
    wife
Has learned with better skill to frame the harmonies
    of life.

My early joys! O what were they to those that thrill
    me now,
When thus with calm, deep tenderness I gaze upon thy
    brow,

Or listen to the lisping tones that fill our home with
    glee,
And in our children's sunny looks still find a trace of
    thee?

Thrice have we watched together, dear, the dying year's
    decay ;
Thrice have our eyes together met the New Year's
    opening day ;
Yet every hour that glided on toward the shadowy past,
But found me at thy side, beloved, still happier than
    the last.

Heaven's blessings on thee, dear one ; time may sweep
    my joys away ;
The bliss that fills my spirit now may know no second
    day ;
Yet will I kneel in thankfulness, resigned to Heaven's
    high will,
And 'mid the wreck of hope rejoice, so thou art left
    me still.

THE PASSING YEAR.

IT passes on, the fading year, with its dim and
    shadowy train,
    Its vanished hours, and by-past days of pleas-
    ure and of pain ;

It passes on, with solemn step, toward that shoreless
　　　sea
Whose tideless waters only stir to whelm mortality.

It passes on ; among the tombs its weary feet have trod,
Too often has its pathway led across the burial sod ;
And many a melancholy eye that marks its swift decay
Is weeping o'er the cherished joys and hopes it bears
　　　away.

It passes on ; and shall it fade without one parting
　　　song
From one around whose sunny path unnumbered bless-
　　　ings throng ?
What have I done to merit such exemption from the
　　　doom
That shrouds full many a worthier heart in sorrow's
　　　darkest gloom ?

It passes on ; and yet its steps crush not a single
　　　flower
That blossoms in my joyous way or cheers my quiet
　　　bower.
It passes on ; and though its trace is left upon my brow,
Yet never was my spirit filled with deeper bliss than
　　　now.

It passes on ; a few brief hours its last farewell will see ;
Then let me breathe my heart's deep thoughts, my own
　　　best love, to thee.

Where shall I find the thrilling words which ought alone
    to tell
The grateful tenderness and love that in my bosom
    swell ?

Since thou first taught my youthful mind to know its
    latent powers,
Thy kindness, dearest one, has been the measure of my
    hours ;
And not a single day has past without its precious store
Of gentle looks and words that made my cup of joy
    run o'er.

It passes on ; when last I watched the sunset of the
    year,
My heart, e'en while it thrilled with joy, shook with a
    sudden fear ;
I dared not hope another year would see such blessings
    last ;
Yet has another fleeted on, far happier than the last.

It passes on, the fading year, and leaves me at thy side,
Regarding thee with woman's love and more than
    woman's pride ;
Would that affection's hidden thoughts upon thy life
    could shed
Such blessings, dear one, as thy care pours ever on my
    head !

THE WIFE'S SONG ON THE NEW YEAR.

" Since my first days of passion, grief, or pain,
    Perchance my heart and harp have lost a string,
  And both may jar; it may be that in vain
    I would essay as I have sung to sing."

Childe Harold.

MY harp has lost no string, love, but rust is on
        its chords,
    And when I seek its melody no answer it
        affords ;
It has alone a single tone, and that is like the dove's,
It will not wake to any touch unless the hand be love's.

My harp has lost no string, love, but still its voice is
        mute,
And said I rust was on the chords of my neglected lute ?
Ah, no ! 'tis but the rosy wreaths that happiness has
        hung
Too thickly o'er it, which have thus the chain of silence
        flung.

My harp has lost no string, love, but ever in mine ear
The voice of calm contentment breathes a melody more
        dear ;
And I forget the witching tales that poesy once told,
While listening to the sweeter ones which truth can now
        unfold.

My heart has lost no string, love, for thou hast watched
        it well ;

Thy gentle hand has guarded it from sorrow's wasting
    spell ;
And lightly do its chords reply to every impulse now,
Aye, far more lightly than when youth was written on
    my brow.

My heart has lost no string, love, it bounds thy voice
    to meet,
And vibrates as exultingly thy coming step to greet,
As when in girlhood's sunny hour it gave itself to thee,
And poured in strains unskilled and rude its deep idol-
    atry.

My heart has lost no string, love, though sometimes it
    may jar, —
The harmonies of life too oft a careless touch may
    mar ;
But when attuned by thy dear hand, not one discordant
    tone
Breaks the full tide of grateful song it pours for thee
    alone.

And yet in vain I seek, love, to sing as I have sung ;
The visions have departed now that once around me
    hung ;
The doubt, the fear, the sickening pang of love and
    hope deferred,
These were the wild emotions that my youthful spirit
    stirred.

I sing not as I sung, love, — grief has full many a strain;
.And poesy delights to shed her balm o'er hours of pain ;

But I have known too much of joy ; she will not deign
    to shed
The balsam that might soothe despair, upon the flower-
    decked head.

I sing not as I sung, love, yet must I weave again
My early song of gratitude, though wearisome the strain :
How can I vary such a lay? I would not change the
    theme
For all the brightest fantasies that ever poets dream.

I sing not as I sung, love, yet shall the new-born year
Find me without my morning gift for one so more than
    dear?
Humble the gift, 'yet who would bid the votary depart
When offering at her idol's shrine her all, — a faithful
    heart?

TO ——.

AND does my spirit yet retain
    Enough of minstrelsy
To breath once more its wonted strain
    Of grateful love to thee ?
Though silence broods with heavy wing
    O'er my neglected lute,
Yet when for thee, love, I would sing,
    How can my heart be mute?

By fancy's vague, uncertain ray,
    Or memory's lamp alone,

Are seen the shadowy forms that play
  Round poesy's far throne ;
How, then, may I e'er hope to be
  Blessed with a poet's sight?
The chambers of mine imagery
  Are filled with earthly light.

Hope, fancy, memory, — what are they
  To one whose heart can find
In every blissful, passing day,
  The joys of all combined?
Thou hast fulfilled mine every hope ;
  The past is nought to me ;
And Fancy in her wildest scope
  Can bring back nought like thee.

The love that once was proudly shrined,
  And worshipped with the lyre,
An humbler, happier home can find
  Beside our household fire.
He asks not now for minstrel songs
  With passion's fervor fraught,
When every word to him belongs,
  And every gentle thought.

I look, beloved, upon thy face,
  And tears my fond eyes fill,
No changes there time's hand can trace,
  Fadeless in beauty still ;
Thy smiles, the sunshine of my heart,
  Still o'er me brightly beam,

And, as I watch the years depart,
  Life seems a summer dream.

But yet to-night my spirit quails
  Before some shadowy fear,
And e'en thy sweet voice, dear one, fails
  My drooping soul to cheer ;
I listen to the solemn knell
  Of the departing year,
As if it were a passing bell
  Above some loved one's bier.

The hand of pain is on my brow,
  My spirit's glow is dim ;
I cannot meet thee, dearest, now
  With love's accustomed hymn ;
Yet, trust me, though I cannot greet
  With song the opening year,
Ne'er did my heart more warmly beat,
  Ne'er wert thou half so dear.

STANZAS.

DEAREST, a mournful strain is all the New
        Year's gift I bring,
    For images of by-gone years throng round me
        as I sing ;
My spirit's joyousness is gone, I can no longer fling
The sunshine of a happy heart o'er every earthly thing.

A shadow lies upon my path which naught can chase
    away,
Save the great Sun of Righteousness with healing in
    its ray;
A shadow from the mountain dark o'er which our feet
    must tread,
To meet again our loved of yore, our treasures of the
    dead.

That shadow lies upon my path, and pleasures 'neath
    its gloom,
Like flowerets grown in darkness, now have lost their
    brilliant bloom;
My days of buoyant happiness have with my youth been
    spent,
Yet will I strive, whate'er my lot, therewith to be con-
    tent!

Alas! the magic cup of life but sparkles near the brim;
The music of this weary world is but a morning hymn;
And like a wingèd dream of night our youthful days
    depart,
Leaving but half-traced images within the saddened
    heart.

Yes, all our joys in after years are like Egyptian feasts,
Where Memory's veiled and shrouded form sits first
    amid the guests;
In vain the gay laugh circles round, the wine-cup man-
    tles high,
The glitter but of unshed tears lights up the listless eye.

STANZAS FOR MUSIC.

Air: " Benedetta sia la madre.''

WHEN the summer sun declineth
T'ward the glowing western sea,
When the star of evening shineth,
Then my thoughts are thine, Marie;
For at such an hour I've wandered
On the pebbly shore with thee,
And o'er many a bright dream pondered,
By thy side, my own Marie.

When the autumn wind is stealing
The green garb from each tree,
Then my heart throbs with a feeling
Which is thine, all thine, Marie;
For 'twas autumn when thy gladness
Filled my quiet home with glee,
And memory's pleasant sadness,
Brings thine image back, Marie.

TWELVE YEARS AGO.

TWELVE years ago! how strange it seems
To wander so far back,
And see so many mile-stones stand
Along life's o'erpast track!

Twelve years ago my steps were light
  Beneath youth's bright sunshine,
For then I was but seventeen,
  Now I am twenty-nine.

Twelve years ago I loved to pore
  O'er tales of wild romance
(Those tales that lull the heart so soon
  In passion's rapturous trance),
And pined to meet on this dull earth
  With beings so divine ;
My longings have been long since done,
  For I am twenty-nine.

I loved Miss Landon's poetry then,
  Hung o'er each witching strain,
And, could my lips have coined such words,
  Had answered such again ;
No empty phrases then I saw,
  I marked no rugged line —
But something more than sentiment
  I seek at twenty-nine.

I did not then sit coldly down
  To learn an author's style,
Fancy and feeling — these alone
  My taste could then beguile ;
I pondered o'er the dreams which youth
  Can feel but not define ;
I can describe, not feel them now,
  Since I am twenty-nine.

Twelve years ago I, loved to sit
  At sunset's gorgeous hour,
And image in the rosy clouds
  My own bright summer bower.
But who when gazing through lunettes
  Air-castles could design?
My chateaux now are built on earth,
  Since I am twenty-nine.

No more ethereal in my tastes,
  I've learned, as I'm a sinner,
To make a breakfast on hot rolls,
  And eat beefsteaks for dinner;
And sometimes, too, I sip a glass
  Of good old racy wine;
I never did such vulgar things
  Ere I was twenty-nine.

'Tis not a pleasant thing to know
  That we are growing old,
For no one likes to watch Time's glass,
  E'en when its sands are gold.
My days of young romance are past,
  Yet why should I repine?
No dream in youth was half so sweet
  As truth at twenty-nine.

"TOUJOURS PERDRIX."

THE LAMENT OF A MAN ABOUT TOWN.

I'M sick of balls, soirees, and parties,
    And long from such scenes to be free;
    Flirtation, I own, is quite pleasant,
But I'm weary of "toujours perdrix."

I go to a wedding on Monday,
    White satin and blushes I see;
A blue-coated groomsman is carving
    The bride-cake — still, "toujours perdrix."

On Tuesday a party awaits me;
    Oysters pickled and stewed there may be,
With champagne and creams for the ladies,
    But still it is "toujours perdrix."

A soiree comes next; 'tis the banquet
    Of reason, not sense; so you see
We have little to eat, but the folly
    And flirting are "toujours perdrix."

I go to a ball, and much marvel
    To see with what infinite glee
The dancers enjoy the dull music
    Which I've heard till 'tis "toujours perdrix."

I'll post to the country, and bury
    My vexation beneath some old tree,

And try whether life in the wildwoods
  Can ever be "toujours perdrix."

I'll flirt with some fair country maiden
  (To woman's heart I have a key),
And try whether rustic flirtation
  Like the city's is "toujours perdrix."

. . . .

I've tried the experiment fairly —
  No more rural pleasures for me ;
Give me back the refinement of cities,
  E'en though it be " toujours perdrix."

The sun in the country has baked me ;
  From dust not a pathway is free ;
The milkmaids are horribly freckled,
  And as wild as if all were " perdrix."

If I must eat of one dish forever,
  And no longer a novelty see,
Why, rather than greens and fat bacon,
  I think I like "toujours perdrix."

LINES ON A PORTRAIT.

I LOVED thee not; yet mournful thoughts are
    rushing
  Upon my heart while gazing on that face,
And tears unbidden to mine eyes are gushing —
  Tears, whose deep source to memory's fount I trace ;

Yet why should I lament thy hapless lot?
For thou wert naught to me — I loved thee not.

I loved thee not ; yet intellect was thine,
  And lofty aspirations after fame ;
For honor in thy soul had found a shrine,
  And thou didst hope to win a deathless name ;
But thou art dead, unnoticed, and forgot ;
Yet what is this to me ? — I loved thee not.

I loved thee not; and hadst thou died in age,
  With troops of tender friends around thy bed,
Had love been there thy sufferings to assuage,
  Had some kind breast upheld thy aching head,
I had not then remembered thee ; no spot
In memory's waste was thine — I loved thee not.

I loved thee not; yet when thy spirit passed
  Thus in thy manhood's prime from earth away,
When those thou lovedst forsook thee at the last,
  And none beside thee knelt to weep and pray,
My heart did thrill in pity for the lot
Of one so gifted, though I loved thee not.

LINES ON THE DEATH OF A YOUNG ARTIST.

HOW shall we mourn thee, gifted one? how wail
　　The fate that snatched thee thus in youth
　　　　away,
Ere in life's wreath one rose-bud had grown pale,
　　Ere one dark cloud had dimmed thine early day?
How speak the sorrow that our bosoms thrilled,
When death the pulses of thy warm heart stilled?

How shall we mourn thee? Thou wert of the few
　　Who walk the earth in majesty of mind;
Genius had given its treasures to thy view —
　　The painter's eye, the poet's thought combined,
The soul to image all things pure and bright,
The skill to give them to our daily sight.

Alas! that hand its cunning has forgot,
　　That eye is closed upon all earthly things;
On thy dull ear the voice of praise falls not,
　　Thy heart is cold to love's soft whisperings.
Called from life's feast too soon, thou hast but quaffed
Of love, joy, fame, one deep and final draught.

Like the Olympian victor, thou hadst won
　　The goal of all thy hopes; and in the hour
When toil was past and glory had begun,
　　Then came the King of Terrors in his power,
And at his touch thou didst in dust lay down
The youthful head girt with its laurel crown.

All earthly gifts were thine save length of days ;
  And dare we ask why God denied thee this ?
Haply the grave that shuts thee from our gaze,
  Closing upon thee in thine hour of bliss,
Was meant to save thee all the varied woe
That waits the weary wayfarer below.

" Thy sun went down at noon," but not in clouds ;
  And while we watch in tears its swift decline,
We know that though death's awful shadow shrouds
  Its brightness now, yet it shall once more shine
Among the host of heaven ; and we, who bear
Life's lessons in our hearts, may hope to greet thee there.

SONGS, FROM CONSTANCE LATIMER.

S thy cheek fair, my brother?
   Are thine eyes bright?
   Hast thou the smile of our mother, —
Her remembered smile of light?
Art thou like the gentle vision
   That comes to my sleeping eye,
When my heart in dreams elysian
   Meets its lost one in yonder sky?

Vainly I ask, my brother;
   No lip can tell;
The imaged form of another
   In my memory still must dwell;
In vain with impatient fingers
   Thy features I seek to trace,
His look in my soul still lingers,
   And in thine I find Julian's face.

HEY tell me Spring is coming
   With her wealth of buds and flowers,
   But I hear no wild bees humming
Amid the leafy bowers;

And till the birds are winging
  With music from each tree,
Till the insect tribes are singing,
  Spring is not spring to me.

They tell me spring is waking
  Glad Nature from her sleep,
That streams, their ice-chains breaking,
  Once more to sunshine leap ;
But the mountain brook rejoices
  In music through the lea —
Till I hear Earth's many voices,
  Spring is not spring to me.

ARTH speaks in many voices ; from the roar
    Of the wild cataract whose ceaseless din
    Shakes the far forest and resounding shore,
  To the meek rivulet which seems to win
Its modest way amid spring's pleasant bowers,
Singing its quiet song to charm earth's painted flowers.

Earth speaks in many voices ; from the song
  Of the free bird which soars to heaven's high porch,
As if on joy's full tide it swept along,
  To the low hum that wakens when the torch
Summons the insect myriads of the night
To sport their little hour and perish in its light.

Earth speaks in many voices ; music breathes
  In the sweet murmur of the summer breeze

That plays amid the honeysuckle's wreaths,
  Or swells its diapason 'mid the trees,
When eve's cold shadow steals o'er lawn and lea,
And day's glad sounds give place to holier minstrelsy.

Earth speaks in many voices; and to me
  Her every tone with melody is fraught;
Her harmony of tints I may not see,
  But every breath awakes some pleasant thought;
While to mine ear such blissful sounds are given,
My spirit dwells in light, and dreams of yonder heaven.

LADY, they tell me thou art fair,
    They say the rose blooms on thy cheek.
  The rose's blush I have forgot,
Its breath alone to me can speak.

Lady, they say thine eye's soft blue
  With heaven's own tint is flashing bright.
Alas! I have forgot that hue,
  My sky is always clothed in night.

Lady, they tell me thou art good,
  Thy heart in virtue's cause beats high.
I know this tale, at least, is true,
  Mine ear assists my darkened eye.

Little I know of beauty's form,
  The dimpled mouth, the snowy skin,

But I can learn, from step and voice,
  If gentle be the heart within.

I know thou'rt one whom all may love,
  Though thy fair brow I ne'er may see,
And can I doubt thou wilt allow
  The blind girl's claim to sympathy?

LIKE the wind-harp whose melody slumbers,
    Unwakened by mortal hand,
  Till the soft breeze calls forth its sweet numbers,
  Like tones from a seraph's land;
So my lips ever echo the feelings
  Which nature alone may impart;
I know naught of passion's revealings,
  Then wake not my slumbering heart.

Like a lake lying far on the mountain,
  Where foot of man scales not its height,
Fed only by heaven's pure fountain,
  And only reflecting heaven's light;
So my soul's quiet depths give back only
  The feelings where childhood has part;
Blessed with friendships my life is not lonely,
  Then wake not my slumbering heart.

THE POETIC IMPULSE.

AWAY, vain yearnings, for a wild ideal!
  Why tempt ye me like visions from above?
Why throng round one who dwells amid things
    real,
Who quaffs the cup of earthly grief and love?

Away, away, and leave me still to follow
  The varied path God gives me to pursue,
The joys of fancy are but false and hollow,
  They shall not win me to forget the true.

Away, nor tempt me with thy bright revealings
  Of Poesy's sweet fairy-land of dreams;
Better for me to nurse the gentler feelings
  Which light my home with calm contentment's beams.

Away, away, ye make my footsteps falter,
  When o'er my lowly way your fair forms come;
To her who serves at the Penates' altar,
  The Delphic oracles must still be dumb.

FRAGMENT.

"The joy untasted."
Byron.

AYE, it is ever thus: in every heart
    Some thirst unslaked has been a life-long
        pang,
Some deep desire in every soul has part,
  Some want has pierced us all with serpent fang;
For who from such a brimming cup has quaffed
That not one drop was wanting to life's draught?

It comes to us in youth — that pining thirst,
  And then we seek to quench it at Love's spring,
Cheating the soul with fancies that at first
  Seem bright and glorious as an angel's wing,
Till time and change o'ershadow them, and leave
The heart in deeper loneliness to grieve.

'Tis with us in our later life; in vain
  We win the sweetest draughts of wealth and fame;
Still in the bosom dwells the unquiet pain,
  Still burns unquenched, unquenchable the flame;
The joy is still untasted, and we wear
Our lives away in hope which brings despair.

And various as the bosoms where it dwells
  Is this vain yearning for some untried bliss;

We little know the secret pang that swells
　　The masker's bosom in a world like this,
For vainly in our fellow-man's calm face
We seek the yearnings of the soul to trace.

.

.

SONNETS TO THE HON. MRS. NORTON.

BEAUTY, transcendent beauty, such as fills
　　The passion-stricken heart with dreams of
　　　　heaven,
Genius to whom such magic power is given
That its least word our inmost spirit thrills;
These, lady, are thy gifts, and life for thee
　　Should have sped onward like a summer's day,
　　Each moment gilded by affection's ray,
Till pleasure's light was quenched in death's calm sea;
This should have been thy fate, fair child of song,
　　Were happiness the meed of high deserving.
Alas! what skill may paint the griefs that throng
　　Around thy soul, its lofty powers unnerving?
Lonely, bereaved, and wronged, yet thou dost borrow
A crowning grace from woe — the majesty of sorrow.

WHERE was old England's chivalry, when thou,
　　Peerless in beauty and in genius, felt
　　The unvenomed shaft of calumny? where dwelt
The spirit that of old inspired the vow

To guard the right, and battle for the weak,
  When thou didst bow thy glorious head in shame,
  As the dark mildew fell on thy fair fame,
And Slander hinted what she dared not speak?
Where were the hearts that should have wakened then,
  When thou wast struck down from thy pride of place,
  Thou bird of song and beauty? That bright face
In ruder times had called forth noble men
To champion thy distress: such times are o'er,
And selfish interest rules where honor reigned before.

SPIRITUAL BEAUTY.

HERE is a form that visits me in dreams —
    A form of delicate and maiden grace;
    And o'er my slumbers bends a gentle face,
Where the soul's speaking brightness ever beams:
'Tis not a face of beauty, yet sweet gleams
  Of pure and holy thought are in her eyes,
And her lip wears a smile that ever seems
  To light the circling air like sunset skies.
Alas! 'tis but in dreams she comes; no more
  That gentle friend shall bless my waking sight,
Until life's changeful April day is o'er,
  And mine eyes close in death's untroubled night:
Then may I hope my lost one's face to see,
And share in happier worlds her immortality.
                18

STANZAS

ON THE DEATH OF A YOUNG LADY.

COULD friends have stayed the dart of death,
  Thou hadst not sure have died;
  Could love recall life's fleeting breath,
  Thou still wert at our side;
But thou wert hurried to the tomb
In all the flush of beauty's bloom,
  In all thy youthful pride;
Affection, powerless to save,
Could only weep above thy grave.

'Twas not the touch of slow disease,
  Sapping life's hidden springs,
Weaning the soul, by slow degrees,
  From all to which it clings;
'Twas not a summons long delayed,
And still reluctantly obeyed,
  Called thee from earthly things:
·A few brief days alone were given
To win thy thoughts from earth to heaven.

The world for thee was glad and bright,
  Thy path was strewn with flowers,
And Pleasure shed her rosiest light
  Upon youth's smiling bowers;
Yet no base fear was in thy heart
When called from all most loved to part,
  E'en in life's morning hours;

For in thy soul was Heaven's own grace,
And angel brightness on thy face.

Fame slants no laurel o'er the tomb
  Where thou dost calmly sleep,
But gentle memories round it bloom,
  And love there bends to weep:
Thou wert of those the world knows not;
Thou art of those, the unforgot,
  Who in our hearts we keep;
A mother's love — O! more than fame —
A mother's tears embalm thy name.

TO ——.

STRAIN of the heart's music! yet one more,
  Though it be low and broken in its tone,
  And blended with the old year's dying moan,
For thee, beloved, I pour.

A strain of the heart's music, full of love,
  Tender and grateful, — love the tried and true;
Yet mingled with a touch of sadness too,
    Like voice of turtle-dove.

For past is now life's glad and joyous spring,
  When every breeze my busy pulses stirred,
And my heart caroled like a forest bird,
    Rising on new-plumed wing.

Now through life's summer-time we journey on,
  Bearing the heat and burden of the day,
  Finding, at every footstep of the way,
    Some loved companion gone.

Hope weaves no more her wild fantastic measure,
  But wraps herself in Memory's mantle gray,
  And chants with quiet voice Truth's simple lay
    Of mingled pain and pleasure.

Yet in my bosom joy doth still abide,
  Aye, joy the purest earth has ever proved;
  For am I not still loving and beloved?
    Still, dear one, at thy side?

The happiness we have together known,
  The bitter tears we have together shed,
  The gentle memories of our blessed dead,
    Cherished by us alone, —

These are the links that bind our wedded hearts,
  These are the thoughts that make me love thee more,
  As years, like spent waves, die upon life's shore,
    And youth departs.

COME TO ME, LOVE.

COME to me, love; forget each sordid duty
    That chains thy footsteps to the crowded mart;
    Come, look with me upon earth's summer beauty,
And let its influence cheer thy weary heart:
           Come to me, love!

Come to me, love; the voice of song is swelling
    From nature's harp in every varied tone,
And many a voice of bird and bee is telling
    A tale of joy amid the forests lone:
           Come to me, love!

Come to me, love; my heart can never doubt thee,
    Yet for thy sweet companionship I pine;
O, never more can joy be joy without thee;
    My pleasures, even as my life, are thine:
           Come to me, love!

BALLAD.

IT was a lady young and fair
    Who sung that mournful strain;
    Her brow wore not a shade of care,
Her cheek no trace of pain;

Yet sung she, e'en as one who knows
    How youthful hearts are torn,
"Love's first step is upon the rose,
    His second finds the thorn."

Bright jewels bound her raven hair,
    And sparkled on her hand,
For earth held nought of rich or rare
    Her wealth might not command;
Yet mark how sad the music flows
    From lips curved half in scorn:
"Love's first step is upon the rose,
    His second finds the thorn."

No brighter, lovelier face appears
    In pleasure's crowded mart;
That proud eye was not made for tears,
    No blight should touch that heart;
Yet, as she sings, some memory throws
    Its shadow o'er life's morn:
"Love's first step is upon the rose,
    His second finds the thorn."

Alas! it is a weary task
    To trace life's hidden cares;
Seek not to raise the smiling mask
    Which maiden pride still wears;
A quaint old rhyme may oft disclose
    How much the heart has borne:
"Love's first step is upon the rose,
    His second finds the thorn."

STANZAS.

OURNFULLY my spirit turns
   To dreams of olden time,
   And oft my heart within me burns
When I hear some old-world rhyme ;
And ever has Poesy been to me
The Atlantis of Time's wide sea ;
I have steered full often my weary bark
For that green isle on the waters dark ;
But never my foot might press its shore,
And I turn to actual life once more
      Mournfully, O, mournfully !

Mournfully doth my bosom pine
   For the fantasies of youth ;
And I would that fancy now could shine
   With a light like that of truth ;
I would lift my worldly laden thought
To the realms with so much beauty fraught,
I would catch again the glorious gleam
That filled my soul with its heavenly beam
Ere my earthly hopes and earthly fears
Brought my feelings back to this vale of tears,
      Mournfully, O, mournfully !

Mournfully do my tear-drops fall
   On the poet's pictured page,
And fain would I the dreams recall
   That gladdened life's golden age ;

But I bartered those treasures long, long ago,
For happiness such as few can know,
Nor would I recall the feverish past,
With its wild unrest and its pang at last;
Yet the voice of song has a magic still,
And its gentle tones can my spirit thrill,
Mournfully, O, mournfully!

THE ENGLISH RIVER.

A FANTASY.

IT floweth on, with pleasant sound,
    A vague and dream-like measure,
And singeth to the flowers around
  A song of quiet pleasure;
No rugged cliff obstructs the way
Where the glad waters leap and play;
Or, if a tiny rock look down
In the calm stream with mimic frown,
The gentle waves new music make,
As at its base they flash and break.
It speedeth on, like joy's bright hours,
Traced but by verdure and by flowers;
But whether sunbeams on it rest,
Or storm-clouds hover o'er its breast,
Still in that green and shady glen,
Beside the busy haunts of men,
    The river singeth on.

It floweth on, past tree and flower,
  Until the stream is laving
The ruins of Strathallen's tower,
  With ivy banners waving.
Methinks the river's pleasant chime
Tells me a tale of olden time,
When mail-clad knights were often seen
Upon its banks of living green,
And gentle dames of lineage high,
With jeweled brow and flashing eye;
While many a squire, whose humble name
Was yet unheralded by fame,
Here wove his dreams of high emprise,
While musical as lovers' sighs,
        The river singeth on.

It floweth on, this gentle stream,
  And seems to tell the story
Of old-world heroes, and their dream
  Of fame and martial glory;
The war-cry on its banks has pealed,
Blent with the clang of lance and shield;
Waked to new life by war's alarms,
Bold knights, and squires, and men-at-arms,
Have sallied forth in proud array
With hearts impatient for the fray;
While the clear streamlet still gave back
The glittering sheen that marked their track.
Though nature's voice is all unheard
When pulses are thus madly stirred,
        The river singeth on.

Yet over e'en the sunniest fate
  Hangs the dark cloud of sorrow,
And sadder scenes the fancy wait,
  Since dreams from truth we borrow;
A well worn path, now grass-o'ergrown,
And hid by many a fallen stone,
To yonder roofless chapel led,
Where sleep Strathallen's buried dead;
Full often that pure stream has glassed
The funeral train as slow it passed:
Hark! as the cowlèd monks repeat
The Requiescat low and sweet,
    The river singeth on.

The vision fades, the phantoms flee,
  And nought of all remaineth;
The river runneth fast and free,
  The wind through ruins plaineth;
The feudal lord and belted knight,
And spurless squire and lady bright,
Long since have shared the common lot,
All, save their haughty name, forgot;
The line is ended, — there is none
To prize the fame his fathers won.
The ivy wreathes the ruined shrine,
And flaunts beneath the glad sunshine;
The fallen buttress, ruined wall,
And crumbling battlements are all
That still are left to tell the tale
Of those who ruled o'er that fair vale;

Nature resumes her lonely sway,
And flowers and music mark the way
The river singeth on.

THE AMERICAN RIVER.

A REMEMBRANCE.

IT rusheth on in fearful might,
    That river of the west,
    Through forest dense, where seldom light
Of sunbeam gilds its breast ;
Anon it dashes wildly past
The wide-spread prairie, lone and vast,
Without a shadow on its tide,
Save the long grass that skirts its side ;
Again its angry currents sweep
Beneath the tall and rocky steep
Which frowns above the darkened stream,
Till doubly deep its waters seem.
No rugged cliff may check its way,
No gentle mead invite its stay ;
Still with resistless, maddening force,
Following its wild and devious course,
        The river rusheth on.

It rusheth on ; the rocks are stirred,
    And echoing far and wide
Through the dim forest aisles is heard
    The thunder of its tide ;

No other sound strikes on the ear
Save when, beside its waters clear,
Crashing o'er branches dry and sere,
Comes bounding forth the antlered deer;
Or when, perchance, the woods give back
The arrow whizzing on its track,
Or deadlier rifle's vengeful crack.
No hum of city life is near,
And still uncurbed in its career,
  The river rusheth on.

It rusheth on; no fire-bark leaves
 Its dark and smoking trail
O'er the pure wave, which only heaves
 The bateau light and frail;
Long, long ago the rude canoe
Across those sparkling waters flew;
Long, long ago the Indian Brave
In that clear stream his brow might lave;
But seldom has the white man stood
Within that trackless solitude.
Yet onward, onward, dashing still,
With all the force of untamed will,
  The river rusheth on.

It rusheth on; no changes mark
 How many years have sped
Since to its banks, through forests dark,
 Some chance the hunter led;
Though many a season has passed o'er
The giant trees that gird its shore,

Though the soft limestone mass, impressed
By naked foootstep on its breast,
Now hardened into rock appears
By work of indurating years,
Yet 'tis by grander strength alone
That Nature's age is ever known.
While towers decay and nations fall,
And Thebes shows but a ruined wall,
Time in the wilderness displays
Th' ennobling power of length of days.
The crumbling buttress tells the tale
Of man's vain pomp and projects frail;
But in the forest's trackless bound,
Type of Eternity, is found
      The river rushing on.

STANZAS.

" Clean forgotten, as a dead man out of mind."
Psalms.

AND is this, then, the common lot?
    The end of earthly love and trust?
    To be by cherished ones forgot
When the frail body sleeps in dust?
Shall hearts which now with love run o'er,
    Retain for us no deeper trace
Than leaves the footprint on the shore,
    Which the next wavelet may efface?

Shall those who only seemed to live
  Within the sunshine of our smile,
To whom existence could not give
  A joy unshared by us the while, —
Shall they 'mid other joys live on,
  And form anew affection's tie,
When we from earth's delights are gone,
  Forever hid from human eye?

Aye; thus it is th' eternal laws
  That rule our nature are obeyed.
Not in mid conflict may we pause
  To linger long where love is laid;
We pile the sod above the breast
  Which pillowed oft our aching head,
Then turn, and leave unto its rest
  Our loved, but half-forgotten dead.

Tears, the heart's desolating rain,
  Awhile upon our path may fall,
But hope's sweet sunbeam smiles again,
  And grief can ne'er the past recall;
Anon the dirge's mournful measure
  Is changed to some less saddening strain,
And soon the echoing voice of pleasure
  Tells grief and love alike were vain.

We form new schemes of future bliss,
  New flowers spring up to cheer our way,
And scarcely from our side we miss
  The partners of life's earlier day;

Alas! how vain our noblest feelings,
How idle would affection seem,
Did not God give us bright revealings
Of life where love is not a dream!

SONNET

TO WILLIAM CULLEN BRYANT, WRITTEN IMMEDIATELY
AFTER THE PERUSAL OF HIS POEMS.

MY thanks are thine, most gifted one; to thee
I owe an hour of intellectual life,
A sweet hour, rescued from the noise, and strife,
And turmoil of the world, which but to see
Or hear óf, from afar, is pain to me.
I thank thee for the rich draught thou hast brought
To lips that love the well-springs of pure thought,
Which from thy soul gush up so plenteously.
The hymnings of thy prophet voice awake
Those nobler impulses that, hushed and still,
Lie hidden in our breast, till some wild thrill
Of spirit-life has power their chains to break;
Then from our long inglorious dream we start,
As if an angel's tone had stirred the slumbering heart.

A LITANY.

HEN the sun of joy shines brightest,
And our steps on earth are lightest ;
When to songs of quiet pleasure
Every pulse keeps joyful measure ;
When no storm-cloud hovers o'er us,
And no darkness lies before us —
Then from dangers lurking nigh,
All unmarked by human eye ;
From the serpent in life's bowers,
Coiled beneath the fairest flowers ;
From the evil thoughts that hide
Even most where joys abide, —
  Good Lord, deliver us !

When a rugged path we tread,
And the heart grows faint with dread ;
When o'er waters wild and dark
Drifts our lone and helmless bark,
While the stars wax dim and pale,
And our hopes of succor fail ;
When to heaven we lift our eyes,
As the waves around us rise,
Feeling that our God is there, —
O ! in answer to our prayer,
  Good Lord, deliver us !

When the hour of death draws near,
And the soul is filled with fear ;

When, with lingering step and slow,
Onward to the grave we go,
Turning from a world of light
T'ward the realms of endless night, —
Then from demons that assail us
When the powers of nature fail us;
From the evil shapes that seem
Fancies of a sick man's dream,
Yet which come, with fearful power,
Tempting us in life's last hour, —
          Good Lord, deliver us!

When the awful trump shall sound,
Startling the world's remotest bound;
When earth's charnel-house shall pour
Its myriads forth to life once more;
When, shrinking, trembling, fearful, all
Before thy glorious footstool fall, —
From the judgments that await
The spirit unregenerate;
From the sinner's guilty shame,
The gnawing worm, the quenchless flame, —
          Good Lord, deliver us!

19

POESY.

HAST thou ne'er marked a fount, from earth up-
    springing,
  Within the shelter of some greenwood glade,
Scarce seen by human eye, yet gladly flinging
  Its wealth of freshness in that sylvan shade ?

The very herbage that its waters nourish
  Serves to conceal it from the passer-by ;
Only the flow'rets on its brink that flourish
  Reveal its windings to the thoughtless eye.

O, thus be Poesy within my bosom, —
  A bubbling fountain ever pure and bright,
Known only by the charities that blossom
  Beneath its influence into life and light !

Within my heart, unchecked, that sweet stream gushes,
  As fresh and pure as in my girlhood's day ;
No beam from glory's sun its surface flushes,
  Love only marks its solitary way.

What though its early fullness has been wasted
  On many a wayside herb and lowly flower ?
It floweth on, and one beloved hath tasted
  Its cooling wave in many a weary hour.

Full well I know that silently it wendeth
  In seeming idlesse to Oblivion's sea,
And yet to daily life its presence lendeth
  A beauty and a bliss enough for me.

DISTRUST.

TOO late! too late! in days of yore,
    Thy voice has thrilled through heart and
        brain,
For then I knelt as never more
    I kneel at woman's shrine again;
Then hadst thou breathed one tender sigh,
    I had lain humbled at thy feet,
E'en though, like Brahma's votary, I
    Could only hope my death to meet.

But I have borne the weight of ill,
    Have suffered all a lover's fate,
Until my heart, benumbed and chill,
    Can only feel thou comest too late;
The joys that blessed our early youth,
    The hopes that o'er my pathway shone,
Love's perfect trustfulness and truth,
    Its sweet unselfishness, are gone.

Within my bosom's secret cell
    Love, lonely hermit, still abides,

But ah! 'neath Memory's cowl too well
   His roseate wreath of joy he hides;
Aye, Love is there, but pale and worn
   His weary vigil still he keeps
Besides the voiceless burial urn,
   Where happiness forever sleeps.

No more I breathe the anguished prayer,
   No more I make the yearning cry;
The haunting demons of despair
   Now couched in sullen silence lie;
Distrust has come our hearts between,
   A sense of wrong in both has dwelt;
We cannot be what we have been,
   We cannot feel as we have felt.

SLIGHTED LOVE.

HE struggle is over;
      Such strife could not last;
      And pride now must cover
   All trace of the past;
My heart has grown stronger,
   Nor shrinks from its task, —
Go, cold one, no longer
   One kind thought I ask.

Thou hast taught me the weakness
   Of woman's fond trust,

When in love's lowly meekness
I knelt in the dust;
And now my brow flushes
With anger and shame,
As my proud spirit crushes
Its once cherished flame.

Our love-dream is vanished,
And coldly I speak
The words that once banished
The blood from my cheek.
Other idols have wooed thee,
All changed is thy lot,
For Fame has pursued thee,
And Love is forgot.

STANZAS.

" I die if neglected."

 TELL me not of lofty fate,
Of glory's deathless name;
The bosom love leaves desolate
Has nought to do with fame.

Vainly philosophy would soar;
Love's height it may not reach;
The heart soon learns a sweeter lore
Than ever sage could teach.

The cup may bear a poisoned draught,
　The altar may be cold;
But yet the chalice will be quaffed,
　The shrine sought as of old.

Man's sterner nature turns away
　To seek ambition's goal;
Wealth's glittering gifts and pleasure's ray
　May charm his weary soul;

But woman knows one only dream —
　That broken, all is o'er;
For on life's dark and sluggish stream
　Hope's sunbeam rests no more.

LINES TO A FRIEND.

LIKE that sweet melody which faintly lingers
　Upon the wind-harp's strings at close of day,
When, gently touched by Evening's dewy fingers,
It breathes a low and melancholy lay, —

So thy calm voice of sympathy meseemeth,
　And, while its magic spell is round me cast,
My spirit in its cloistered silence dreameth,
　And vaguely blends the future with the past.

But vain such dreams while pain my bosom thrilleth
　And mournful memories around me move,

E'en friendship's alchemy no balm distilleth
  To soothe the immedicable wound of love.

O, well thou knowest this truth, for thou hast tasted
  The draught which leaves such bitterness behind ;
Thou e'en in life's glad spring hast idly wasted
  Feeling's sweet perfume on the unconscious wind.

Alas ! alas ! passion too soon exhaleth
  The dewy freshness of the heart's young flowers ;
We water them with tears — but nought availeth,
  They wither on through all life's later hours.

SONNET.

NO more, — no more, my heart ! give out no more
  Thy solemn music to the inconstant wind,
  Suffer not every careless hand to find
Thy hidden stops of harmony, nor pour,
As thou wert wont to do in days of yore,
  Thy sweetest tones on ears that yield no heed :
  O, be not thou like the responsive reed,
That, ever as the light air wandereth o'er,
  Utters its wild and broken melody ;
For I would have thee like the ocean shell,
  Breathing a monotone of that deep sea
Whose moaning waves within my breast must swell,
  Marking with ebb and flow my destiny,
Until death's icy touch the restless surge shall quell.

THE INCONSTANT.

PLEDGE to thy lady; aye, fill high the bowl
To the Cynthia that rules o'er the tides of
thy soul, —
To her whose light hand wanders over thy heart,
Bringing out the rich music its chords can impart;
Aye, drink to her now, lest a new love awake,
Ere thy lip meets the wine bead that swells but to
break.

Pledge to thy lady, but breathe not her name;
That draught quenched already a fast-waning flame;
Ere next at the banquet thou pourest the red wine,
Thy love will be pilgrim at some newer shrine;
Another will weave thee a fresher rose-chain,
To be worn a brief moment, then flung off again.

A CHARACTER.

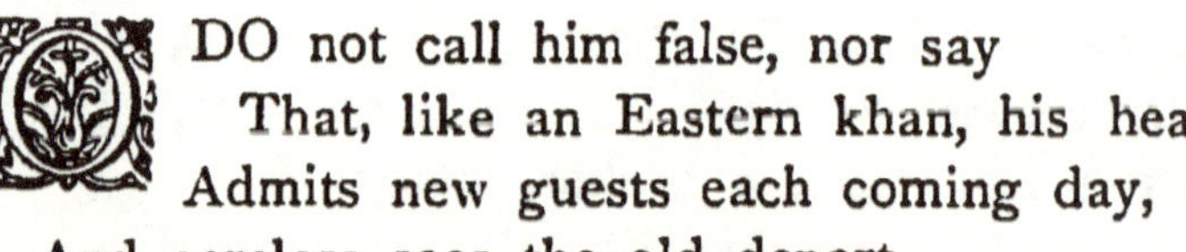

I DO not call him false, nor say
That, like an Eastern khan, his heart
Admits new guests each coming day,
And careless sees the old depart.

'Tis rather like some idol fane,
Where crowds of pilgrims pass the gate,
And kneel in homage brief as vain,
While but one priestess there may wait.

RECKLESS MIRTH.

AYE, give me wine, and let me quaff
  To the light-winged loves around me ;
Fill high the bowl, and we will laugh
At the rose-chains that once bound me ;
Call in the guests, and I will smile,
  With a brow as free from sorrow
As if my heart was glad the while,
  And looked for as glad a morrow.

Aye, give me wine : to me 'tis fraught
  With a spell of daily gladness,
For it drowns the voice of that lonely thought
  Whose whispers are full of sadness.
Then serve the feast, and we well drink
  To the present's fleeting pleasures ;
Let me drain the cup, for I would not think
  Of the past with its buried treasures.

Aye, give me wine : I'll cull to-night,
  From the wreath by passion braided,
Some blossoms rainbow-hued and bright,
  Some leaflets still unfaded ;
For while young beauty's beaming eye
  On my blighted brow reposes,
I'll pledge the love that awakes no sigh,
  And gather life's thornless roses.

· I WILL NOT LOVE THEE.

WILL not love thee; I have ever cast
 'Too many passion-flowers on life's dark tide,
Then, like a truant school-boy, idly passed
My vacant hours to watch them onward glide.

I will not love thee; why should I reope
 My bosom's secret treasury for thee,
And cull its richest gems, without one hope
 To see them shine amid thy blazonry?

I will not love thee; thou shalt never find
 My hopes to thee, like incense, offered up;
I will not fling sweet odors to the wind,
 Or melt another pearl in passion's cup.

I will not love thee; though I know thee all
 That women envy and that men adore,
Though on my brow thy smiles like sunbeams fall,
 My heart must worship, but must love no more.

INQUIETUDE.

METHOUGHT the icy hand of Time had chilled
 The gushing fount of passion in my breast;
Methought that reason's power, for aye, had stilled
The bitter struggles of my heart's unrest.

Cold, calm, and self-possessing, I had deemed
　In quiet now to view life slip away,
Forgetting much that once my soul had dreamed,
　And lengthening out in peace my little day.

Safe in indifference, I had vainly hoped
　To scorn the sympathy I might not share,
And little thought mine own hand would have oped
　My bosom's portal to returning care.

How burns the blush of shame upon my cheek,
　How bends to earth in grief my haughty brow,
When thus I find myself disarmed and weak
　Before the ideal shapes that haunt me now!

O God! how long, misled by erring thought,
　Shall I grope darkly on in feeling's maze?
When shall I be by Time's sad lessons taught,
　And reach my home of rest by quiet ways?

A GENTLE HERITAGE IS MINE.

GENTLE heritage is mine,
　　A life of quiet pleasure;
　My heaviest cares are but to twine
Fresh votive garlands for the shrine
　Where bides my bosom's treasure.
I am not merry, nor yet sad;
My thoughts are more serene than glad.

I have outlived youth's feverish mirth
  And all its causeless sorrow ;
My joys are now of nobler worth,
My sorrows, too, have holier birth,
  And heavenly solace borrow ;
·So, from my green and shady nook,
Back on my by-past life I look.

The Past has memories sad and sweet,
  Memories still fondly cherished,
Of joys that blossomed at my feet,
Whose odors still my senses greet,
  E'en though the flowers have perished ;
Visions of friends long past away,
Whose love once blest life's earlier day.

The Future, Isis-like, sits veiled,
  And none her mystery learneth ;
It may be that her cheek is paled
With sorrows yet to be bewailed ;
  Perhaps before her burneth
A lurid fire that must destroy
My every bud of hope and joy.

I would not lift the veil that hides
  Life's coming joy or sorrow ;
If sweet content with me abides
While onward still the Present glides,
  I think not of the morrow ;
It may bring griefs ; enough for me
The quiet joy I feel and see.

SONG.

LOVE her? No! for passion blendeth
   Ever with the heart's young dream ;
  And earth's evil shadow lendeth
Darkness to life's purest beam ;
Still with jealous hopes and fears
   Love has marked his weary lot,
Tracing every step by tears ;
   Then be sure I love her not.

Love her? No! such fire ne'er burneth
   Save when sighing fans the flame ;
While the bosom wildly yearneth,
   Nursing hopes it dares not name ;
Since desires the soul may stir,
   Vague and vain, yet unforgot,
I would guard sweet thoughts of her,
   But be sure to love her not.

Love her? No! my heart inurneth
   Ashes she can ne'er illume ;
And the lamp that in me burneth
   Shines, a lamp within a tomb ;
On my brow the seal is set,
   Sorrow never sets in vain ;
Time may teach me to forget,
   But I cannot love again.

Love her? No! pure, deep devotion
   Such as angel hearts might prize,

Stills my bosom's wild emotion
    When I meet her earnest eyes;
Like a high and holy star
    Cheereth she my lonely lot;
I may worship from afar,
    But be sure I love her not.

SONG.

HAVE won thee to love me, all cold as thou
        art;
I have won thee to love me, untamable heart!
For this every joy of my life has been given,
For this I have risked every promise of heaven;
I have won thee to love me, — I hold thee in thrall,
And the sight of thy bondage repays me for all.

I have won thee to love me, untamable heart!
I have won thee to love me, and now let us part;
Thou mayst throw off my fetters with haughty disdain,
But the scar and the aching must ever remain;
My toils may seem frail as the wood-spider's net,
But Love's spell is upon thee, — thou canst not forget.

NEVER FORGET.

NEVER forget the hour of our first meeting,
　　When 'mid the sounds of revelry and song
　　Only thy soul could know that mine was greeting
Its idol, wished for, waited for so long;
　　　　Never forget.

Never forget the joy of that revealment,
　　Centring an age of bliss in one sweet hour,
When love broke forth from friendship's frail concealment
　　And stood confessed to us in godlike power;
　　　　Never forget.

Never forget my heart's intense devotion,
　　Its wealth of freshness at thy feet flung free,
Its golden hopes whelmed in that boundless ocean
　　Which merged all wishes, all desires, save thee;
　　　　Never forget.

Never forget the moment when we parted,
　　When from love's summer-cloud the bolt was hurled
That drove us, scathed in soul and broken-hearted,
　　Alone to wander through this desert world;
　　　　Never forget.

THE ÆOLIAN HARP.

HARP of the Winds! how vainly art thou swelling
    Thy diapason on the heedless blast!
    How idly, too, thy gentler chords are telling
  A tale of sorrow as the breeze sweeps past!
Why dost thou waste on loneliness the strain
Which were not heard by human ears in vain?

And the harp answered : "Though the winds are bearing
  My soul of sweetness on their viewless wings,
Yet one faint tone may reach some soul despairing,
  And rouse its energies to happier things;
O! not in vain my song, if it but gives
One moment's joy to anything that lives."

O heart of mine! canst thou not here, discerning
  An emblem of thyself, some solace find?
Though earth may never quench thy life-long yearning,
  Yet give thyself, like music, to the wind;
Thy wandering thoughts may teach thy love and trust,
And waken sympathy when thou art dust.

" SOMETHING BEYOND."

HEART ! weary heart ! what means thy wild un-
        rest ?
        Hast thou not tasted of life's every pleasure ?
With all that mortals seek, thy lot is blest,
    Yet dost thou ever chant in solemn measure,
            " Something beyond ! "

Heart ! weary heart ! canst thou not find repose
    In the sweet calm of friendship's pure devotion ?
Amid the peace which sympathy bestows,
    Still dost thou murmur with repressed emotion,
            " Something beyond ! "

Heart ! weary heart ! too idly hast thou poured
    Thy music and thy perfume on the blast ;
Now beggared in affection's treasured hoard,
    Thy cry is still, — thy saddest and thy last, —
            " Something beyond ! "

Heart ! weary heart ! O cease thy wild unrest ;
    Earth cannot satisfy thy bitter yearning ;
But onward, upward speed thy lonely quest,
    And hope to find, where heaven's pure stars are
        burning,
            " Something beyond ! "

20

THE MOURNER'S APPEAL.

LOWERS, happy flowers! methinks your tender
    eyes
  Look kindly on me in my deep distress;
Dwells there no healing virtue in your sighs?
  Have ye no balm the weary heart to bless?
Can ye not give from out your glowing hearts
  A freshness like the joy of childhood's hours?
Or must I sadly feel, as youth departs,
  Life's dial only once is wreathed with flowers?

Stars, holy stars! pure watchers of the night!
  Is there no beam that points the way to hope?
Amid a world of so much gladsome light,
  Must I forever in thick darkness grope?
O chase this vague, wild horror from my thought;
  Let me but feel Heaven pities my deep woe;
My future years are with such anguish fraught,
  I would look upward, — peace dwells not below.

Since first my soul took cognizance of life,
  I've looked on Nature with a lover's eye;
Amid the world's vain toil and bitter strife,
  I still have felt her gentle influence nigh:
Yet now when in my agony I come,
  Fleeing to her in refuge from despair,
Her shrine is cold, her oracles are dumb,
  No sympathy nor solace wait me there.

'Tis that mine eyes are dimmed with frequent tears,
  Else would I see a balm in every flower,
And find a light to chase my gloomy fears
  In every star that gems the evening hour;
'Tis that my soul is dark with sinful doubt,
  And finds no promise in a world so fair,
Else would each star and fragrant bud give out
  Its pledge that God, our Hope, is everywhere.

SONNET

TO THE AUTHOR OF "VESTIGES OF CREATION."

SELF-MISSIONED leader through Creation's
        maze !
      Dost thou interpret thus God's mighty scheme
Weaving the cobweb fancies of a dream
O'er each gray vestige of His mystic ways?
When thus midst chaos thou didst blindly grope,
  Gathering new links for matter's heavy chain,
Dwelt there not in thy soul the secret hope
  That some strong truth would rend the bond of pain
Which fixed thee to Progression's iron wheel?
  O teach not suffering earth such hopeless creed,—
Too heavy were her curse if doomed to feel
  That in her frequent hour of bitter need,
Her lifted eye of prayer could only see
Necessity's stern laws graven on Eternity.

SONNET

ON A PICTURE OF THE TWO MARYS AT THE TOMB OF CHRIST.

" Last at his cross and earliest at his grave."

NOT to the holy men in whom the flame
  Of inspiration all serenely burned,
  When from his lips God's mystic truths they
    learned, —
Not unto them the risen Christ first came ;
Theirs were the gifts of prophecy and prayer,
  And eloquent teaching of his holy name ;
'Twas theirs his ministry of good to share,
  To bear his cross and to despise the shame ;
But they who humbly sought to do his will,
  Content to bear meek-hearted woman's doom, —
They who had lingered last on Calvary's hill,
  And earliest sought their master's hallowed tomb, —
To them 'twas given their risen Lord to see,
And catch the first bright gleam of immortality.

SONNET.

ALAS for those who quench the holy spark
  Of inspiration in their secret soul,
  Yielding their natures up to earth's control,
Until the mental sight grows dim and dark,

And thought no longer seeks a lofty mark,
  No longer toils to reach a noble goal,
  While the heart drains life's enervating bowl,
And freights with all its hopes some helmless bark !
Alas ! alas ! on earthly shrines we lay
  The incense we should offer up to Heaven,
We lavish on an idol of to-day
  The love that for infinitude was given,
Till from our souls the light fades slow away,
  And clouds of doubt and fear are o'er our spirits
    driven.

THE STAR-FLOWER.

KNOW you whence sprung this starry flower,
  With golden heart and azure rays,
  Which blooms in every woodland bower
When fades the glow of summer days?

Then list the legend long since heard
  Beside the red man's winding river,
What time the wilds and forests lone
  Were held by right of bow and quiver.

They tell of one, — a youthful brave
  (His name would far outrun my rhyme) ;
His fame, in savage warfare won,
  Would rival those of classic time.

They tell how in the ambushed strife
  An arrow pierced his fearless breast,
And how, on Susquehanna's marge,
  They laid him with his sires to rest.

But when the burial rites were done,
  And he in forest glade was sleeping,
There came a gentle Indian maid,
  Whose starry eyes were dim with weeping.

She built her lodge beside the grave,
  And there, as passed each dreary morrow,
She still her faithful vigil held,
  And dwelt alone with love and sorrow.

Full soon, beneath Annunga's[1] care,
  The turf was decked with many a flower,
Until death's dreary home appeared
  As fair as love's own chosen bower.

There lingered last the buds of spring,
  There first glowed forth the summer's bloom,
And autumn's gayest flow'rets shed
  Their glories round that woodland tomb.

All day within her silent lodge
  The mourner shrunk before the light,
For earth beneath the sun's glad ray
  Seemed to her tearful eye too bright.

[1] Annung, *i. e.* The Star.

But when the shades of evening fell,
  Deepening the tint of leaf and blossom,
And stars came looking meekly forth,
  Glassed in the river's tranquil bosom, —

Then knelt she by that hallowed spot,
  And wept the livelong night away,
Until heaven's sparkling crown grew dim,
  And faded in the morning ray.

When earth was wrapped in wintry shroud,
  And leafless trees stood grim and gaunt,
Like giant spectres set to guard
  The spot where grief had made her haunt, —

Still dwelt she in her forest lair,
  Which cowered beneath the branches low,
And seemed, amid those dreary wilds,
  A speck upon the waste of snow.

Thus came and went the changing times,
  While still the maid her watch was keeping,
Till grief its weary task had done,
  And life was worn with frequent weeping.

But in that season[1] when the haze
  With purple light the distance fills,
As if old Autumn in his flight
  Had dropped his mantle on the hills ;

[1] The Indian summer.

When forest trees with regal pomp
　　Their wealth of gem-like leaves display,
And earth in gayest garb puts on
　　The glory that precedes decay, —

Then prostrate on. her lover's grave,
　　With long black hair all lifeless spread,
Shrouding her in its pall-like gloom,
　　They found the gentle maiden dead.

And where her quivering lip was pressed
　　When breathing forth her life's last sigh,
They, wondering, saw a nameless flower
　　Look meekly upward to the sky.

Such blossom ne'er before was found
　　In woodland brake, or tangled dell ;
It sprung beneath Annunga's sigh,
　　Born from the heart that loved too well.

THE RUINED MILL.

LONE and roofless thing it stands
　　In sunshine and in shower,
　　Stretching abroad its palsied hands,
　A wreck of giant power ;
Each mouldering beam and crumbling stone
With velvet moss is now o'ergrown,
　　While many a wind-sown flower

Is peeping through the broken floor,
Seeking the place it held of yore.

The bright-eyed toad looks fearless out,
    And newts to covert steal,
While the spider weaves his web about
    The cogs of the massive wheel;
And where the miller once gayly stood
The adder rears her hissing brood,
    Nor fears his iron heel;
Man's rule within the place is o'er,
And Nature wins her own once more.

O'er the broken dam the brook leaps free,
    And speeds on its course along,
Wooing the wild flowers daintily
    With its smiles and pleasant song;
No longer chained to the busy mill,
It wanders on at its own sweet will,
    The hoary rocks among,
Then creeps around the old tree's foot,
To brighten the moss on its gnarled root.

I sate me on a gray old stone
    And watched the lapsing stream,
Till outward things before me shone
    Like pictures in a dream;
Amid the mists of reverie,
I rather seemed to feel than see
    Earth's bright and sunny gleam;

Once more the angel of my youth
Touched all things with a sweeter truth.

That bright ideal ! O, how well
  My spirit knew its power,
For early had I learned its spell
  In childhood's sunny hour ;
It gave new glory to the skies,
New music to earth's melodies,
  New charms to every flower ;
But rarely now the gentle sprite
Awakes me to such deep delight.

Yet there, in that secluded spot,
  Beside the ruined mill,
Came back the fancies, long forgot,
  Which fain would haunt me still ;
That stream an image seemed to be
Of mine own gushing poesy,
  Wasted with wanton will,
Without concentrate power to sway
A leaflet on its loitering way.

PORTRAITS.

A GENTLE maiden, whose large, loving eyes
　　Enshrine a tender melancholy light,
　　Like the soft radiance of the starry skies,
　Or autumn sunshine, mellowed when most bright;
She is not sad, yet in her look appears
Something that makes the gazer think of tears.

She is not beautiful; her features bear
　　A loveliness by angel hands imprest,
Such as the pure in heart alone may wear,
　　The outward symbol of a soul at rest;
And this beseems her well, for love and truth
Companion ever with her guileless youth.

She hath a delicate foot, a dainty hand,
　　And every limb displays unconscious grace,
Like one who, born a lady in the land,
　　Taketh no thought how best to fill her place,
But moveth ever at her own sweet will,
While gentleness and pride attend her still.

Nor hath she lost, by any sad mischance,
　　The happy thoughts that to her years belong;

Her step is ever fleetest in the dance,
  Her voice is ever gayest in the song ;
The silent air by her rich notes is stirred
As by the music of a forest bird.

No poison-breathing passion flowers are twined
  Around the brow where Heaven has set its seal ;
Her soul, in crystal purity enshrined,
  No touch of earth-born vanity can feel ;
Already half-enskyed and consecrate,
The child of God awaits her blessed fate.

There dwelleth in the sinlessness of·youth
  A sweet rebuke that vice may not endure,
And thus she makes an atmosphere of truth,
  For all things in her presence grow more pure ;
She walks in light, — her guardian angel flings,
A halo round her from his radiant wings.

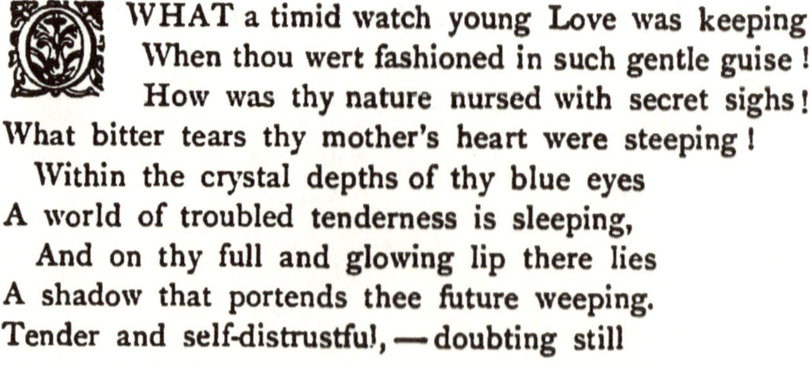

WHAT a timid watch young Love was keeping
  When thou wert fashioned in such gentle guise !
  How was thy nature nursed with secret sighs !
What bitter tears thy mother's heart were steeping !
  Within the crystal depths of thy blue eyes
A world of troubled tenderness is sleeping,
  And on thy full and glowing lip there lies
A shadow that portends thee future weeping.
Tender and self-distrustful, — doubting still

Thyself, but trusting all the world beside,
Tremblingly sensitive to coming ill,
  Blending with woman's fondness manhood's pride, —
How wilt thou all life's future conflicts bear,
And fearless suffer all that man must do and dare?

PROUD, self-sustained, and fearless, — dreading
      nought
    Save falsehood, loving everything but sin, —
  How glorious is the light that from within
Illumes thy boyish face with lofty thought !
A child art thou, but thy deep eyes are fraught
  With that mysterious light by genius shed,
And in thy aspect is a something caught
  From the bright dreams that cluster round thy head.
I know not what thy future lot may be ;
  But when men gather to a new crusade
Against earth's falsehood, wrong, and tyranny,
  Thou wilt be there with all thy strength displayed, —
Thy voice clear ringing 'mid the conflict's roar,
And on thy banner writ in stars, " Excelsior."

SUCH as thou art the loved disciple seemed
    To the bright visions of the men of old,
    When on their speaking canvas ever gleamed
His tender face within the pitying fold

Of the meek Saviour's arm, as if His breast
Gave its own softness to the cheek it prest.

Such look is thine, my gentle one; I meet
    Upsearching reverence in those pure eyes,
And on my soul rush yearnings sad and sweet,
    While hopes and memories together rise, —
Hopes that for thee on time's wild waves are tost,
Memories that linger with the loved and lost.

There beams a tender sadness in thy face,
    Which, though ofttimes exchanged for sunbright glee,
Yet comes back ever with a winning grace,
    Drawing our hearts, as by a spell, to thee,
And telling of the deep and trusting love
That o'er thy spirit broodeth like a dove.

THE OLD MAN'S LAMENT.

FOR one draught of those sweet waters now,
    That shed such freshness o'er my early life !
    O that I could but bathe my fevered brow,
  To wash away the dust of worldly strife,
And be a simple-hearted child once more,
As if I ne'er had known this world's pernicious lore !

My heart is weary, and my spirit pants
  Beneath the heat and burden of the day :
Would that I could regain those shady haunts
  Where once with hope I dreamed the hours away,
Giving my thoughts to tales of old romance,
And yielding up my soul to youth's delicious trance !

Vain are such wishes ! I no more may tread
  With lingering step and slow the green hill-side ;
Before me now life's shortening path is spread,
  And I must onward, whatsoe'er betide ;
The pleasant nooks of youth are passed for aye,
And sober scenes now meet the traveller on his way.

Alas ! the dust which clogs my weary feet,
  Glitters with fragments of each ruined shrine

Where once my spirit worshipped, when with sweet
  And passionless enthusiasm it could twine
Its strong affections round earth's earthliest things,
Yet bear away no stain upon its snowy wings.

What though some flowers have 'scaped the tempest's
      wrath?
  Daily they droop by nature's swift decay.
What though the setting sun still lights my path?
  Morn's dewy freshness long has passed away;
O give me back life's newly budded flowers!
Let me once more inhale the breath of morning's hours!

My youth! my youth! O give me back my youth!
  Not the unfurrowed brow and blooming cheek,
But childhood's sunny thoughts, its perfect truth,
  And youth's unworldly feelings; these I seek!
Ah who can e'er be sinless and yet sage?
Would that I might forget Time's dark and blotted page!

PATIENT LOVE.

KNOW thou lovest me not; I know
    My image now must seem
A footprint in the drifting snow,
  A shadow on the stream;
Yet on thy memory will I trace
A name that years can ne'er efface.

I know that all thy dreams of life
  With brighter hopes are fraught,
Yet 'mid the future's weary strife
  Will come a gentle thought,
Winning thy heart in sadness back
To pleasures in thy by-past track.

I would not bind thee by a spell,
  Were mine a Circe's skill ;
I could not love thee half so well
  But for thy curbless will ;
The fettered eagle ne'er should be
An emblem meet for one like thee.

I twine no garlands for thy brow,
  I weave no silken tie ;
Thou wert not worthy of my vow :
  Couldst thou in bondage sigh ?
My heart's deep faith I would not yield
To one who bore a rusted shield.

Go forth in hopefulness and pride,
  And while earth's joys are thine,
I ask not thou shouldst turn aside
  To friendship's lowly shrine,
Where kneeleth one who there always
For thee in humble meekness prays.

No thought in mirthful hour I claim ;
  But when thy sorrows come,

21

Then wilt thou think upon my name,
    And seek thy spirit's home.
Let others share thy pleasures brief :
I only ask to bear thy grief.

To thee I am as nothing now,
    And so I fain would be ;
I bide the coming time when thou
    Shalt fondly think of me,
And turn, when brighter hopes depart,
To rest upon my patient heart.

SONNET.

BRING to thee no gift, no outward sign
    Of the indwelling love that fills my heart ;
    No symbol-language meetly may impart
An emblem quaint for tenderness like mine.
I bring to thee no gift ; I could not twine
    Flowers as unfading as affection's bloom,
    And Earth holds not in all her caverned gloom
A gem that like unfailing truth may shine.
I bring no gift ; for long ago I gave
    All that was worthiest both of heart and brain ;
And thou hast learned, in love and trust, to brave
    The poet's waywardness, perchance with pain,
But yet with hope ; as from the stormiest wave
    The diver ever seeks his purest pearls to gain.

DREAMS.

" So he giveth his beloved sleep."

Psalm cxxvii.

HE giveth his beloved sleep;" O blest
The boon that stills the fevered pulse of pain,
Shedding refreshing dews o'er heart and brain,
And to the sorrow stricken bringing rest.

" He giveth his beloved sleep;" how vain
Were all earth's blessings if bereft of this !
How would we faint e'en 'mid continuous bliss,
Could we no moment of repose attain !

He giveth sleep, but ah ! he giveth more ;
When the worn frame in peaceful slumber lies,
The spirit soars beneath enchanted skies,
And finds youth's fountain on a brighter shore.

From angel pinions come the sunny gleams
That make the world of sleep a world of light ;
Day brings its sins and sorrows, but the night
Still wooes us heavenward through the land of Dreams.

ILLUSIONS.

" Shadows we are, and shadows we pursue."

NUMBER the riches by thy memory hoarded,
  Relics of joys thy by-past years have known:
How many real things are here recorded?
How much true light was o'er thy pathway thrown?

'Twas fancy's hand bestowed the fairy treasures
  That made thee rich in boyhood's golden time,
Imagination deepened all youth's pleasures,
  Illusion brightened all thy manhood's prime.

Seen through the wave of time above them sweeping,
  Hope's broken fanes in softer splendor gleam;
The retrospective eye forgets its weeping,
  The past wears all the glory of a dream.

How can we say this joy or that was real,
  When all have passed like visions of the night?
How can we know the true from the ideal? ·
  Which glowed with inward, which with outward light?

It needs not we should ask: the grave's dark portal
  Soon shuts this world of shadows from our view;
Then shall we grasp realities immortal,
  If to the truth within us we are true.

STANZAS.

NAY, fear me not; deem not that I would meet thee
  With bitter word, cold look, or chilling tone;
I could — I think I could now calmly greet thee
  With the bland smile of courtesy alone;
Why should I not, since thou wert not the friend
On whom my heart did so much wealth expend?

'Twas my own fancy conjured up a creature
  High-souled and earnest, pure and passion free,
Made it assume thy shape in form and feature,
  Gave it thy thrilling tones, and called it thee;
It was no fault of thine that I was schooled
To know myself by my own nature fooled.

I did mistake thee, yet thy thought is cherished
  Amid the heart's rich relics of the past;
Though all that made its charm has long since perished,
  'Twas an illusion pleasant to the last,
And gentle memories in my bosom dwell
Of friendship's faded dream and broken spell.

So on thy heart, in hours of lonely sadness,
  Will beam the image of a loving eye,
That once could brighten at thy mood of gladness,
  Or darken into sorrow at thy sigh,
Till to thy soul comes back its haunting pain,
Its quenchless thirst for sympathy again.

I would have saved thee from this yearning sorrow,
  And shared the pangs that wring thy fevered brow,
But thou hast willed it thus: the cheating morrow
  Still wins thy fealty from the truthful now;
The false mirage that in the desert gleams
Can tempt thee ever from life's freshening streams.

I think of thee as of a friend departed
  To some far region which I ne'er may tread;
The air thou breathest is not for the true-hearted,
  Therefore art thou more distant than the dead.
Alas! the surest trust our heart can feel,
Is in that love where Death has set his seal.

SONNET.

HOW are men worn with heaviness of heart,
  And wasted with fierce turmoil of the soul!
  Surge after surge our passions wildly roll,
Sweeping o'er each sweet hope till life depart.
Earth holds no balsam for the bitter smart
  Of feelings wounded as by insect stings,
  Of instincts crushed beneath earth's baser things,
And tortured till they learn the torturer's art.
  Fame has no clarion note to drown the cry
That from our nature's anguished depths comes up!
Love — alas! from Love's empoisoned cup
  We drink the honeyed draught by which we die.
O God of mercy! bid this tumult cease:
Thy hand alone can shed the dews of holy peace.

SONNET ON HEARING MUSIC.

THE wind's sad song through ocean's echoing
cave,
The wave's deep sob a foundered bark above,
A mother's wail beside the span-long grave
Which holds the earliest blossom of her love,
The dove's low plaining through the high-arched grove
Where falling waters blend their monotone
With rustling leaves, and that deep-cadenced moan,
While evening's breath the closing blossoms move, —
The sweetest, saddest music ever heard
From earth's rich harp, with all its thousand strings,
Comes to my fancy, and my soul is stirred
As by the waving of an angel's wings
When that deep thrilling melody hath spoken
Its tale of hallowed grief, its death-song of hearts broken.

STANZAS.

NAY, fathom not Time's rushing stream
When swollen its tide with tears,
And count not over faded dream
To measure out thy years..

O! even for the darkest lot
Hath life some blessed thing,

As earth holds not the sterile spot
  Where verdure may not spring.

But we in bitter discontent
  The wayside blossom spurn,
And for some bright and far-off star
  With wild, vain longings yearn.

When sunbeams cross our pathway dark,
  We joy not in their ray,
But set a dial up to mark
  How swift they pass away.

Yet would we take the joy that is,
  Nor dream of what might be ;
Time could be meted out by bliss,
  Not marked by misery.

For even in our daily paths,
  With thorns and brambles strown,
The seeds of many an Eden flower
  By angel hands are sown.

STANZAS.

"Ephraim has turned to his idols : let him alone."

"LET him alone!" he clingeth to his idol,
  Binding his soul beneath earth's heavy chain :
  And now no longer shall God's mercy bridle
His wild desires, his passions fierce as vain.

"Let him alone!" his gifted soul now spurneth
  Its lofty destiny for meaner things;
To earthly dreams in its blind faith it turneth;
  Life's murky air has stained its snowy wings.

"Let him alone!" the Spirit hath departed,
  Which, often grieved, shall strive with him no more;
Now must he onward, until, weary-hearted,
  He loathes the idol which he loved of yore.

"Let him alone!" the awful doom is spoken;
  Leave him to quaff the cup his hands have filled;
O! know we not, by many a bitter token,
  What poisons by our passions are distilled?

THE WAYSIDE BROOK.

NOT in the depths of the forest glade
  Where the elm-tree flingeth its graceful shade,
  Where the noontide ray through the alder's bough
Just scatters its sheen on the wave below,
Where no footfall crushes the daisied brink,
Where the wild-bird stoops on its flight to drink,
Where the wood and the upland with melody ring, —
Not there, O brook! do thy waters spring.

Nor yet where the gray old rocks are piled
In the rugged pass of some mountain wild,

Where the mossy stones seem striving to keep
Thy glad stream back from its joyous leap,
While thy silvery foam in the distance gleams
Like a snow-white pennon when morning beams,
And the rush of thy tiny waves might sound
Like a trumpet-call mid the caves around.

O! not for thee is the shady nook,
Or the mountain channels, thou wayside brook!
By the dusty road thou art speeding along,
Wasting unheeded thy smiles and thy song.
No beauty hast thou for the traveller's eye,
Thou wakest no spell as thou glidest by,
Thy freshness is failing with each summer day:
How canst thou sing on thy lowly way?

Brook of the wayside! though footsteps may crush
The daisies that bend where thy glad waters rush;
Though dust from the highway thy brightness may dim,
Yet ceaseless thou singest thy low chanted hymn.
Brook of the wayside! while musing I trace
Thy humble course onward in freedom and grace,
A lesson of life can thy music impart,
Thou type of the meek and the lowly in heart.

THE VOICE OF THE BROOK.

IT cometh to me ever,
  That melancholy voice,—
When the joyous tones of morning
  Would bid my soul rejoice,
When the noontide ray has silenced
  The song of bird and bee,
When the star of evening waketh
  Earth's vesper melody ;
It cometh to me ever,
  That low and tender song,
Which the hidden brook is pouring
  As it flows unseen along.

It cometh to me ever,
  That solemn undertone :
When sounds of mirth are in the air
  It seems a far-off moan ;
But when sad memories awake,
  And earth seems lone and drear,
Its voice of melody gives out
  A hymn of holy cheer ;
And sometimes, too, in moody hour
  It falleth on my ear,
With a sound as of the rustling wings
  Of guardian angels near.

It cometh to me ever :
  In the silent hours of night,

When my spirit comes unwilling back
  From dreamland's worlds of light,
Where its golden gates are closing,
  And I linger still to hear
The music of those angel harps
  That claimed my sleeping ear,
Then comes the moaning of the brook,
  With fancy's music blending,
Like the wail of human love and grief
  'Mid seraph choirs ascending.

It cometh to me ever:
  Howe'er the air is stirred
With noisier sounds of busy life,
  That singing brook is heard;
It cometh like the mystic voice
  Which e'en mid care and strife,
Still whispers to our secret souls
  A dream of holier life, —
The voice which, when on danger's brink
  Our heedless feet have trod,
Has taught us that within us dwelt
  The oracle of God.

SONG.

SUNSHINE dancing on the ocean,
  Insects sporting on the air,
  Wingèd seeds in breezy motion,
All things bright and frail as fair, —

Such be emblems meet for me,
In my glad inconstancy.

Gems in earth's dark bosom burning,
　Pearls in ocean's depths that lie,
Flowers that to the sun are turning
　While they perish 'neath his eye, —
Symbols these of faith may be
But I seek them not for me.

Who that plucks earth's fragrant blossom
　Thinks of gems that lie beneath?
Borne on ocean's placid bosom,
　Who would seek her pearlèd wreath?
No! the joy I feel and see,
This shall be enough for me.

'Tis because my heart has tasted
　Life's full cup of joy and pain,
And with spendthrift folly wasted
　Faith that cometh not again, —
'Tis for this I scorn to be
Slave to thankless constancy.

HOW WILL YE THINK OF ME?

WHEN Life's false oracles, no more replying
  To baffled Hope, shall mock my weary quest;
  When, in the grave's cold shadow calmly lying,
This heart at last has found its earthly rest —
  How will ye think of me? O gentle friends,
    How will ye think of me?

Perhaps the wayside flowers around ye springing,
  Wasting unmarked their fragrance and their bloom,
Or some fresh fount in the lone forest singing
  Unheard, unheeded, may recall my doom:
    Will ye thus think of me?

Or let the day-beam glancing o'er the ocean
  Picture my restless heart, which, like yon wave,
Reflected doubly, in its wild commotion,
  Each ray of light that pleasure's sunshine gave:
    Will ye thus think of me?

Will ye bring back my memory's art, the gladness
  That sent my fancies forth like summer birds?
Or will ye list that undertone of sadness,
  Whose music seldom shaped itself in words?
    Will ye thus think of me?

Remember not how dreams, around me thronging,
  Enticed me ever from life's lowly way,

But O ! still hearken to the deep soul-longing
  Whose mournful tones pervade the poet's lay, —
    Will ye thus think of me ?

And then, forgetting every wayward feeling,
  Bethink ye only that I loved ye well,
Till o'er your souls that " late remorse " is stealing
  Whose voiceless anguish only tears can tell :
    Will ye thus think of me ? O gentle friends !
      Will ye thus think of me ?

STANZAS FOR MUSIC.

WITHIN my bosom's secret shrine,
  There dwells a form which is not thine ;
  For long before I saw thy face,
Love there had found his dwelling-place ;
And cherished still that love must be,
Although I since have looked on thee.

I know not if thine image dwells
In wizard memory's haunted cells,
But somewhere in my heart it bides,
And through each lonely chamber glides,
Until it almost seems to me
No other there had claim to be.

That inner shrine thou canst not hope
Ever with magic key to ope,
But still within' my cloistered breast
Thou hast so long been welcome guest,
That now it almost seems to me
I could not live if wanting thee.

THE PEASANT GIRL'S WISH.

WOULD.I were a lady! Methinks if I were clad
In silken garments every day, I never could be sad ;
No peasant's coif should cover then my soft and glossy curls,
But every tress should find its place 'mid bands of snowy pearls.

O would I were a lady! I would not sit within
Yon cottage porch the livelong day so wearily to spin ;
A stately coach should bear me with my greyhound at my feet,
And with a proud but winning smile the gentles I would greet.

O would I were a lady, to sit beside the board,
Where costly dainties deck the feast, and the rich wine is poured !

How would I queen it o'er the guests! while youths of
    high degree,
If I but kissed the golden cup, would pledge me on
    their knee.

O would I were a lady! to lead the courtly dance,
While many a gallant gentleman was watching for my
    glance !
I'd smile on crowds of lovers, and each should play his
    part,
Till one by noble deeds had found his way into my
    heart.

O would I were a lady! They tell me I am fair,
With merry eye, and sunny brow, and braids of glossy
    hair ;
But O! how much more beautiful is beauty when bedight
With silken robe and sparkling gem, like a stately lady
    bright !

THE OLD MAN'S LAST WISH.

THE Psalmist's span of life had past
    Full twenty years or more,
    And still the old man's footsteps tracked
The sands on Time's wide shore,
While Death's dark wave impatient swelled
    Those footprints to sweep o'er.

22

Aye, more than ninety years had shed
  Their sunshine and their shade,
Since first upon that aged head
  A father's hand was laid;
And now not one was left of all
  With whom his childhood played.

The memory of that far-off Past
  Had faded from his sight;
The mists of many years had dimmed
  Life's golden morning light;
And he was now content to watch
  The closing shades of night.

But when at length Death's summons came,
  While breath was ebbing fast,
Those veiling mists were rent atwain,
  As by a mighty blast,
And once again the old man lived
  In that long-hidden Past.

Once more he saw the homestead where
  His youth had passed away,
The trees that interlaced above
  Its roof so old and gray,
The sheltering porch whose trellised vines
  Gleamed in the sunset ray.

And strange unto his failing eyes
  The Present quickly grew,
The old familiar faces near

Now wore an aspect new,
And ever on his sinking heart
A gloom their coming threw.

"O take me home!" 'twas thus he spake
To all who gathered nigh;
"Beneath the roof where I was born,
There would I choose to die;
Then take me home! O take me home!"
Was still the old man's cry.

For memory's voice within his soul
Sang like a spirit-bird,
Until the tones of other years
Alone his cold ear heard;
And all his nature's time-sealed depths
Were by that music stirred.

And brighter still, and brighter grew
These visions to the last:
"O take me home!" was still his cry
While life was fleeting fast,
And with this prayer upon his lips
The weary spirit passed.

When on the grave's dark verge at last
The time-worn body lies,
And visions of a brighter world
Float past the glazing eyes,
O! who can tell what shape may take
These dreams of paradise?

Still to the struggling spirit clings
  The heavy weight of clay;
It hath not yet put on its wings
  To soar from earth away;
What marvel if its visions wear
  The glory of youth's day,
And life's bright morning-star appears
  Like heaven's first golden ray?

THE POET'S PRAYER.

LEAVE me not, love! ('twas thus a poet chanted
    His heart's fond pleading to the midnight air,)
  Leave not the dwelling by thy presence haunted,
The home thou long hast filled with visions fair.

O leave me not! although thy fleeting pleasures
  Are but as snow-flakes in the sun's warm ray,
Though thy best gifts are only fairy treasures,
  A golden glitter fling o'er things of clay, —

Yet leave me not; all earthly hopes have perished,
  And e'en thine hour of promise has gone by,
But I would fain the fond illusion cherish
  Which still in joy or sorrow brought thee nigh.

Perhaps my hand (like hers in olden story)
  Let fall the burning drop that broke thy rest,

Marring by base distrust thy veilèd glory,
  And scaring thee too rudely from my breast;

Yet leave me not! although thy shrine be broken,
  Though all its votive wreaths are long since gone;
Faith lingers there, albeit the prayer, unspoken,
  Dies on her lip like sorrow's half-breathed moan.

STANZAS.

" The night cometh, when no man can work."

YE who in the field of human life
    Quickening seeds of wisdom fain would sow,
    Pause not for the angry tempest's strife,
  Shrink not from the noontide's fervid glow;
Labor on, while yet the light of day
Sheds upon your path its blessèd ray,
    For the night cometh!

Ye who at man's mightiest engine stand,
  Moulding noble thought into opinion,
O stay not for weariness your hand,
  Till ye fix the bounds of truth's dominion;
Labor on, while yet the light of day
Sheds upon your toil its blessèd ray,
    For the night cometh!

Ye to whom a prophet-voice is given,
  Stirring men as by a trumpet call,

Utter forth the oracles of Heaven, —
  Earth gives back the echoes as they fall;
O speak out, while yet the light of day
Breaks life's slumber with its blessèd ray,
    For the night cometh!

Ye who in home's narrow circle dwell,
  Feeding Love's flame upon the household hearth,
Weave the silken bond, and wake the spell
  Binding heart to heart throughout the earth;
Gentle toil is yours; the light of day
On nought holier sheds its blessèd ray;
    Yet the night cometh!

Diverse though our paths in life may be,
  Each is sent some mission to fulfill;
Fellow-workers in the world are we
  While we seek to do our Masters will;
But our doom is labor while the day
Lights us to our task with blessèd ray,
    For the night cometh!

Fellow-workers are we; hour by hour,
  Human tools are shaping Heaven's great schemes,
Till we see no limit to man's power,
  And reality outstrips old dreams:
Toil and struggle, therefore, work and weep;
In "God's acre" ye shall calmly sleep,
    When the night cometh!

WEARY SPIRIT.

TO ————.

WEARY spirit, fold thy drooping wings;
   O resign thy sad and hopeless quest:
   Not on earth dwells the pure love that flings
Light to lure thee to thy heaven of rest.

Weary spirit, crush the hope that springs
   Ever within thee as its fellow dies;
Treasured in heaven, with Eden's precious things,
   Dwells the ideal that eludes thine eyes.

O give o'er thy heart's vain wanderings now;
   E'en if led aright by fancy's beams,
Couldst thou, while the earth-veil dims her brow,
   Recognize the Psyche of thy dreams?

Weary spirit, cease thy idle quest;
   Listen to thy heart's deep voice at last;
Nestle on some kind and loving breast
   Till life's mystery be overpast.

Round thee lies the earnest and the real,
   Life's affections clustered near thee stand,
While at heaven's high gate thy bright ideal
   Waits to greet thee in yon spirit-land.

In thine inmost heart the bright dream cherish,
Feed the flame that pointeth to the skies,
But let not earth's flowers unheeded perish,
While the far-off stars attract thine eyes.

STANZAS, WRITTEN AFTER LISTENING TO MUSIC.

WITHIN a lonely chamber
A silent harp was hung;
The gathered rust of many years
Upon its chords was flung,
And human hand might never rove
Those voiceless chords among.

Within that lonely chamber
No human foot might tread;
The pleasant things once treasured there
With by-gone years were fled,
And shadowy forms now peopled it,
Like spectres of the dead.

But to that cell deserted
There came a gentle dream,
And the gloomy darkness vanished
Before that silvery gleam,
While the ghastly phantoms in its light
Like angel visions seem.

And to those silent harp-strings
  There came a breath of song,
A vague and wandering breath that swept
  Its rusted chords among,
And once again its ringing tones
  Were poured forth deep and strong.

The gentle dream soon vanished,
  And the breath of song swept by ;
Again in gloom and darkness
  That haunted cell must lie,
And the voice of that long-silent harp
  In wailing sad must die.

Not so! not so! though darkness
  May fill that haunted cell,
No more the chain of silence
  Upon that harp may dwell,
But ever must it echo now
  To Music's mystic spell.

"DOUBT ME NOT."

"DOUBT me not," thou! though all beside might
    falter
When comes the test hour of their love and
    truth,

Though all the old familiar faces alter
    Till nought remain to thee of by-gone youth,
Yet doubt not me ; the loyalty Love taught
Is still unbroken by a wandering thought.

By the wild love, which, reckless of a morrow,
    Cherished its sweet but hopeless dream of thee ;
By the vain yearnings of my young heart's sorrow ;
    By weary days, and nights of agony ;
By the deep scars that in my soul remain,
To mark how close it clasped its heavy chain ;

By all the spendthrift tenderness that flung
    Its richest gifts unasked before thy feet;
By the high impulse that so early strung
    The minstrel harp whose voice to thee is sweet ;
By the devotion of a heart whose pride
Was loving thee when every hope had died ;

By these sad memories of a blighted past,
    And by the peacefulness of present days ;
By the calm joys thy hand has round me cast,
    As one by one each flower of youth decays ;
By the deep love thy soul has caught from mine,
Through years of wedded love, — I still am thine.

Forever thine, in life, in death, the same :
    The love that prayerful sorrow sanctifies
Was born for heaven, and, like the mounting flame,
    Points ever upward to th' immortal skies ;
There only shall my heart's deep truth be shown,
There only shall we know, and there be known.

EPITAPHS ON A YOUNG LADY.

I.

CALLED from life's banquet ere one rose grew
    pale
    Which love had wreathed around thy youthful
    brow,
Death summoned thee to joys that never fail,
And made thee thus the angel thou art now.

II.

Gifted with all that life could bless,
    Thine early death we must deplore;
For earth hath now one saint the less,
    Though heaven hath gained one angel more.

SONGS FOR MUSIC.

NOT thus! O look not thus upon me!
   Nor breathe for me that plaintive strain;
That glance, those tones have almost won me
Back to my early dreams again.

Some spell my every sense enthralleth;
   Fain would I yield my spirit up
To softness that upon me falleth
   Like dew within the floweret's cup.

O turn away those eyes' soft pleading,
   And thou, bewildering voice, be still:
That gaze my inmost soul seems reading,
   Those tones my bosom wildly thrill.

Nay, tempt me not: my heart has taken
   Its vow of silence long ago;
And never more its pulse must waken
   One fever-throb of joy or woe.

Away! my life is all too real;
   Youth's love-dreams may not rule its fate;
Why comest thou then, O bright ideal,
   To mock me thus, too late — too late!

HEN thou art absent, my heart telleth o'er
   The tender thoughts it cherished for thee,
   Hoarding up, miser-like, the precious store,
Which, spendthrift-like, 'twould fain give lavishly.

But when again thou comest, methinks I tremble
   Such priceless gifts of fondness to bestow,
And then love's boundless wealth I would dissemble,
   Lest thou insatiate with thy riches grow.

WILT thou remember, when years are gone by,
   O! wilt thou remember the hour we first met,
   When, 'mid words of calm greeting, one glance
      of thine eye
Awakened the passion that haunteth us yet?

O! wilt thou remember how coldly we turned,
   With thoughts full of gladness and spirits elate,
Nor knew, till our glances on each other burned,
   That our souls in that moment encountered their fate?

E parted in sadness, yet shed not a tear;
   We parted in coldness, for cold ones stood near;
   No vow did we utter, no truth did we plight,
Our hearts hid love's bloom, and our hearts hid its
      blight.

We parted in coldness, while light laugh and jest
Concealed the keen aching that woke in each breast ;
We took but one look, 'twas our fondest and last ;
In that moment a life-time of bitterness past.

We parted in sadness : when years have gone by,
Will the heart be as cold as the lip and the eye ?
Ah, no ! pride may stifle the sigh of regret,
But our brief dream of passion we cannot forget.

WAKE, lady, wake, while the night-dew is weeping
   Its tear-drop o'er earth's faded roses ;
   Wake, lady, wake, while the violet is sleeping
On banks where the starlight reposes.

Wake, lady, wake, for the moments are flying,
  That only to true hearts belong ;
All things in silence and slumber are lying :
  Waken to love and to song.

WE knew we were parting forever ;
   We knew time could never restore
   The bonds we were destined to sever,
  The love we had cherished of yore ;
We knew our best joys had been tasted,
  We knew we could never wend back
To the fountain whose freshness was wasted
  In the sands of life's overpast track.

As the maiden in elfin story
  Anointed her long-cheated eyes,
And beheld that all fairy-land glory
  Was falsehood in glittering guise;
So we now, with soul disenchanted,
  Our brief dream of passion may see,
But alas! by its memories haunted,
  We weep from its thrall to be free.

THE CHILD'S DESTINY.

N angel was watching a slumbering child ;
   His presence had brought there a beautiful
       dream,
So the babe in its innocent loveliness smiled,
  And o'er its bright face passed a summer gleam ;
But the brow of the angel grew sad, for his eye
Marked the shadows of destiny gathering nigh.

"O ! would it were mine," sighed the angel, "to strew
  O'er thy life's future pathway my bright Eden flowers,
And to shed on thine eyelids the soft honey-dew
  Of a slumber like this of thy calm infant hours !
But already hath gone forth the changeless decree,
And the chaplet of sorrow is woven for thee.

"Yet thine eye shall be touched with a holier light
  When that chaplet is pressing thy weary brow,
And the anguish that fadeth thee, never shall blight
  The beauty God gives as thy birthright now ;
The fires of affliction thy soul shall refine,
For the touch of grief hallows a nature like thine.

"Then will I come to thy troubled sleep,
  And sing thee a song of my native heaven ;

Bright visions of beauty thy spirit shall steep,
  And a cherub's voice to thy lips be given,
Till thy look and thy song, in thy life's saddest years,
Shall unlock the deep fountains of sympathy's tears."

TIME'S CHANGES.

REMEMBER the time when thine eye's starry
        light
    Was as gladdening to all things as sunshine
        in spring ;
When thy smile made an atmosphere round thee as
    bright
  As the sudden unfolding of some cherub's wing :
O ! beautiful wert thou with youth on thy brow,
But trust me, beloved, thou art lovelier now.

Thine eye's starry lustre is softened by tears,
  And the bloom of thy beauty has faded away ;
But ne'er in thy gladdest and sunniest years
  Did the high soul within shed so holy a ray :
·O ! beautiful wert thou with youth on thy brow,
But trust me, beloved, thou art lovelier now.

Life's roses have vanished, life's freshness has fled ;
  Thy future no longer Hope's pencil may paint ;
But the halo that sorrow has cast round thy head
  Has made of our Hebe an exquisite saint :
O ! beautiful wert thou with youth on thy brow,
But trust me, beloved, thou art lovelier now.

SONG.

THOU art changed; thou art changed! though
　　the tender smile plays
　　O'er thy lip as it did in our love's golden days
Though thine eye still grows bright when my footstep
　　　draws near,
Though thy voice still as tenderly falls on mine ear,
Though no outward sign showeth thy heart is estranged,
Yet my soul's deep voice whispers, thou'rt changed, aye,
　　thou'rt changed!

Though the warm flush of feeling still mantles thy cheek,
No more for me only its warm blushes speak;
Though thy hand still as fondly seems resting in mine,
Yet its touch sends no thrill from my heart's pulse to
　　　thine;
I cannot say how I first knew thee estranged,
But my soul's prophet voice whispers, changed — O!
　　thou'rt changed.

SONNET.

A BRUISED and broken heart, O God! I bring
　　To lay upon thine altar; it has striven
　　Rebellious 'gainst thy will, and madly given
Its precious things to idols, and doth cling

E'en yet to earthly love, whose venomed sting
  Has poisoned all the charities of life,
  Turning its life-blood into tears and strife.
O let me nestle 'neath the Dove's pure wing!
Send down the Comforter, that He may lay
  The balm of healing on my aching brow,
And with his radiant presencè chase away
  The dark and frowning shapes that haunt me now,
For I am fainting 'neath my great despair,
Crushed by the burden of a granted prayer.

SONNET

ON RECEIVING SOME VIOLETS IN MIDWINTER.

THE cloud-flecked sunshine of an April day,
  The changeful beauty of its lights and shades,
  Falling athwart the newly herbaged glades,
Or marking out some tiny streamlet's way;
A pleasant fancy of each pleasant thing
  That comes when storms have vanished from the sky;
A vision of the fairy-footed Spring
  Stooping to kiss the violet's half-shut eye, —
These are the dreams that paint my chamber walls
  With many a woodland haunt in wintry hour;
And sweet bird-voices and low insect-calls
  Seem to make musical each sylvan bower;
Such genial influence on my spirit falls,
  Waked by the faint, sweet perfume of a flower.

"DUM SPIRO, SPERO."

DUM spiro, spero;" while I breathe, I hope:
  O! God be thanked above all else for this,—
  The only gift within the world's wide scope
Which in its ceaseless promise bringeth bliss.

"Dum spiro, spero;" life and hope entwined:
  Grief may o'ershadow us and pain destroy,
But in our inmost spirit is enshrined
  This sweet expectancy of coming joy.

"Dum spiro, spero:" till our latest breath
  Our human nature hath its cherished dream;
But Immortality is born of Death,
  And bliss eternal dims Hope's earthly beam.

LINES

ON SEEING A SEAL WITH THE MOTTO "SEMPRE LO STESSO."

SEMPRE lo stesso," always the same,—
  Such be the motto affixed to thy name;
  "Sempre lo stesso," always the same,—
Thy thoughts mounting up like the heaven-pointing
  flame;
"Sempre lo stesso," when duty's lone star

Shineth above thy life's waters afar ;
" Sempre lo stesso," when troubles arise,
Looking still upward for help from the skies ;
" Sempre lo stesso," when joy shineth bright,
Remembering the day comes, and also the night ;
" Sempre lo stesso," when grief's frequent cloud
Threatens thy young hopes in darkness to shroud ;
" Sempre lo stesso," when fails thy last breath,
True to thyself, to thy God, to thy faith ;
" Sempre lo stesso," in life and in death.

LINES

ON BURNING SOME OLD JOURNALS AND LETTERS.

AYE, let them perish: why recall
    Dreams of a by-gone day ?
Why lift Oblivion's funeral pall
    Only to find decay ?
The heart of youth lies buried there,
    With all its hopes and fears,
Its burning joys, its wild despair,
    Its agonies and tears.

A light has vanished from the earth,
    A glory left the sky,
Since first within my soul had birth
    Those visions pure and high ;

Or is it that mine eye, grown dim,
  Hath lost the power to trace
The glory of the seraphim
  Within life's holy place?

Methinks I stand midway between
  The future and the past;
The onward path is dimly seen,
  Behind me clouds are cast:
Why should I seek to pierce that gloom,
  And call the buried host
Of haunting memories from the tomb, —
  Each one a tortured ghost?

I could not look upon the page,
  With eloquence o'erfraught,
Where, ere my head had grown so sage,
  My heart its wild will wrought;
I could not, would not ponder now
  O'er my youth's wayward madness,
Which left no stain on soul or brow,
  Yet shrouded life in sadness.

Aye, let them perish! from the dream
  Of passion's wasted hour
There comes no retrospective gleam,
  No spectre of the flower;
The treasured wealth of Eastern kings
  Enriched their burial fire,
And thus my heart's most precious things
  Shall build its funeral pyre.

LAMENT (OF ONE OF THE OLD RÉGIME).

 THE times will never be again
          As they were when we were young :
      When Scott was writing "Waverleys,"
      And Moore and Byron sung ;
When Harolds, Giaours, and Corsairs came
      To charm us every year,
And "Loves" of "Angels" kissed Tom's cup,
      While Wordsworth sipped small beer ;

When Campbell drank of Helicon,
      And didn't mix his liquor ;
When Wilson's strong and steady light
      Had not begun to flicker ;
When Southey, climbing piles of books,
      Mouthed "Curses of Kehama,"
And Coleridge in his dreams began
      Strange oracles to stammer ;

When Rogers sent his "Memory,"
      Thus hoping to delight us,
Before he learned his mission was
      To give feeds and invite us ;
When James Montgomery's "weak tea" strains
      Enchanted pious people,
Who didn't mind poetic haze,
      If through it loomed a steeple ;

When first reviewers learned to show
      Their judgment without mercy ;

When "Blackwood" was as young and lithe
  As now he's old and pursy;
When Gifford, Jeffrey, and their clan
  Could fix an author's doom,
And Keats was taught how well they knew
  To kill, "à coup de plume."

No women folk were rushing then
  Up the Parnassian mount,
And seldom was a teacup dipped
  In the Castalian fount;
Apollo kept no pursuivant
  To cry out, "Place aux Dames!"
In life's round game they held good hands,
  And didn't strive for palms.

O, the world will never be again
  What it was when we were young,
And shattered are the idols now
  To which our boyhood clung;
Gone are the giants of those days
  For whom our bays we twined,
And pigmies now kick up a dust
  To show the "march of mind."

LINES SENT TO A FRIEND, WITH A PER-FUMED "SACHET."

AS odors, prisoned in soft silken cells,
   Give out their subtile essence to the air,
   Betraying where the soul of sweetness dwells,
And waking summer dreams of flowerets fair, —

Thus, when life's daily blossoms round thee fade,
  And hope's sweet song falls fainter on thine ear,
Thus would I have love's memories pervade
  Thy heart and home through many a wintry year.

I would not be within thy soul enshrined,
  A drooping, sad-eyed spectre of the past;
But let one thought of me, vague, half-defined,
  Float round thee, like sweet perfume on the blast.

THE JEALOUS LOVER'S EXCUSE.

FORGIVE the doubt! the flower that springs
   Only beneath the sunbeam's light,
   Trembles at every cloud which flings
  Its portent of the coming night;
Thus when on others lightly fall
The smiles which are my life, my all,
What marvel if my heart's wild thrill
Should seem to presage future ill?

Forgive the doubt! the breeze that sweeps
  O'er ocean's ever ruffled brow
Sends its vibration to the deeps
  Which lie so cold and still below;
Its breath scarce stirs the sea-gull's plume,
Its swell may seal a proud ship's doom;
So words that to thy lip come free
May stir the depths of woe for me.

Forgive the doubt! the moon that rides
  At noon of night her pearly car,
Knows not that all earth's myriad tides
  Await her influence from afar;
Thus, bright one, thou, whose look can still
Each impulse of my wayward will,
Unconscious of thine own sweet art,
Dost reign and triumph in each heart.

THE PROPHECY.

BY the pride on thy lip, and the light in thine
      eye
      I know thou hast visions, pure, noble, and high;
Thou hast dreams of a future illumined by fame,
Where a halo of glory encircles thy name;
Already in fancy thou seest the glad hour
When thy look shall command, and thy word shall have
      power:

But thy doom has been spoken ; thou'rt under a spell ;
" Unstable as water, thou shalt not excel."

There is love in thy heart, too, for tenderness lies
Like a reflex of heaven in the depth of thine eyes ;
There is love in thine heart, and sweet words on thy
      tongue,
And the charm of warm feeling around thee is flung ;
So lovely without and so kindly within,
Thou wilt look but to charm, thou wilt woo but to win :
Yet thy doom has been spoken ; thou'rt under the spell ;
" Unstable as water, thou canst not excel."

STANZAS.

AYE, rear thine altar to Ideal Love,
    And heap with costliest sacrifice the shrine ;
    The fairest chaplet fancy ever wove
From thought's most precious jewels, there should
    shine.

Aye, rear thine altar high, and on it lay
    All that thy nature has of highest, best ;
Bid thy mind coin new wealth there day by day,
    And in thy lavish offering be thou blest.

But write no name upon the altar-stone,
    Shape out no image of thy soul's bright dreams,

Adore the unseen spirit-god alone,
　Nor crown a mortal brow with heaven's own beams.

The fantasies that thrill thine every vein,
　The pearls that melt in passion's burning cup,
Youth's many-colored dreams, half joy, half pain,
　Its vows so true, so lightly offered up, —

O mingle not these sweets of daily life
　With the rich gifts thy soul's ideal claims!
Thy human nature has its woes and strife,
　Its strong requirements and its cherished aims.

The love that from an earthly fountain springs
　Alone can satisfy that human quest;
The bird that highest soars, on strongest wings,
　Yet stoops to earth to find a quiet nest.

But recognize thy yearnings, vague and vain,
　As dim remembrances of that bright world
Whence thou wert missioned on some task of pain,
　Or haply for a parent's errors hurled.

Till God has loosed thy being's weary bond,
　That angel light will flash o'er heart and brain,
Filling thy soul with aspirations fond
　And winning thee to thy lost heaven again.

THE GARDEN.

WHAT a world of beauty lies within
The narrow space on which mine eye now rests !
And yet how cold and tintless seem the words
That fain would picture to another's sense
Those tall, dark trees, whose young, fresh-budded leaves
Give out their music to the summer wind ;
Or that green turf, with golden drops besprent,
As if Aurora, bending down to gaze
On scene so lovely, from her saffron crown
Had dropped some blossoms as she sped along !
What joyous language could be found to paint
Yon vine with its lithe tendrils dancing wild,
As if inebriate with th' inspiring blood
That courses through its old and sturdy heart ?
What rainbow-tinted words could sketch the flowers
Which through the copse-like leafiness gleam out ?
First in her beauty stands the festal rose,
Wearing with stately pride night's dewy pearls
Yet fresh upon her brow, as if to show
That none might woo her, save the evening-star,
Yet e'en now hiding in her heart of hearts
The bee that lives on sweetness.
                          At her feet,
With eye scarce lifted from earth's mossy bed,
The pansy wears her purple robe and crown,
As modestly as a young maiden queen,
Abashed at her own state.
                          The hoyden pink
(Like some wild beauty scorning fashion's garb),

In her exuberant loveliness, breaks loose
From the green bodice by Dame Nature laced,
And bares her fragrant bosom to the winds.
The honeysuckle, climbing high in air,
Swings her perfumed censer toward heaven,
Giving forth incense such as never breathed
From gemmed and golden chalice, or carved urn
In dim cathedral aisles.
                              All things around
Are redolent of sweetness and of beauty,
And, as beside the casement I recline,
Prisoned by sickness to the couch of pain,
Their mingled odors to my senses come,
Like the spice-scented breath of Indian isles
To the sick sailor, who, 'mid watery wastes,
Pines for one glimpse of the green earth again,
And sees the cheating calenture arise
To mock his yearning dreams.
                              Yet thus to lie,
With such a glimpse of Eden spread before me,
And such a blue and lucid sky above,
As might have stretched its interposing veil
'Twixt sinless man and heaven's refulgent host,
When heaven seemed nearer to the earth than now,
And the Almighty talked amid the trees
With his last, best creation, — thus to lie,
E'en though in bondage to bewildering pain,
And fettered by unnerving feebleness
To one small spot, is happiness so much
Beyond my poor deservings, that each breath
Goes forth like a thanksgiving from my lips.

Hark ! merry voices now are on the breeze,
While glad young faces smile through leafy screens,
And where the arrowy sunbeams pierce their way
Like random shafts sent 'mid the clustering boughs,
The sheen of snowy robes is gleaming out ;
Thus by her own pure brightness I can trace
The fleeting footsteps of that blessed one
Who to my glad youth like an angel came,
Folded her pinions in my happy home,
And called me " Mother."
                        To my o'erfraught soul
These images of all my home joys come
Like rose-leaves strewn upon a brimming cup,
And in its very fullness of content
My heart grows calm, while every pulse is hushed
With a most tremulous stillness.

FRAGMENT.

THE fire within my soul burns dim and low,
    Like some neglected cresset's dying glow,
    And my heart's pulse beats fitfully and slow,
  E'en as a bell in ruined turret hung,
  When by the gusty night breeze feebly swung,
  Making no pleasant sounds, as to and fro
  Through the thick air its dull vibrations go.
The light is darkened on my spirit's shrine,
  And silent are the oracles of thought ;

Hushed are the echoes of that voice divine
Whose faintest tone my inner sense once caught;
　　No bright descending angel flings
　　From off his glorious wings
The hues of Paradise o'er earthly things;
No heavenly dreams like seraphs round me throng,
Filling life's temple with the voice of song.
　　　　Fain would I lift
My soul in adoration, but no more
Upon my lips I feel the precious gift
Of eloquent utterance, as in days of yore;
Yet there are times when o'er my dull brain floats
A strain of fleeting music, and the notes
Seem like articulate words; then would I fain
Forget the weary weight of wasting pain,
And pour forth all the love that now lies mute,
Like the tones hidden in a stringless lute.